Reviews for *Gnosis:*

"*Gnosis,* by Philip Gardiner, is a refreshing creation of true spiritual teaching—as well as being a good read. Gardiner possesses that rare ability to weave history, mythology, and spiritual tradition into writing that is both understandable and enjoyable to those out of the gnostic loop, as well as to steadfast initiates. His source material is irreproachable and his intentions are totally above board. *Gnosis* contains a wealth of information worthy of Frazer, Blavatsky, and Crowley—minus those writers' ponderous style (Frazer), mystification (Blavatsky), and idiosyncrasy (Crowley). 'The Knowledge Dictionary' is really good and lists concepts, people, and ideas that are of benefit to beginners and advanced students of gnosis and the occult. Gardiner also includes a timeline of serpent worship, which is just as instructive and enjoyable to read. *Gnosis: The Secret of Solomon's Temple Revealed* definitely belongs in a gnostic library. It will be a real eye-opener to people unfamiliar with religious and cultural development—just as it provides remarkable backup information for readers who have already progressed beyond the mass delusions perpetrated by state religion and new age nonsense."

—*Gnostic Communications* internet magazine

"I can confirm that the basic premise—that Solomon's Temple never existed—is true. I also agree that Gardiner writes with clarity, and most readers will enjoy his book. Please consider this book if you are at all interested in why myths grow into war and all the other things we suffer."

—Robert Baird, author

"*Gnosis* will fascinate readers with its complex insights into spirituality—insights that are more advanced than the simplistic fairytale-like bits of wisdom handed down by conventional religious dogma."

—Joseph Iorillo, *Dark Wisdom* magazine

"Philip—Thank you for all that you do! I have so enjoyed your work and can't begin to tell you what an impact it has had on me personally as well as professionally. I look forward to your future projects as well as updates on your Website. Your contribution on this journey is immeasurable."

—Robert T. Rasnake, 32nd degree Freemason, MA, NCC, LPCC counseling psychologist

GN⊕SIS

The Secret of
Solomon's Temple Revealed

By

Philip Gardiner

Best-selling author of
The Serpent Grail

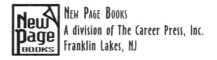

NEW PAGE BOOKS
A division of The Career Press, Inc.
Franklin Lakes, NJ

GNOSIS
EDITED BY ASTRID DERIDDER
TYPESET BY EILEEN DOW MUNSON
Cover design by Dutton and Sherman
Interior images courtesy of Philip Gardiner
Printed in the U.S.A. by Book-mart Press

To order this title, please call toll-free 1-800-CAREER-1 (NJ and Canada: 201-848-0310) to order using VISA or MasterCard, or for further information on books from Career Press.

The Career Press, Inc., 3 Tice Road, PO Box 687,
Franklin Lakes, NJ 07417
www.careerpress.com
www.newpagebooks.com

Library of Congress Cataloging-in-Publication Data

Gardiner, Philip.
    Gnosis : the secret of Solomon's Temple revealed / by Philip Gardiner.
        p. cm.
    ISBN-13: 978-1-56414-909-1
    ISBN-10: 1-56414-909-9
        1. Gnosticism. 2. Wisdom (Gnosticism) 3. Temple of Jerusalem (Jerusalem)
    I. Title

    B638.G38 2006
    299'.932—dc22

                                                    2006012346

Dedicated to
Joshua and Angeline,
for being the perfect son and daughter.

■ ▪ ▪

Acknowledgments

I would like to acknowledge the help I received from my wife—she is a constant source of enlightenment. I would also like to thank my parents, John and May, for their perpetual support. My thanks to the unnamed subjects of all my experiments, and to those who contributed their wisdom over the years. My special thanks to the many authors who have assisted and heralded me, such as Andrew Collins, Graham Phillips, Graham Hancock, Crichton Miller, Nick Pope, Karen Ralls, Ernest Scott, and many more. I would also like to thank Astrid deRidder, my wonderful editor, for making me look good.

Contents

INTRODUCTION

Eritis sicut dii scientes bonum et maulum.
(You will be like God, conscious of Good and Evil.)

Many people have no understanding of what the word *gnosis* means; others think that it simply means *knowledge* and leave it at that. Yet there is a deeper meaning. It is a word that gives rise to the title *Gnostic*, or one who has special knowledge. The true definition of the term *gnosis* is *the direct mystical experience of the Divine in the self*. It is the realization of the true nature of ourselves, and cannot be discerned through intellectual dogma or doctrine, but only through experience.

The beliefs and ultimate secrets of the Christian Gnostics are a mystery to most people. They practice a spirituality that is distinctly more Eastern than the traditional Western version of Christianity. As Mathew says in the book of Thomas: "For whoever does not know self, does not know anything, but whoever knows self, already has acquired knowledge about the depth of the universe." These are the words of Christ according to Thomas, and these few words reveal the depth of the gnostic belief system. This passage seems to say that the most important place to search for truth, the Divine, and for ultimate knowledge of the universe, is within ourselves.

The Indian Upanishads say that "It is not by argument that the self is known. Distinguish the self from the body and mind. The self, the *atman*, the highest refuge of all, pervades the Universe and dwells in the hearts of all. Those who are instructed in the self and who practice constant meditation attain that changeless and self-effulgent atman. Do thou likewise...."[1] The *atman* is the true inner reality, the spirit, or the Son of God element within each one of us. Alchemists say that the atman does not die. It is without end of days, and it is absolutely perfect. The goal of gnosis is to discover this true inner reality, which gives us insight into the universe itself.

"I shall give you what no eye has seen, what no ear has heard, what no hand has touched, and what has never arisen in the human mind."[2] These were the words attributed to Christ by Thomas. Gnostics believe that Jesus Christ was nothing other than the atman—the true inner reality of ourselves, talking in unity throughout history and mankind. The words of Christ match those of other leading historical and religious avatars, because it is an archetype that exists within each of us. The true Christ is the true Us, and if we can obtain the wisdom and knowledge of this true Us or Christ, then we shall be able to see "what no eye has seen" and hear "what no ear has heard." We shall truly touch "what has never arisen in the human mind" because what we shall see is much more than just the creation of humanity.

The secrets of the ancients are more profound than most people suspect. The truth behind some of the most enigmatic problems of mankind's history—including the Temple of Solomon—are held within the mind of man. These problems were previously identified by our ancestors, but the answers have been lost. Modern man strives to explain man's existence with rational and logical thought. But in so doing, modern man has all but destroyed this secret knowledge and can no longer understand the language of our ancestors, who so diligently recorded their discoveries regarding our existence, life after death, and the ultimate evolution of our own consciousness.

Because of mankind's attempts at manifesting the mystical into the physical world, we have lost the knowledge of these mysteries, creating puzzles that we must now solve. We shall never find the bones of the apostles, for they never truly lived as real people. We shall never hold a fragment of the true cross, for it never carried out its crucifixion. We will never find the Holy Grail, for it exists only within the mind of man. And we will never find the Temple of Solomon, for it is man himself.

At any other time in history I would have been burned at the stake for presenting the knowledge contained in this book. That still might happen. Many before me have attempted to reveal gnostic secrets and have been silenced, or have been forced to conceal the truth behind incredibly symbolic language that few could understand. Only those who know the secrets have the eyes to see and the ears to hear. Men whom we would today call *alchemists* and *occultists* hid their understanding behind language and imagery that was multilayered, and it has taken many years of searching to uncover the truth. The language of these adepts, whether written, spoken, or in art, has become known as the *esoteric*, in that only those who understand will be able to decipher the hidden meanings, which is the definition of true *gnosis*.

To those who have little knowledge of gnostic traditions, the concept that our ancestors held arcane secrets that remain relevant today might seem quite ridiculous. However, there is more relevance to you and everything you know in these ancient and sacred secrets than in anything else you will ever come across. The knowledge within this book is so powerful that it will change your life. It is not the knowledge that is wrong, rather it is your perception of it.

You may be wondering how I came to this knowledge. It is a long story, but I shall endeavor to keep it to a minimum. I began my journey many years ago, researching and reading hundreds of books on history, religion, esoteric philosophy, and all manner of alchemic and occult literature. I was trying to balance the information I discovered with the science of modern times.

I always believed that there was more to life than meets the eye. In my previous role as a marketing expert, I knew that there were subtle and ongoing propaganda machines in motion around the world. These ranged from marketing firms to public relations departments of international companies and organizations. There are crossovers between all these organizations. These crossovers use the techniques or marketing and propaganda to manipulate the masses into distinct and controllable animal pens. I say *animal* because, quite simply, this is the base part of man that marketing experts play on. They strive to be the biggest influence upon the basic evolutionary desires of each sector of mankind. Whether selling products or political rhetoric, they pull on those same animal instincts that reside within our minds. For instance, when selling a product to children, they use strong but basic language, colorful and primary images, and simple music and sounds. When they sell to the elderly, they use softer language, subtle pastel shades, and retrospective music. This process has been used for thousands of years, and all the techniques of sales and persuasion have been developed to draw on the same instincts of man's basic nature.

These experts have used enticement and threat. They have said that mankind can achieve entry into a Christian heaven or be cast down with the heretical pagans to hell. You can vote for the good political party or the evil one, and get tax cuts or pay rises. You can live in a paradise on earth with flashy sports cars; expensive holidays; and a big, white mansion, or you can be part of the lower classes and struggle just to survive. This is the capitalist's version of heaven and hell.

Over the course of thousands of years, man has learned about the subtleties of his own nature, and yet is still confused and puzzled that a master of marketing or propaganda can bewilder him. Marketing and propaganda has become the tool of the expert, and this expert must understand human nature as well as any psychologist. Paradoxically, it is the role of the real psychologist to correct the confused mind of someone who has succumbed to the constant cycle of desire, refusal, dejection, and depression created by the marketing expert. We have failed to realize that the products we produce and sell to one another are fleeting and do not offer true enlightenment. These products are merely material things. We have failed to follow the most basic directive of the ancient philosophies—to find balance.

It is with this background that many people in the marketing world end up feeling cynical and deflated. I began to reject the commercial and capitalist world that I helped to create, and which seemed to be taking over the entire planet. I wanted to run away and evade the all-pervasive and encroaching rot of greed. I wanted to achieve balance in my life.

With all of this in mind, I wanted to know if there were any men and women in history who felt as I did—that there are mysterious theories and thoughts hidden within literature and art. Eventually, after years of learning signs, symbols, and ciphers, I began to see a subtle undercurrent in remarkable places and from incredibly ancient times. It seems that our ancestors discovered remarkable secrets, and I was slowly uncovering them. More correctly, I was coming to a deeper understanding as to the truth behind the secrets.

During my research I contacted hundreds of people and found that many people had similar thoughts. I was soon invited to become a member of a secret society. (I will not reveal the name of this gentlemen's club, suffice to say it goes back many hundreds of years and is not the Freemasons.) In truth, the invite was more of a demand. I had been given a book by an elderly gentleman. The book had been printed anonymously in the 1930s, but predicted the outcome of the second World War. My initial thought was simply that the book's publishing date was incorrect, and that it had been printed after the war. However, not all events stated in the book came to pass, just the major ones, and all my research indicated that the book had been published in 1933. How then, did the author know that certain events would take place? The answer was given to me by the elderly gentleman. The events were part of a much bigger plan, he said, and there were various outcomes possible— all of which led to the setting up of an international organization. (Many conspiracy theorists call it the New World Order.) This was, the gentleman claimed, now called the United Nations. Now that I knew this, he said, I have no choice but to join the secret society.

The old gentleman died and left me wondering what to do. Should I join the society, or should I just ignore the whole thing? In truth, I was without option. The elderly gentleman had proscribed my membership in his last will and testament. I was a member of the secret society whether I wanted to be or not. On the lowest level, the whole thing seemed rather silly and contrived, but as time passed I noted subtle changes in the language of the levels and found that I understood more of the texts and works of art that had previously confused me. This was evidence of my growing knowledge. There seemed to be layer after layer of hidden messages and teachings that nobody on the outside understood or believed. I believe that this is the road to wisdom, a method which has been used for centuries. I traveled around the world to see if my newly acquired knowledge was supported by the artifacts and imagery of various nations and religions. Everywhere I went, I saw confirmation.

This is the short version of my path to the light. This is a journey that has just begun, and a journey that has taught me the amazing secret of Solomon's Temple. I sincerely hope that, in this book, I will be able to express the wonder and sense of awe I felt when I came to the startling realization that there truly is a higher consciousness, and that this state is obtainable to all. I hope you too will feel outrage that these deep and real elements of our own existence have been kept from us by the manipulators of the world. The reason for this deception is simple—the release of our own mind gives us a freedom from controlling influences. This is truth in and of itself: our minds, senses, and very thoughts are under the influence of others.

I would like to point out that there is so much ground covered in this book that I simply cannot go into lengthy details for each and every aspect. With this in mind, I hope that such a thirst is created in the reader that you are moved to go and drink at the well of ancient wisdom for yourself. These wells are the old texts of the religions of the world—the Bible, the Koran, the Upanishads, and more. These texts are not just for the religious-minded, they are everyone.

If I have any advice for the journey ahead, it would be this: Forget what you believe, ignore all that you are told, and come to this book with a fresh and open mind. If you fail to comprehend all that is written, read the book again. This knowledge is so deeply rooted that it can easily be missed, and quite often a second reading will finally bring it to the surface. I have included an extensive Knowledge Dictionary at the end of the book to aid you. This dictionary is a reinterpretation of various beliefs, symbols, and texts with the new interpretations discussed in this book. The stark reality will be obvious that, from alchemy to Taoism and from gnostic Christianity to mystical Sufism, the truths discussed in this book are at the root of all wisdom. The truths are in every culture of the world.

Good luck on your journey into real wisdom and true gnosis.

—Philip Gardiner

For more knowledge, information, and texts, please visit
www.philipgardiner.net.

Chapter 1

THE SERPENT

St. John's chalice with serpent and book of knowledge.

I n order to fully comprehend what gnosis is, we must first understand the background and history of this hidden world. We must come to an understanding of the idea that our present orthodox history is basically incorrect. Over the last few centuries there has been an ongoing revision of history by those people in power, both ecclesiastical and political. As any good historian will tell you, the history of the world has been written by the victors. The victory could be a military conquest, a political campaign, or a religious movement—either way, the losers are generally silenced and eradicated from the history books. Sometimes they are made to look foolish, or even vilified.

When we are told by the history books that "the war was won by the glorious and good," we must be wary. The story has usually been exaggerated out of proportion by the victorious, and is no longer an accurate version of the truth. This is especially true concerning the victories of Christianity. For instance, it is commonly reported that Patrick went to Ireland and defeated the serpents, eradicating the island of all indigenous snakes. This is blatantly untrue, as Ireland has never had any snakes. The facts in this case have been hidden from us by those in authority—namely the Roman Catholic Church. What is occurring is a multilayered symbolic statement. This story is actually an allegory, meaning that Patrick eradicated Ireland of all devil worshippers. (The snake or serpent was commonly associated with pagan worshippers.) This story proves the existence of a serpent-worshipping cult in Ireland, which was replaced by the new cult of Christianity, and is linked to the worship of what we shall discover to be the *wisdom of the serpent*. It also refers to the fact that Patrick overcame the power of the serpent, and thereafter mastered it.

St. Patrick and the snakes.

As I revealed in my previous book, *The Serpent Grail*, the serpent cult was prevalent across the globe in ancient times. The snake often has a wonderful and physical *Elixir of Life* in its venom. This venom is packed with proteins that have scientifically proven beneficial properties, which actually aid the extension of life and improve health. I showed how the ancients understood this, utilized it, and included numerous references to it in their texts, art, and structures. Eventually the mixing of blood and venom from the snake in a ritualized bowl gave rise to the holy mixing bowl we know today as the Holy Grail. The serpent symbolizes wisdom— often called ultimate wisdom. Why would a slithering snake, which moves across the ground, eats its victims, and casts off its skin, be seen as a symbol for the ultimate knowledge?

In *The Serpent Grail*, I claimed that serpent worship was prevalent around the world in ancient times and actually gave rise to the many disparate religions and cultures of humanity. In the following passages, I will very briefly remind you of a few elements I believe to be relevant from the history of serpent worship and mythology. I will not, as yet, explain the reasoning behind each and every strange occurrence or text, as this is a simple but often slow process of trickling information into the mind, allowing the retained memories to jump out occasionally once new insights are gained. Think of them as small sparks of enlightenment, and you will be close to the truth. In essence, we shall be moving through the various stages as if we were initiates in the mysteries of gnosticism.

Ancient Worship

The worship of the serpent[1] goes back in history to Greek, Roman, Egyptian, and even Sumerian times. Snake worship can be found as far apart as Australia, Europe, South America, and the African Continent. Serpent worship is involved at almost every level of any given culture.

In Africa, the snake was often pinned to a cross or tree as a sacrificial offering, just as Jesus was pinned to the cross in the New Testament. Moses also lifted and pinned the Brazen Serpent, which was thought to have been on a Tau-cross. The Tau-cross eventually came to signify hidden treasure, and as we continue our initiate journey, we shall come to the realization that this symbolism is due to the hidden knowledge manifested in the symbol of the upwardly moving serpent on the cross.

In a state census taken in 1896, it was remarked that more than 25,000 different forms of the Naga snake (the Indian mythical Cobra) were prevalent in the northwest province of India, and many experts believe that snake worship can be traced back through India to Persia and Babylon, as well as various other early civilizations.

The snake is intricately linked with magic and mythology in almost every culture. It is seen as the personification of wisdom and goodness, and alternatively as the personification of evil—thus revealing the duality that is implicit to it's nature. This also implicates the duality of the energy serpents known as Ida and Pingala, which traverse the spine in the Hindu tradition known as the Kundalini. The Kundalini is commonly seen as one of the paths to true wisdom.

Disagreement exists regarding the sexual symbolism of the snake. Some people believe that snakes are masculine, because when a serpent stands upright when threatened, it is phallic in nature. At the same time, when snakes are associated with water, they are often given a female connotation. I disagree with much of what is assumed in this area. Natural things cannot always be attributed or related to human sexuality, although there are definitely instances of serpent/god/phallus relations. Some of these are historically proven, but have more to do with the *union of opposites* within ourselves rather than a sexual union between male and female. This internal union has been depicted throughout history as a sexual union, even though it is not implicitly sexual in nature. It is often represented as the *Hermaphrodite* or *Androgyny* figure. However, it is important to remember that, just because there is one association of the phallus with a serpent god, not all snakes are associated in that way. It may well be that the phallus is just a symbol of the power and fertility of the snake. I believe that this means the snake itself (whether the real physical snake or the energy serpent of Hinduism and others) was a *carrier* of fertility, rather than just being a *symbol* of fertility.

Some experts believe that the ancients considered caves, wells, and other such openings in the earth to be entrances to the womb of the Goddess, from which all life erupted and into which all things were laid at death. The snake is said to live within the earth, which is often symbolized as the body of the Goddess. In this way, the snake is aware of all her secrets and wisdom, including those of life, death, and rebirth. This is an indication of why the serpent was seen as the phallus and an allusion to the sexual potency of the male, as well as the feminine watery serpentine spirit of wisdom. It is the union of power and wisdom.

Water has been regarded as sacred by many cultures, and shrines were often created at water sites. Eventually, these places evolved into all manner of churches, temples, and mosques, being commandeered by various organized religions. Many serpent or dragon-related myths have remained associated with these sacred places over time, including the stories surrounding the Sinclair family, now commonly associated with their ownership of Rosslyn Chapel in Scotland.

The Sinclair family (who are intrinsically involved in the Templar Grail myths) have their familial origins in Scandinavia. This northern region cannot escape its serpent past. Whether Vandals or Lombards, they were all "addicted to the worship of the serpent."[2] Olaus Magnus, a Swedish ecclesiastic writer and historian, informs us that snakes ate, slept, and played with ordinary people in their own houses. This serpent worship becomes obvious when looking at the dragon standards of the Danes and Vikings. These dragons were later brought to Wales and into Arthurian legend by Norse invaders. In *The Worship of the Serpent*, John Bathurst Deane lets us in on the secret behind the Danish sacred vessel and its primitive idolatry. The relic is a "celebrated horn found by a female peasant, near Tundera in Denmark, in the year 1639." The vessel is said to be of gold and embossed in parallel circles, seven in number. In circle one, there is a naked woman kneeling with extended arms—on each side, the figures of serpents. Circle two has the figure in prayer to the serpent; while in circle three she is in conversation with the snake. This has to be a grail, a horn of plenty, a horn of offering and receiving from the sacred snake.

It is said that the women of the Vandals (who worshipped the flying dragon) kept snakes in hollowed oak trees and made them offerings of milk. The women prayed to the snakes for the health of their family. Keeping them imprisoned, feeding them, and then requiring healing from them may be an indication of how deeply the Vandal society was entrenched in serpent worship. Deane claims that the Lombards similarly worshipped both a golden viper and a tree on which the skin of the "wild beast was hung." In approximately A.D. 682, the Bishop of Benevento suppressed this belief by cutting down the tree and melting the golden viper into a sacramental chalice.

Christ shall be lifted up as the Brazen Serpent! Lichfield Cathedral.

The Normans were descended from Vikings and considered the yggdrassil tree important, with the serpent as the Ouroboros around the heavens. They incised dragons and snakes on their sword hilts and shields. This was most often with the symbol of the Tau-cross (before they were Christianized).

The crest of Henry St. Clare (the first Earl of Orkney) from the 14th century uses the head of a great serpent. The engrailed cross (seen at Rosslyn Chapel) also has some remarkable connotations. The engrailed cross is now a Sinclair symbol, but the original definition of *engrail* implies *generation*. The Sinclair family—the Holy Light—was the Holy Generation, the keepers or protectors of the Grail. At the center of the engrailed cross is the Templar cross. Although the Sinclair family denies the connection, the element of the Templar cross is there. The Templar cross begins the outward journey from the center in horseshoe-like curves, and so becomes symbolic of immortality.

The engrailed cross.

The tomb of Sir William Sinclair, which sits inside Rosslyn Chapel, depicts a chalice and octagonal cross, as well as a rose. The chalice is the

Grail, the cross is the number eight for immortality, and the rose is the blood of the serpent (Christ) and symbolic of the mother goddess Ishtar and her hidden wisdom.

Because the movements of a snake are typically sinuous and wave-like, similar to the course of a river, three letters are attributed to the snake—*M*, *W*, and *S*. The use of these letters has to be closely watched, especially when they are used in conjunction with snake mythology or Alchemy (such as *M*ary or *M*are for water, *W*ater itself, and *S*erpent). The snake is not implied every time these letters are used, just when in association with other snake symbolism.

Many cultures around the globe believe that water contains a spirit-serpent, which in these cultures is linked implicitly with water cults. Serpents are often seen as the resident guardians of a pool, pond, or well. This is particularly true in Celtic culture, where they are depicted with gods and goddesses. For example, Brighid is associated with many serpent deities, such as Neit. These watery serpents were guardians of the *W*isdom associated with *W*ater. There is a *W*ell, situated in Pembrokeshire, England, which is said to have contained a golden torque (said by some to be symbolic of the snake), guarded by a hand-biting serpent. At the *M*aiden's *W*ell in Aberdeenshire in Scotland, there was reputed to be a winged serpent present.

Some experts believe that the snake was originally a symbol of the virgin goddess giving birth to the cosmos, unaided by any male principle, almost an androgynous element of creation. In some early myths, the goddess gives birth to the universe, and afterwards the original singularity of the goddess split into the separate form of god and goddess. It was from their sexual union that creation was thought to arise. It is, therefore, the *re-union of these opposites* that is required for true wisdom and creativity.

Creation Myths

THE PELASGIAN CREATION MYTH[3] BY DR. JAMES LUCHTE
ADAPTED FROM ROBERT GRAVES'S *THE GREEK MYTHS*

In the beginning, Eurynome,
The Goddess of All Things,
Rose naked from Chaos.

She found nothing upon
Which to rest her feet, and thus,
She divided the sea from the sky.

She danced lonely upon
The waves of the sea.

She danced towards the South, and
The Wind set in motion behind her
Seemed something new and strange
With which to begin a work of creation.

Wheeling about, she caught hold of
This North wind, rubbed it between
Her hands, and behold!
The great serpent Ophion.

Eurynome danced to warm herself, wildly
And more wildly, until Ophion, enchanted,
Coiled about her divine limbs
Becoming one with her.

As she lay with the Ophion,
Eurynome was got with child.

Eurynome assumed the form of a dove,
Brooding upon the waves and with time,
She laid the Universal Egg.

At her bidding, Ophion coiled seven times
About this egg, until it hatched and split into two.

Out tumbled all things that exist, her children:
Sun, moon, planets, stars, Earth with her mountains
Rivers, trees, herbs, and all living creatures.

Eurynome and Ophion made their home upon
Mount Olympus where he vexed her by
Claiming to be the author of the Universe.

Forthwith, she bruised his head with her heel,
Kicked out his teeth, and banished him to the
Dark caves below the Earth.

Eurynome opened her gaze and her arms to her
Children, giving each its name which she read
Off its own singular power and being.

She named the sun, moon, planets, stars and
The Earth with her mountains and rivers, trees,
Herbs and living creatures.

She took joy in her creation, but soon found
Herself alone desiring the face, voice,
ear and warmth of another of her own.

Eurynome stood up and once again
Began to dance alone upon the waves.

In the Pelasgian creation myth, the goddess created the first living creature from air—the giant serpent Ophion—and became a female serpent to mate with it, giving birth to the World Egg. She then became a dove (which later became a symbol for the spirit of god or Holy Spirit) and floated on the primordial ocean, while Ophion coiled around the egg seven times until it hatched and created the heavens, the earth, and the underworld.

Lightning was known as the *sky-serpent* or *lightning-snake*. The thunderstorm was believed to be the mating of the Sky Father and the Earth Mother, bringing the fertilizing rain. The lightning strike itself was a masculine thrusting and fertilizing power.

The Greeks believed that the mushroom was the result of the mating of the God and Goddess, the lightning snake, and the earth. Many have pointed towards this mushroom as being the Elixir of Life. If this mushroom is an elixir, then it was created symbolically by the snake. According to John Bathurst Deane in *The Worship of the Serpent*, the site of a lightning strike was once considered to be a place so full of power that it was designated an *abaton* (abyss) or *forbidden place of the serpent* (ab). This itself links the serpent with the electrical or electromagnetic energy of the Earth, as it is commonly seen in the Chinese Dragon Paths and the Serpent Ways or Ley Lines of Europe.

In the Dionysian mysteries, a serpent representing the god was carried in a box called a *cista* on a bed of vine leaves. It is believed that this may be the infamous cista mentioned by the early writer Clement of Alexandria, which was exhibited as containing the phallus of Dionysus. The cista mentioned in the mysteries of Isis is also said to have held a serpent, also known as the missing phallus of Osiris. Again, according to Deane, the fertility festival of the women of Arretophoria included cereal paste images "of serpents and forms of men," revealing the dual aspects of female wisdom and male power.

A serpent is said to have been found beside the sleeping Olympias, mother of Alexander the Great. Philip of Macedon, the husband of Olympias, is reputed never to have coupled with the *Bride of the Serpent* again. Alexander is sometimes connected with the images of the horned serpent, which is a symbol used for the enlightenment experience. Alexander, the great general and war hero, claimed his authority through the prevalent serpent power of his day.

The Greek and Roman god of healing, Aesculapius, is also said to have fathered a son by a woman who is depicted in the temple at Sicyon as sitting on a serpent. This clearly means that Aesculapius was seen as the serpent, making the connection even stronger. Barren women often sought help at the temples of Aesculapius to sleep in the precincts of the *abaton*.

Serpent Seasons

In classical Greco-Roman mythology, the year was divided into three seasons to represent the three aspects of the Mother Goddess. These three aspects were ruled by the totems of lion, goat, and serpent. The serpent represented the autumn or death aspect of the Goddess. This is the point of entry into another realm. The lion and goat are aspects of the lower nature of mankind—the non-spiritual side of our consciousness. The snake is sometimes seen as ruling the winter portion of the year. The sun god Apollo was often depicted as slaying the python at Delphi with his sun ray arrows. (Although this image may be a myth to explain the conquest of patriarchal gods over the female snake goddess.) In truth, this myth explains the powerful serpent energy of Apollo slaying the female or negative aspect of the serpent.

The snake can also be seen as the Lord of the Waning Year and the dark twin of the Sun Lord. The two lords fight to rule of the land at the beginning of summer, and again at the beginning of winter. This may have given rise to the later myths of the valiant hero being slain by the dragon instead of defeating him, as in the story of Saint George and the dragon.

In the Pagan world, the slain lord will rise every year, and the light and dark (winter and summer, day and night) will rule in balance. Later myths see death as a final ending, and the light and dark are in total opposition.

The Sun Lord also dies nightly, and passes through the underworld realm of the serpent or dragon. The Egyptian god Ra, as the solar cat, was seen as battling the serpent of darkness known as Zet or Set. Similar stories are told in many myth systems of sky gods fighting serpents, such as Marduk and Tiamat, Apollo and the Python, and Zeus and Typhon. In the Old Testament, the sea monster Leviathan appears. This was probably the original totem deity of the Levite clan, whose name means *son of Leviathan*. Leviathan may have been a dual deity combined with Jehovah, each ruling half of the year. First century medallions show Jehovah as a serpent god.

In Greek myth, Ge (the earth goddess) gives the Tree of Immortality as a wedding gift to Hera. It is located in the Hesperides, a mythical island in the far west, and guarded by the daughters of night and the serpent Ladon. The apples of the tree represent the sun, which sets or dies nightly in the west, and journeys through the underworld lair of the serpent or dragon, to be reborn each dawn in the east. The story of Adam and Eve is said by some to be a regeneration of this myth.

Slaying the serpent came to represent the triumph of light over dark, or one religion overcoming another. Often it involved pinning of the serpentine earth energy to a specific location. Apollo slew the snake at Delphi, while Saints Michael and George slew dragons in England. Saint Patrick, as I pointed out earlier, is said to have banished snakes from Ireland. The Virgin Mary is often depicted as trampling the serpent underfoot, as are many more saints and Christian figures. But we should ask ourselves, how or why did the serpent come to be represented as evil? How did this animal become associated with death?

Folklore has it that, when Saint George kills an adder in early spring, it brings good luck for the year. But if he lets it go, he brings bad luck. This was symbolic of killing the serpent winter, which suggests that the serpent was losing its life of symbolism and was being replaced with the Christian attributes of Satan.

Prophecy and Divination

Snakes are associated with divination throughout the world. The Greeks kept oracular snakes in temples; the Arcadian word for *priest* literally means *snake charmer*.

According to the historian and writer Philostratus, the Arabs could foretell omens through the sound of birds, but only after they had eaten the heart or liver of a snake. Both Arabs and Hebrews derive their word for *magic* from the word for *serpent*.

Worship of the serpent goddess was widespread in predynastic northern Egypt. The asp had the title of *uzait*, meaning *the eye* for its Otherworld sight and wisdom. The goddesses Hathor and Maat were both called *the eye*. The *uraeus* headdress, worn by the pharaohs, symbolically gave the wearer the power of the Third Eye. The snake was meant to strike at any enemy coming into the presence of the ruler. All Egypt's queens were given the title of *Serpent of the Nile*.

In North America, the Native American Indians would choose a warrior to undergo the ordeal of allowing a snake to bite him several times during a sacred dance. If he survived, he was considered to have gained great wisdom and insight into the workings of the cosmos. This is typical of the trials of shamanic initiation, and is a symbolic act of the power of the inner serpent energy, which can be seen in myths the world over.

Many *serpent plants* (plants given the title of serpent or snake for their ability to alter consciousness) have been used to bring about trance states and engender Otherworld journeys.

The Druids often used snake stones, said to be formed by adders breathing on hazel wands, for healing and divination.

The Triple Realm

In Egyptian mythology, the pyramid texts speak of the snake as celestial and earthly, as well as subterranean—which means it has a trinity aspect. The divine phallus—the serpent—was in perpetual copulation with Mother Earth and represented the *axis mundi*, passing through all three realms of hell, earth, and heaven. This is symbolic of opening up a pathway within ourselves to allow an internal dialogue between our lower nature and our higher senses or consciousness. Due to the fact that the serpent lives underground, it is often seen as a link with the underworld. Snakes were often found in graveyards, where they were thought to communicate with the dead.

The serpent or dragon is seen as guarding a wealth of underworld treasure in many circumstances—under a lake, in a cave, or on an island. Cherokee Indian legends tell of great wisdom that will come to the warrior who takes the jewel from the head of the serpent king, Uktena. This brings to mind the idea that the snake has a jewel set in its head, which is common in several different mythologies. It was said that the Elixir of Life was an emerald jewel that fell from the forehead of Lucifer the serpent angel, whose name means *bearer of light*. In Hindu mythology, the serpent was said to have a jewel in its forehead. The jewel here, of course, is a symbol of intense wisdom.

The idea of the snake's healing power has been attributed to the shedding skin. The ancient Chinese saw the human process of rejuvenation as a person splitting their old skin and emerging once more as young. The Melanesians say that to slough ones skin means eternal life. We can find similar reasoning in both Judaism and Christianity.

St. Paul's snake, Malta.

The whole concept we will be discussing in this book, though, gives us another interpretation. To truly achieve gnosis or intense wisdom, we must kill off our old self. This old self is full of what Christians call *sin*, and I call *the cause of suffering*. We must eradicate this part of ourselves (the egocentric self) and thereby release the real Us, as if shedding the skin of the dead serpent.

Snakes have been identified with the patron god of healers, Aesculapius. The Caduceus of Aesculapius, a symbol of medicine and healing, shows two intertwining snakes. The daughter of Aesculapius, Hygeia, is sometimes depicted with a serpent at her breast, or even a snake in a chalice. She, of course, gave us our word *hygiene*. Buddha is said to have taken the form of a snake to stop disease among his people. The Norse god Siegfried bathed in the blood of the dragon he slew and became invulnerable. The blind emperor Thedosius recovered his sight when a grateful serpent laid a precious gem upon his eyes, and Cadmus and his wife were literally turned into snakes to cure the ills of mankind.

During the medieval period, the snake was generally regarded as a symbol of evil, yet still had links with healing. Adder stones, thought to be formed from the skins of fighting adders, were used to heal cataracts. Dried snake heads were used to cure snake bites, and snake skins were worn about the head to prevent headaches or around other parts of the body to ward off rheumatism. Adder venom was even used to induce abortions. Old ideas developed that medical skill could be gained by eating some part of a serpent, the idea being that we could assimilate the snake's healing qualities.

On the slopes of Aventine, one of the seven hills of Rome, there used to be a temple to the earth goddess Bona Dea, which was said to be a kind of herbarium. Even here, in this sacred place of healing, there were snakes. They were kept as symbols of the healing art, and possibly kept for other more practical reasons, which are often ignored by dogmatic historians.

In Kashmir, the ancient serpent tribes were famous for their medical skill, and attributed this to their health-giving snakes. The ancient Psylli of Africa and the Ophiogenes of Cyprus were worshippers of the serpent, and this association alone enabled them to heal people. The infamous father of medicine, Galen, admitted to having requested help from the Marsi people who inhabited the central mountainous area of Italy. The Marsi were snake hunters, charmers, and excellent druggists. They were said to have immunity from snake poison, and sold venom antidotes. Galen eventually learned of a prescription that contained 75 substances, including flesh of a viper. Aristotle claimed that the Scythians used a deadly poison arrow made from decomposed snake tissue and human blood.

The snake is deeply rooted in the mythology of the world. There is no other animal on the planet with such strong and widespread mythology, tradition, medicinal value, and folklore. From ancient pre-civilization to modern medicine, the use or the symbol of the serpent is ever present. There simply must be more to this massive and worldwide phenomenon than an ability to slough off skin. There must be a bigger reason for archetypal figures to imitate its act of rebirth and rejuvenation. This reason is very simple—the snake has within it the ability to heal and extend life, as no other mineral, animal, or plant on this planet. It has been used for this purpose for thousands of years. It was the first and, in my opinion, will be the last. But there is even more. The snake is the physical manifestation of an amazing and universal wisdom that goes to the very heart of mankind's psychology.

Front of Prudence holding wise serpent.

Reverse of Prudence, revealing bearded male head, hence duality in wisdom.

How much longer can we ignore the ramifications of the role of the serpent in mankind's history? We began in *The Serpent Grail* to walk towards the truths that lie behind the use of this amazing animal in the myths, traditions, religions, and folklore of the world. The snake or serpent is at every level of our belief systems. It is derided and held aloft; it kills us and cures us. It is the perfect symbol of duality. How can this reptile have anything more to do with mankind than the healing aspect? It is at the heart of human evolutionary consciousness.

Chapter 2

THE KUNDALINI

We now know just how widespread the worship of the serpent was in ancient times. We also know how the beliefs in the properties of the serpent varied from the straightforward physical aspects (such as the sloughing of the skin) to the more mystical and metaphysical (such as the associated ideas of rebirth and wisdom). In *The Serpent Grail* we covered the physical aspects of this worship, as well as some of the aspects regarding higher consciousness. But now we must understand the metaphysical relationship of the serpent to the ancient wisdom traditions. Through this we shall build the elements in our mind, which will help us to accept those sparks of enlightenment.

First, we must come to some basic understandings of the origin and belief surrounding *serpent energy*, which can be found on the Asian subcontinent. India is the home of an ancient and great religion that we have found to be at the root of much Western belief—Naga worship. The Naga were cobra deities or devas (Shining Ones). They guarded wonderful treasures in subterranean or subaquatic realms; the treasures were, and still are, the amazing secrets of various wisdom traditions. They are the keys to a higher consciousness—what we term the *superconscious state*. The snake or serpent guards these elements of wisdom in hidden places, which we could equate to the unconscious world. It is through the symbol of the serpent energy that this superconscious state is obtainable—the unconscious becoming and being conscious.

The serpent energy, which is said to enable our access to this superconscious state, has many names and appearances: Solar Force, Solar Fire, Serpent Fire, and the Holy Spirit, as well as appearing as the fire of the Persian Zoroastrians, who gave us the Magi of the New Testament. It was the fire that licked above the heads of the disciples in Acts 2 as the Holy Spirit came upon them, and is none other than the origin of the biblical saying "Christ is all and in all."

Through the centuries, the adepts of this wonderful and spiritual belief have been passing on their wisdom to travellers such as Apollonius of Tyana. Some people believe that Yeshua, the supposed blueprint of Jesus Christ, was taught the beliefs of the serpent energy. Alexander the Great, who is known to have had serpentine tendencies, travelled to the east and seemingly took with him an authority bestowed by the serpent fire. In modern times, seekers from the west have made the journey to seek out ultimate knowledge among the spiritual elite of India. From Madame Helene Blavatsky to George Harrison, the famous, infamous, and completely unknown have seen something in India that struck a chord with their desires to learn about their own inner reality and the ultimate truth.

What lays at the center of the worship of the serpent is an intricate system, which mankind has found to actually heighten awareness of the self. This system involves elements many will already be aware of, and others will fail to understand. This failure to comprehend the teachings of the East is simply due to a cultural divide between the Christian Orthodox, capitalist, and greed-orientated west and the self-realising, patient, and introspective East. The language of both cultures has, over time, developed a vast gulf of misunderstanding. The Indo-European root of the English language has split from its origins so much that understanding the Indian language or the English language will be difficult, if not impossible, for either side. Add to this the esoteric depth and local customs and dialects, and we basically have little chance, without aid, in comprehending each other. But we must start somewhere, and so we shall begin by breaking down the various elements of the Kundalini system— which is related to various wisdom traditions and is central to the secret of the Temple of Solomon.

The Chakra Systems

The word *chakra* is Sanskrit, and means *wheel*. Some describe it as wheels of energy that are found at certain chakra locations on the body. There are seven basic locations, that are believed to relate metaphysically to the endocrine glands which are found along the spine.

In Hinduism and many other beliefs, the coiled serpent is said to rise up the spine through the various metaphysical glands or chakras, enlightening the individual as each vortex is energized. The serpent is said to twist through three-and-a-half turns, and if we take into account the dual nature of serpent energy, this becomes the number seven.

The spinning chakra vortices are the source of multicolored auras, which mystics say envelops the body like a sphere or egg. This may be the source of the egg illustrations commonly found in alchemical texts. It is in this way that each chakra produces the colors of the *septenary spectrum*.

Evidence for the reality of auras and possibly the chakras can be found in the existence of Kirlian photography and the many well-documented accounts of people who are able to see them. These people include a fair number of doctors and physicists.[1]

Kirlian Photography

It was discovered by Semyan Kirlian in 1939, when either he or another (it is disputed) received an electric shock while undergoing electrotherapy. The shock caused a spark, and Kirlian became curious as to what would happen if he put light-sensitive material in the path of the spark. After much experimentation, Kirlian managed to photograph an aura around his hand. Biophysicist Victor Inyushin of the Kirov State University in Russia concluded that the photograph showed the existence of what he called *biological plasma*. This concept relates to healing powers, where better photographs have been achieved using the hands of healers. *Plasma*, in this context, is the name given to the collection of positive and negative ions, and is neither solid, liquid, nor gas. It has no electrical charge, due to the fact that there are equal amounts of positive and negative ions. In other words, it is neutral, as these positive and negative ions are in equilibrium and cancel each other out. This balance has remarkable implications for the experience of enlightenment, which is the root of the word *shining*. It was discovered that Kirlian auras increase at the same time as cyclic solar flares, therefore bringing a remarkable union between human enlightenment (or illumination) and the physical illumination of the sun. The outer sun and the inner sun are working together.

This healing energy relates to electromagnetic—or what some would term *paramagnetic*—energy. It is found particularly in the round towers of the world, and especially in volcanic rock. It is believed that the energy is imparted to the rock over millions of years of constant grinding and crushing. This same energy has been shown to make plants grow faster and to help heal sick people. Although still on the fringes of science, this new psuedo-science (as it is often called) is creeping into the mainstream.

In many cases, the auras are said to have seven layers, with each layer getting progressively denser. We can associate these layers with the seven levels of the chakra. At this stage I want to divert our attention for a moment to the use of the number seven in many areas of myth, religion, and folklore. This is something that we shall return to periodically throughout the book.

As the reader will be aware, the number seven has become (in the West) a lucky number,

Pharmaceutical sign in Paris showing serpent and Grail.

and is of great importance to our lives, as there are seven days in the week, seven colors in the septenary color system, and much more. But it is only when we combine various uses of the number in religion, folklore, and myth that we begin to see just how important this number was to the ancients, and possibly how this may relate to the chakra system. The following is a brief list of the use of sevens.

Sevens

- The biblical Joshua walked around Jericho (the first civilization, according to some, and home to the largest group of Shamans) seven times. It took seven stages to bring the sinful world, or lower nature, crumbling down.

- Seven heavens are to be found in the Koran, the Bible, and in the traditions of the Shaman and Druids. These seven heavens relate to the levels of enlightenment associated with the Hindu chakra system.

- There are seven steps to heaven, which is a popular belief found on many ziggurats and pyramids.

- There are seven deadly sins and seven virtues. These are methods of balance as we move up the chakra system— negatives and positives—balancing out desires with wisdom.

- Life has seven cycles, according to tradition. This emerges from the cycles of enlightenment as we grow older.

- There are seven sacraments according to the Christian Church.

- The seventh son of the seventh son is, by Jewish tradition, believed to have great healing powers.

- Magic boots that allow the wearer to walk seven leagues in one stride. The story goes back to the mythical magic of the giants or men of renown. These are the *Egregores* or *Watchers*, also known as Shining Ones.

- Seven days in a week match the days in creation. The creative principle of man must follow the seven-fold path.

- The Hebraic *to swear on oath* means to come under the influence of the seven, which could possibly infer the seven planets.

- The seven Argive heroes of Greek legend.

- The seven champions of English legend.

- The seven seas and the seven wonders of the ancient world.

- There are seven gifts of the spirits. These are obviously linked to the seven levels of the chakra system, enlightening the spirit within.

- The seven-headed snake in the images from the Naga worship of India, and those of Sumeria atop the sacred tree.

- There are seven Japanese gods of luck.

- There are seven joys and sorrows of Mary.

- The seven sages of Greece or Wise Men of Greece.

- There are seven sciences.

- Man has seven senses, according to the ancients. They are under the influence of the seven planets of classical times, and as we shall discover, these are in reality the seven planets within us: fire moves us, earth gives the sense of feeling, water gives speech, air gives taste, mist gives sight, flowers give hearing, and the southwind gives us our sense of smell.

- There are seven elementary hues to the spectrum. When blended together, they form white.

- We also see the same theme of seven at the microcosmic level: The atom has up to seven inner orbits called *electron shells*, and these seven orbits, shells, or levels reflect the levels of the electromagnetic spectrum.

- We see the same use of sevens in man, who is believed to stand between the macrocosm (universe) and the microcosm (atomic or subatomic world), for aligning the human spine are the seven chakra vortices, which reflect the seven levels of consciousness and existence.

The ancients believed that our thoughts and actions mirror the chakra level at which our own energy is working. If we are thinking on a purely base level, then our energy vortices will be wheeling or whirling at the lowest chakra level. The more creative or intelligent we become, then the higher the chakra level of energy.

It is also believed that, at each level, the whirling energy chakra has poles of energy, both positive and negative. In order for our energy to be raised upwards, these polarities must come into a balanced union, or fuse to reveal the neutral energy state. It is a little like trying to walk up the stairs with one foot—it is extremely difficult to get to the top if we do not employ both feet! The element of this fusion becomes apparent to those who have achieved the enlightened state, as they experience both energy states at one time. They experience the full being, known in kabbalistic terms as the *chesed*.

The apex is said to be the center of the seventh chakra, known by the Hindus as the *bindu*. It is said to be located at a point just above the head, and has been described by psychics as a mini-vortex that grows taller and brighter (similar to a flame) when people are in a joyous state. (I believe that this reflects the raising of the energy of the serpent.) Indeed, Kirlian photography has picked up this peculiar aura in spiritually enlightened individuals—indicating a heightened electromagnetic activity. This also matches with the image described in Acts 2 of the Bible, where the disciples are said to have flames licking above their heads and are born again or illuminated. Today we see the ancient depiction of this effect on our images of wizards, with their tall, conical hats.

In the seven-level chakra system, the bindu is the octave point, and could also paradoxically be referred to as *level 9*, which in occult lore is often symbolized by the *lemniscate* or *infinity symbol*—a horizontal figure eight. The lemniscate is derived from an intertwined serpent, and is often found above the head of the adept in occult symbolism. Similar imagery comes down to us in the halos around the heads of saints or holy people. This is revealing, as the dot at the center of a circle is still seen as the highest and most important symbol of the Freemasons.

Shining aspect of angelic being from Kykkos Monastery in Cyprus.

The seventh chakra level is associated with the pineal and pituitary glands in the brain, which are thought to activate during meditation. This is why these particular chakra centers and related endocrine glands were considered important to the ancients. Much of this ideology has been incorporated into great and monumental structures around the globe, including the Great Pyramid at Giza and other pyramids scattered across the world.

There is compelling evidence that the ancients understood that these seven levels are also expressed in the tiny building blocks of matter we called *atoms* or *subatomic particles*. It's no surprise to find that, intuitively, our ancestors were correct, even if they were not instructed in this knowledge. In this respect, I personally believe in the intuitive aspect as related by the author Jeremy Narby in *The Cosmic Serpent*. Having spoken to many subjects over the years who have experienced altered states of consciousness, I have found a remarkable number who saw what they could only describe as atoms, particles, and sometimes DNA. Research across the globe has now shown this to be a universal experience.

The nucleus of an atom has up to seven energy layers or orbits surrounding it—much like the layers of an onion, or the seven auras seen by mystics. It would make sense for the pattern to be continued from the microcosmic to the macrocosmic—from atom to man. The specific level on which the electron finds itself at any particular time depends entirely on the amount of energy (more specifically light-energy) that it is absorbing or emitting. In order for the electron to escape the atom, the energy levels must rise so that eventually, the electron is so excited or energized that it can escape the atom. The vortex created by this energy whirling around is similar to the chakra vortices. In this way the mind can actually affect matter on the subatomic level. These escaped and charged electrons are then caught by other atoms, and information is passed from one atom to the next. This is how information at the atomic level is passed, and this is the science of the chakra system. An action that was once described in religious terms is now defined in science.

If it is true that there can be mind over matter, in that our concentrated thoughts can affect atoms and even subatoms, then it may be true that what we are really doing is transferring energy by thought. In this way, the chakra system of improved mental capabilities affecting our own self and our own health may have more truth than previously assumed. Our thoughts may raise the energy discovered in the atom. Partner this with the theory of quantum entanglement (whereby particles across any distance can entangle with each other) and we might have the amazing ability to alter matter from a distance by mere thought. What the ancients have been telling us all along may be true.

What we must do, in order to improve our own lives, is not so much escape from the atom, but look inside the atom. The many wisdom traditions of the globe all tell us, in their own way, to escape the cycles or vortices of reality and find the *eye of the storm*, which is the central location in any vortex. This is the escape from *samsara*, the constant cycles of life. To reach the center is to achieve *nirvana*.

Experimentation

During the research and writing of this book I was contacted several times by a young researcher who was keen to test these ideas. This young man did so, and the following e-mails briefly summarize his reactions. I would like to point out that this is by no means the right path towards enlightenment, but certain aids can help in gaining insight into the workings of the mind.

> 24th Sept. 2004
>
> You asked in the last e-mail to keep you up to date regarding them [the reactions]. Well since then I've had two more noteworthy experiences. Another thing is that I've had a dream in which I saw a lion and a bear I think chasing me or something. I didn't really remember the dream clearly. There were also golden coins I think in it

which I had to feed to either one. I think it has a connection to it because David in the old testament also fought or killed a bear and a lion, and if this as the mystic Neville Goddard claimed was an archetypical story recorded that would happen to everyone that starts to experience the process, like seeing these things as visions, there may be the connection.

■

2 Nov 2004

Hi. Last night I started experiencing another effect I think is from gold, [this is the term given to the substance used] probably in conjunction with Kundalini energy. I started noticing the typical effect of prana...pressure and slight heat, this at three spots: base of the spine, upper back of the head, and left side of the neck. With that, at the solar plexus area (same spot actually where I felt effects before, which I think is the solar plexus), again the distinct energy flow which felt similar to what I felt before there...some kind of love/acceptance feeling but this time more fluid, less fixed into a wellbeing feeling and very emotional. Quite different from the other prana effects at the three spots previously described. With these feelings, I started noticing an inner vision/sight again, which actually seemed to be in tune with what I was feeling as coming from the solar plexus. Now what I saw was, a sort of basement, crypt, cellar setting, and I could feel the setting not just see it, and a corpse...no not a corpse, but something that felt very old, very ancient, and looked like a dust composed human shape, like a very worn mummy kind of thing, almost like a husk of dust and earthy substance. It came alive. Well, it felt like becoming alive, I was feeling it become animated by that energy, and it felt like being me, I felt like being regenerated. Not resurrected, just made alive, that's the best description of it. Literally there was a feeling of that dead thing being me and becoming alive. At that point I was reasoning along the lines of: "oh no not now I don't want this to happen now," and I used will to put a lock on energy flow and broke off the experience, with which all faded. I actually don't really want it to happen yet but I guess it might continue sometime, but it's all very emotional. I wanted my physical body to feel more okay and feel more comfortable before letting it continue, and not have it happen when I don't feel physically right for it. Also with that experience, I think right before the vision, but I'm not sure it could have been during or afterwards, I had a very strong prana surge, the kind that felt like sexual energy, which originated around the genital area and wanted to rise into my body, and actually felt like wanting to make me have an energy orgasm and an erection, which is typical for that kind of energy. This experience to me has a distinct connection with the rebirth. What I saw looks as alluding to it. It all felt very emotional. Felt kind of unusual too. And it's so different from normal dreams or mental sights, just because of the heavy feeling connection.

■

10 Dec 2004

The last post I sent about my experiences was one where I said I had a distinctive feeling at the solar plexus and vagus nerve, base chakra and bindu chakra (upper back of the head), and I saw an inner sight of a cellar/crypt like setting, with a corpse or corpse like remains, that seemed to come alive and be animated and it felt like being me, I really had the feeling along with the energy sensation at the solar plexus. A few days ago I flipped some pages in the book *The Red Lion* and read that Hans Burgner after he partook of the potion awakened to find himself in a crypt. I was suggested to read some Neville Goddard by someone, and in one of his transcribed lectures I read that when he awoke from the dream of reality, he found himself in his skull, and felt like he awoke for the first time in a long time. I also had a very distinctive feeling of something like that during that experience. Like I was made alive again. But some time after that experience happened, I had something else happen. I saw myself as a full grown body, as another me, again in that paradise like other realm setting. It was with that inner sight again and very distinctive, I didn't get a full clear sight or rather said right now in the here I don't recall it all, but I saw it thrice (or four times, not sure about the fourth) and the first and second time were quite clear and real, actually feeling more real than here. The first time I really was startled when I saw it. Not only had I not expected it, but it/I also looked good. It/I looked like a very perfected refined version of me here, and there was a feeling associated with it, with that observance, that I can only describe as princely. I also knew it was me, just like when I had these other sights. I also had golden-blonde hair and there was a red sheen or red hue to it all. Now I don't have continuous awareness of that body or of me as that state, but sometimes, I do have the impression that I am shifting towards in, and this world seems again more like, not a dream, but like a play, I'm distancing from, and sort of shifting out. This state-awareness usually is easier to manifest after I took or am under a shower. I think it's the water steam that does it. I think steamed hot water is special energetically.

I even read a reference to it being used alchemically to increase the stone in virtue. It may perhaps be the heat that charges and evaporates the ormes in water. Back to the body—I think this is an energy body or template, which may need to be merged with the physical, or maybe connected to it by more ormes ingestion.

■

As we can see, the subject went through an incredible experience—and was lucky enough to be lucid enough to explain his experiences, emotions, and reactions. But our ancestors did not need to revert to drugs to access this world of energy and information. They simply developed ways of entering the third state or neutral state, which exists between the opposites. This is elementary balance, running between the powerful push and pull of the negative and positive charges within the atomic world. It would take a superconscious state to enable the conscious control of this level of reality. It appears from all the ancient texts and symbols that this is precisely what the wisdom traditions are telling us. Each and every one tells us to reach within and find the real *Inner Reality*, and to bring this into a kind of balance. In each case, this spiralling energy is seen as or symbolized by the serpent. It is a universal archetype.

References to the chakra system can also be found on ancient Sumerian, Assyrian, and Persian cylinder seals. Most common are the illustrations of a tree-like column, complete with seven or more branches on either side—the sacred tree. The tree is usually flanked by two figures, which may represent the two opposites. The tree is the World or Shamanic Tree, which is none other than the Tree of Life or the Tree of Knowledge. The tree symbolises the spinal column, while the branches represent the chakra vortices.

The secret of the Kundalini (and other important and similar systems) exists in rising upwards through the chakra locations. In one form or another, this has been known for thousands of years. It was of profound importance to the ancients. It was so important that massive and complex structures (not to mention thousands of ancient texts and works of art) have been created, protected, and revered by millions of individuals, century after century. But this system is just a stepping stone to the opening of the *Third Eye* or *Eye of Ra*. Once opened and activated, this amazing human system could lead thousands of people on mystical journeys that have long puzzled mankind.

Chapter 3

THE SHINING

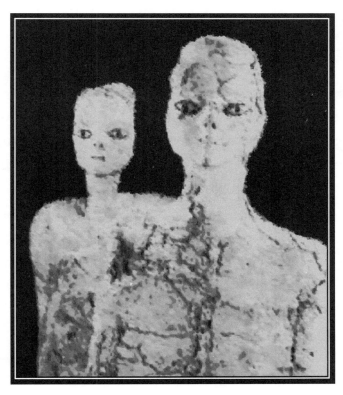

"The Shining Ones" watercolor by P. Gardiner.

N ow we must turn to a term that I have found in my book *The Shining Ones* to be universal and always related to the enlightenment experience. It is related to a brotherhood that spanned the globe with their religious impulse, originally derived from the enlightenment experience. This experience comes directly from the internal chemical, electrical, and biological reactions to our own thought processes. It is, in essence, something we can create ourselves, and this is quite simply the divinity within ourselves. It is spoken of—in hidden language—by many ancient and modern writers.

In this chapter we shall bring ourselves up to date with this term. We will become familiar with its place in ancient cultures and the reasoning behind its use. For more on this subject, I must guide you to the book *The Shining Ones*, which goes into some depth on the matter.

The Shining Priests

The Shining Ones are a secret religious brotherhood that date back to at least 5,000 years before Christ, and who aided in the formation of the modern world. All religions, ancient monuments, and governments (including royal families) have their background in the Shining Ones.

The early messiahs were gurus and shaman who understood how the world worked in their own unique way; they received much of their knowledge while in the trance state and the inner-enlightenment experience. Later, their descendants used that information and knowledge to their advantage. Then came the priests and kings, with their cyclical birth/death/resurrection rituals that mimicked the roles of the internal actions required to achieve enlightenment. From there, organized religions developed, which became the perfect way to control the people. Those who controlled were not true adepts of the experience—they were copyists who manifested the magic for power.

On my journey to uncover the Shining Ones, I learned that history (as we know it) is a lie. History is, as Justice Holmes said, "what the people who won say it is." The truth has been warped beyond recognition over vast periods of time to fit with each generation's idea of what is reality. When we leave old religions behind, we are simply given a new one, which is usually more relevant to our age and to the political aims of the current power brokers. But the new belief systems are commonly based on the same old lies and the belief that man is too simple to understand secret knowledge. Our belief systems, whether religious, scientific, or political, have been manipulated by secret (and sometimes sinister) groups of individuals who can trace a history going back thousands of years. They have a name, they have a power base, and they have a secret (locked away within their initiated few), which has major implications for the future of mankind. This secret is the internal process of enlightenment, which has been jealously guarded from the masses. These secrets hidden by the elect have been taken literally over the ensuing years, so that today we search for a fake bloodline of Christ, go on voyages to find Atlantis, or dig to find Joseph of Arimathea's grave.

Once we decipher the Shining Ones' clues, we can see how the mysteries of the ancient world could be solved, from the megalithic standing stones to the Holy Grail, and alchemy to the truth behind religion and our present political systems. We must forget the false interpretations of myth and religion we have heard so many times, and know them for what they really are: the secret language of the Shining Ones taken literally by those individuals still searching for truth. Behind this elite religious group, which formed the entire religious establishments of the globe, past and present, is a fundamental process within the mind and brain of enlightenment—*the shining*.

We have seen how the number seven has been important and related to the Kundalini and chakra systems. We have also seen how the seven colors of the spectrum, when combined, create the color white. This external or macrocosmic perception of light is exactly the same internally, when all seven levels of the chakra system are achieved. Basically, an enlightened person becomes white light or shining. This is the color of wholeness or *Oneness*, which we shall find later on to be important in the search for Solomon's Temple.

White or Shining Figures

White, bright, or shining words or figures are indicative of the way of truth. White appears again and again in stories relating to our ancient and mystical monuments. In popular myth and traditional fairy stories, white ladies usually dwell in great white towers or atop mysterious snowcapped

The Great Pyramid, photo courtesy of John Bodsworth.

mountains. These towers or mountains are nothing more than the full achievement of the highest chakra system—they are the World Tree, and the white is the shining at the top.

In the German *White Lady* myth she is called Bertha, which was the name of the Great Goddess of Nature. In the city of Megiddo in ancient Palestine there is a horned altar to the Mother Goddess (from around 2,000 B.C.). The stone is purposefully sculpted white lime. In China, there is the infamous grand story of *Lady White Snake*. The Great Pyramid at Giza was covered with whitewashed plaster and possibly topped with gold. The Egyptians called it the *Light*, and it would have been visible for hundreds of miles, calling and reminding people to worship the Great Light or Shining One.

Borobudur (on the island of Java) means *Temple of the Countless Buddhas* or *Temple of the Infinite Enlightened One*. There is a huge ziggurat-shaped pyramid with three stone circles of bell-shaped *stupas* on top. The idea of the temple was for the initiated to walk around the false mountain and read or see the reliefs, which stretched for 5 kilometers around the lower square base. When the initiate understood the reliefs, he or she could move up to the top of the heaven mountain and become holy. This shape is derived from a burial mound on the plains of Central Asia, which is indicative of the rest of the burial mounds of Europe. Seen partly as a *mandala* (Sanskrit for *circle*), the circles symbolize wholeness as well as the cycle of life. The cross between the stone circles, the pyramid, the burial mound, and the procession running up to the top links all the major constructions of the globe together, as if those who built the Borobudur structure (in around A.D. 900) knew the various paths of religion around the globe and were party to their planning and sacred architecture. The temple is truly a massive structure of the inner process we must all go through to achieve enlightenment. It is truth, and we must not skirt around it or ignore it. Reality, we are told, is more than that which you can touch.

The people of Borobudur moved further east and influenced China and Japan, or at least that is what some archaeologists believe. It may be true that they were all from the same root anyway, and just did things a little differently. A similarity that occurs in mystical thought is that the ancient stone sites in Java (including Borobudur) are claimed to be situated on *energy spots* and to be in located lines. These are as the *Ley Lines* of Europe. One remarkable thing to remember about Borobudur is that, when it was first built, it was painted white, and it shined like a celestial city in the sky.

In North America, oral tradition claims that sacred and holy people exist on tall mountains, and are called the *Great White Brotherhood*. These are the *Lemurians*, or people from the days of the past who are advanced souls and who help us through our evolution. They are guiding us through the generations, with a set goal in mind for mankind. They inhabit etheric monasteries and make themselves visible in the light at certain times in history. Could there be a subtle clue in this tradition as to the influence and historical identity of these people who hold our lives in their hands? What is their goal and how do they carry out their purposes? If they exist (and conspiracy theories are impossible to prove incorrect by their very nature), then they have produced Buddha, Jesus Christ, Muhammad, and any number of other enlightened beings, all for our improvement— whether literally or symbolically.

We have linked the color white, and by extension the white horse, with all that is good and godly as far back as the Hindu story of Vishnu returning to earth on a white, shining horse. This may be a clue to the whereabouts of the Shining Ones in our past. Wherever such a horse is depicted was likely a place where the ancient priesthood was situated. Ancients believed that the horse was symbolic of the sun god. The image was placed upon the Mother Earth in union, and it depicted the presence of mystical learning. It would follow that the Shining Ones themselves would wear garments of white as an outward sign of their inner enlightenment. We must be careful, though, not to include everybody as Shining Ones just because of the color associations. The situation, role, and time must be taken into account.

Ancient bards wore white. They were the tellers of tales, and the keepers and makers of history. It was these people who creatively wove our history and religions. They made these stories more real in the minds of the ordinary people. The stories they told and the morals they posited became real. The tales of King Arthur and his round table inspired thousands of knights and kings, and moved nations into action. (It was also used and abused by the ruling class to feed propaganda to the masses.) Queen Elizabeth I was just one monarch to claim descent from Arthur, and even the current monarch is still regarded as a descendent of the true bloodline. Bards were employed by the ruling class. They were also wandering oracles who were held in awe by the common people. In many cases it became a crime to upset a bard. They were surely deeply involved in manipulating the people, or at least being manipulated themselves.

The Romans noted that the inheritors of the stone circles, the Druids, also wore white. With the background of the Druids steeped in myth, and the fact that in all probability their ancestors were the people who built the stone monuments all over Europe and Central Asia, there can be no doubt as to the reason why they wore the "Shining" color.

The eye of god shining within the triangle trinity, Rome.

Elsewhere, the priests of Osiris were adorned with a white crown over their Third Eye to guide them. The Priests of Jupiter also wore white. The Magi and Persian priests wore white, and said that their gods did also. The Romans carried the serpentine Caduceus staff, which was white.

From discoveries of chalk and limestone balls at or around stone circles, it has been hypothesised that the stones were painted white to shine like the Great Pyramid. In Ireland, white quartz central stones occur in a number of circles. Even today, many stones (when struck by the sun on the solstice) shine a brilliant white without any paint. The chalk may have also been used as a marker for the floor, so that our ancient friends could map the shadows for their predictions and time calculations. The mandala of the Hindu and Buddhist beliefs was a circle of life. The priests frequently drew the mandala on the floor with special powder for various initiation rites. Was this practice carried out on or around stone circles? Was this a nomadic stone circle? Was it universal? I believe that it was probably an initiation device.

The psychologist Carl Jung said that the mandala was a "universally occurring pattern associated with the mythological representation of the self." It is still used today as a therapeutic tool. The Maoris of New Zealand represent their deities as standing stones in the ground; the Kafirs of India worshipped stones; Mithra, the great bull god, was born of a rock; and Moses said we all came from a rock. The rock or stone was therefore a physical manifestation of the Shining Divinity.

To fully realise the extent of the term *shining* in ancient texts and culture, I have detailed a quick list of some of the deities and beings with which the term is either associated, or where it is used as a title. It is only by realising the universal use of the term that we can comprehend the wide nature and meaning of it.

- Actaeon—meaning *Shining One*. He was depicted as horned.

- Aelf—Anglo Saxon term meaning *Shining Being*, and giving rise to the term *elf*, who are now seen as wise, elegant, and sublime characters.

- Agni—a Hindu god whose name means *Shining One*. He illuminates the sky. In this we can see the cross association with the sun.

- Akh—Egyptian term meaning *Shining Soul*. Note the use of the term in the names of certain pharaohs, such as Akh-en-Aten, the Egyptian king who is said to have worshipped the Outer Sun only.

- Anannage—from the Sumerian creation myths, the Great Sons of Anu or Great Sons of the Shining One. They were the original Shining Ones, similar to the Hebrew Anakim and the Angakok of Greenland.

- Angel—Semite word *El,* meaning both *angel* and *shining*.

- Archangel Michael—He who is Shining.

- Barbes—Waldensian pastors, meaning *Shining Lights*.

- Bodhisattvas—Buddhist Holy Men and regarded as Shining Ones.

- Devas—Sanskrit for *Shining One*; minor deities of Hinduism and Buddhism, and relating to aspects of the inner self, where the true shining exists.

- Du-w—linked phonetically with Yahweh; means *Shining One* or *One Without Darkness*.

- Dyaus Pittar—Shining Father.

- Elijah—Shining Prophet.

- Elohim—The biblical term for *Lord*, but actually meaning the plural *the Shining Ones*, indicating that these were originally a group of respected humans of Sumerian origin, as can be seen in the etymology of the language. Also a term for the *heavenly host* or *the stars of heaven*.

- Emanuel—derives from the Egyptian Ammun-u-El, meaning *Amum is Shining*. Emanuel, therefore, gives us *The Shining One Is With Us*.

- Fatima—daughter of the Prophet Mohammed; meaning *Shining One*. She was said to be virginal, and her title was *bright blooming*.

- Gaumanek—a Shaman term for the enlightenment process; means *to be illuminated* or *to shine*.

- Helios—a Sun God depicted on a shining horse.

- Hu—means *Shining Light*, and is the root of many names of god/deities, such as Lugh, Dyhu, Taou, and Huish.

- Isis—the great Queen of Heaven (a term used for Mary, Mother of God). She governed the Shining Heights.

- Kether—a kabbalistic reference to the crown, meaning *Crown of Pure Brilliance*, or *Shining One*.

- Lampon—the horse of Diomedes, also called the *Shining One*.

- Melchior—one of the Magi who visited Jesus at his birth. He was King of Light or Shining One. These Magi supposedly derived their knowledge from the Brahmans of India.

- Moses—emergent serpent. He came down from Mount Sinai with Shining Skin and was Shining Forth.

- Ra—the Great Egyptian Shining One in the sky.

- Raphael—Shining Healer.

- Seraphim—supposedly angelic beings, but having all the attributes of humans, with faces, hands, and legs. Their wings were symbolic of the Shaman flight. They existed in light, and were thus termed the *Shining One*s.

- Skinfaxi—the Norse mythological horse means the *Shining Mane*.

- Tuatha de Danaan—Sons of the Tribe of Danu or People of Danu, related to the Anannage. D'anu the Shining One is the origin of the name *Denmark*, and various other European sites. They were the mythological inhabitants of Ireland, having arrived there from Egypt, according to some. The name *Dan* is male and *Danu* female—two versions of the same deity.

- Shining Ones—the remnant of the biblical Raphaim (*rapha*=healing, hence Raphael the archangel was the *shining healer*) was Og the giant, linked with Ogma from Sumeria, which in turn was linked with Cerne Abbas, which in turn is linked with Dyaeus, which means the *Shining Ones*. Therefore, King Og of Bashen in the Bible is the remnant king of the Shining Ones.

- Quetzalcoatl—means *Light of Day*, suggesting he is very bright.

- Helios—depicted as a shining horse.

- Lampon—the horse of Diomedes is the *Shining One*.

- The Nile—said to be the healer of mankind who 'shines when he issues forth from the darkness.'

- Beards—Giants are said to have beards, as this relates stature, power, manhood, and enlightenment, and is common throughout the history of the Shining Ones. Pharaohs of Egypt (including Queens) wore either real or false beards. Baal wore a beard, which relates to our image of the Christian God having a beard. The men of Islam wear beards. Samson loses power when his beard is destroyed. Samson was a member of the

Nazerites, who all had beards. The Essene wore beards. El, the Canaanite god, also has a beard and is the image of a bull. Jupiter is associated with Adonis, which was the other title used by the Jews for God, and means the *Shining One*. Quetzalcoatl had a beard. Druids had beards.

Shining Moses with horns in the Spanish quarter of Rome.

- Crosses—North American shaman are suspended by their wrists in the style of crucifixion, taking them in a trance to the Otherworld and coming back with powers. Odin was sacrificed on the Tree of Life and visited the underworld. Hindu temples and in the shape of a cross. Burial tombs all over Europe are in the shape of a cross. The Great Pyramid at Giza forms a cross on the ground at summer solstice. Hindus form a cross by stretching their arms out as an initiate tries to gain salvation. Quetzalcoatl's symbol was a cross. The Golden Fleece of classical myth stood for immortality, and it was hung on a tree.

- Trinity—three Shaman worlds. Three kinds of devas or Shining Ones in Hindu. Triad of Hinduism: Brahman, Vishnu, and Shiva. The Christian Trinity: God the Father, the Son, and the Holy Spirit (Ghost—being an old pagan idea). Book of Dead in Egypt includes three streaming rays of Shining Light hitting the soul of the initiated. Thrice Great Hermes comes out of the balancing act between Thoth, Tammuz, Hermes, and Mercury. Zoroaster would return three times. Three Magi brought three gifts to the birth of Jesus. Jesus was crucified on a mountain with three crosses. There are three chatras on Hindu temples.

- Duality—Shaman ideas of light and dark, good and evil, the balance. Japanese and Chinese yin-and-yang duality. Mother/Father relationships in all cultures.

- Bull—Shaman bull image for sacrifices. Egyptian sun god Ra in the image of a bull. The bull is seen throughout Old Testament. El is symbolized in the image of a bull. The Latin *apis*, meaning *bow*, is identical to the Apis, the sacred bull of Egypt.

- Rebirth—the Bhagavad Gita says, "I have been born many times." The Bible says, "You must be born again." The Egyptian Book of the Dead says, "I have the power to be born a second time." Egyptian rebirth rituals abound. Zoroaster, Osiris, Horus, Adonis, Dionysos, Hercules, Hermes, Baldur, and Quetzalcoatl all descended into hell and rose again on the third day. Vishnu said, "Every time that religion is in danger and that iniquity triumphs, I issue forth for the defence of the good and the suppression of the wicked; for the establishment of justice, I manifest myself from age to age."

- The virgin birth and the cave—Isis immaculately conceived Horus. Virgil said the messiah would be born of the Virgin Lady. Zoroaster was born of a virgin. Abraham was born in a cave. Muhammad was enlightened in a cave. Fatima the Shining One gave birth to three sons and is said to have been a virgin. In China, the virgin birth consists of treading in the footprint of God, which the mother of Hou Chi did and was born like a lamb. He was born amidst sheep and cattle, similar to Jesus.

- Circles—the mandala is a circle. The chakra wheel is tied up in energy points of the body and may be similar to the wheels on the ground of energy points. The promised land of the Aztecs was the place of the circle, or Anáhuac. Stone circles are named in the Bible as gilgal. There is an ancient traditional belief that evil spirits may not pass through a circle of candles.

In conclusion, we have a term that is universally used by (and in association with) some of the world's leading religious characters. It is a term used for the true attainment of enlightenment, and as such, the leading deities and kings must be Shining. It is also a term intricately linked with the serpent, both in etymology and in usage. The snake is the means by which we can attain the shining enlightenment. This is the same serpent that is the prana/Kundalini energy spoken of by the mystics of India in relation to the road to illumination.

Before we move on into the secret interpretations of the ancient gnostic, occult, and alchemical societies, we must ask ourselves whether there is any scientific backing to the process of enlightenment. We have already seen how the mind could possibly gain insight through consciously perceiving and manipulating the very core of the atom, but it is time to look a little deeper into this amazing part of human evolution and the emerging discoveries in science.

Chapter 4

THE VOID

The arched portal into a better place, a cemetery in Rome.

B efore we begin to look at the term *void* or *nothingness* and its meaning, we need to review the term *energy* and its relationship to the Kundalini (or similar systems) and gnosis. *Energy* is a term used by both scientists and mystics, but in different ways, and neither would necessarily agree with the other about the use of the term. For the purposes of this book, I have decided to look at both sides and see if there is a common ground between them.

This energy, as I am calling it, is nothing more than the *Serpent Fire*, *Solar Force*, or *Pranic Energy* of the serpent-worshipping mystics of the world. It is similar to the Kundalini power base, and drives the enlightenment process forward. Without the energy of the Serpent Fire, there could be no true gnosis, as true gnosis is the energy of the mind in balance. This passes on information at a subatomic level and raises energy. It is very easy to say that we must have this energy, but we must also learn how to control it. And yet what is this energy? We have touched upon the atom and how it may be possible for thought to control the energy within the atom through a process possibly related to quantum entanglement, but is there any truth to this idea?

Over the course of human history there have been thousands of individuals who have claimed to have experienced enlightenment or illumination, giving rise to the term *shining*. If it is true that mankind, across the world and across time, has been having these experiences, then they must be brought on by some kind of energy. This energy is both the electrical charge within the nervous system to the brain, and the chemical/biological reactions within our brain brought on by numerous methods of meditation, prayer, and dervish. These methods have been discovered and perfected by initiates and adepts of many cults and creeds. These methods really work; they create altered states of awareness by the electrical, biological, and chemical reactions they generate. The question that scientists are asking is simply whether the reactions are purely biological functions accidentally discovered by mankind, or if they are mystical and spiritual capacities of a higher self. The answer to this can be found within the individual, but we may find other insights by digging a little deeper.

We can see exactly why the ancients across the world chose the *tree*, *axis*, or *spine* as the conductor of this serpentine energy when we read samples of modern-day experiences. In the book *Spontaneous Human Combustion*, Jenny Randles and Peter Hough write:

> I suddenly felt some activity at the base of my spine. A feeling like shuddering, surging energy began travelling up my back. I felt as if every nerve trunk on my spine had begun firing. I could feel vortexes of electricity around places that have been described as chakras.

And again:

> Suddenly, surges of energy—like electric charges— streaked up my spine. These gradually evolved into a steady current of hot energy flowing from the tip of my spine to the top of my skull.

We can see, with Randles and Hough's use of these examples in their book on spontaneous human combustion, that this energy is a very real phenomenon. It can be quite dangerous if it is not used correctly. This is, of course, something spoken of in ancient literature—the dual nature of the serpent. We can see how this *Serpent Fire* was a powerful energy to control, and therefore a powerful symbol used by the pharaohs of Egypt as the *Uraeus* serpent on the brow. The quantum reaction of this uncontrolled energy actually causes real fire, as the atoms are agitated to such an extent that the molecular makeup of the human body can no longer contain the energy. And all of this can be caused by the human mind (in the case of those who caught fire) that is simply not in control of its own energy release.

Gopi Krishna is now infamous for his writings on the Kundalini, and is one of the very few people to have experienced what he believes to be true enlightenment through this energy. He tells us in his writings that he was often dismayed that there was nobody to help him control the process, and more than once or twice he suffered the negative sides of the Serpent Fire, including intense burning sensations. This has been put down to the burning male side of the Kundalini, which needs to be balanced with the water or female side. These are terms used for positive and negative mental controlling devices required to obtain optimum self-control.

Over time and across the world, this real and human natural phenomenon has spurned the writings and religions of hundreds of cultures. It was a mystery, both good and bad, both beneficial and dangerous. The correct balancing of this energy gave us God-head. It came to be known as the *Holy Ghost* or *Spirit* in Christian literature; in Hebrew texts it was *Rauch Ha Kodesh* or the *Holy Wind*; in Indian myth it had many names, among them *Prana* and *Liquid Fire*; in medieval alchemy it became *Serpent Fire* or *Solar Force*; in China it was *Ch'i*; in Mayan myth it was *ch'ulel* or *life essence*; in Polynesia it was *Mana*, the *Vital Force*; and to the Scandinavians it became known as *Wodan* after their God Odin. Across the world a great *brotherhood in the shining* arose, only to eventually fall into the base world of greed, desire, and control. This is almost a paradoxical situation (that enlightenment can eventually bring about such awful things) but the fact remains that human nature is based on evolutionary desires, and these desires often cause the sins of man if they are not balanced with love. The descendants of the initiator of the creed, known by most people as *the mystic*, fall away eventually from the originator's true goal, and rule instead by their own lower nature.

There are many more terms for *illumination*, but the point is that the energy is universal. Mankind has discovered this energy; he has tamed it and controlled it, and given it names that relate to his gods. He has then gone on to abuse it, as seems to be a common theme in humanity. In all cases, this energy is part of our natural makeup, and is said to be our guide and key to access the Otherworld. We are guided by the process I call *quantum entanglement* or *zero point energy*.

Zero Point Energy

In ancient Sanskrit there is a term known as *Sunya'* which, simply put, means *zero*. It is related to a modern concept known as *the void*. How is this ancient metaphysical concept of *nothingness* related to a modern quantum world we call *the void*? And how is this related to the ultimate knowledge of mankind?

In his book *Zero: The Biography of a Dangerous Idea*, Charles Seife tells us, "Today it's a timebomb ticking in the heart of astrophysics." The book follows the term *zero* from its Eastern philosophical concept to its acceptance in European science. The peculiar significance is that the Eastern philosophy of zero is actually related to both consciousness and the astrophysicists concept of black holes. The limitless energy of the vacuum, known today as *zero point energy*, is based on the same philosophical concepts.

Imagine a large sea or lake. We know that this body of water is made up of tiny molecules, which themselves are made up of atoms. Inside these atoms we discover a miniature solar system, not dissimilar to the macrocosmic solar systems so prevalent in the universe. This miniature solar system is made up of a nucleus (which is equated with the sun) with electrons revolving around it (as though they are mini-planets). The space between these tiny stars and planets is the science of the void, and is not different than the void of space between the sun and its orbiting planets. In fact, the majority of both the miniature solar system and that of the macrocosmic solar system is made up of this void. Incredibly, if we were to travel even farther into the center of the nucleus, we would find exactly the same thing again.

This relationship between the miniature and the macrocosmic reveals to us the truths behind the concepts of "as above, so below" from the infamous Hermetic *Emerald Tablet*, which has been attributed to Hermes Trismegistus. In fact, I claimed in *The Serpent Grail* and *The Shining Ones* that this void is the true reality of existence and that the matter of the electron, particle, or even atom is nothing more than creation from within the void. The void is the true creative element, and it is the neutral space between the opposites. The *nothingness* (or neutral state) some know as the *void* or *zero point energy* is in reality *thought*—just like the continuum of the Buddhist philosophies. It is the quantum realm of our real consciousness. I have shown how, through the entanglement of particles (known today as *quantum entanglement*) these thoughts can be entangling with other particles. Thus we have what the alchemists called the *Universal Mind*, or in popular terms, *God*.

The world of the mystic and the enlightenment process, I believe, is nothing more than the accessing of this *Universal Mind*, *Akashic Record*, or *zero point energy*. This is through the ability to be conscious at the point of quantum entanglement—to be aware of the unconscious world and the numerous connections between our mind at the subatomic level and the subatomic universe. Between the worlds, in the neutral awake/sleep state (also known as the *hypnagogic*) is where the superconscious mind can access the divine.

The vesica piscis, or the world between.

This thing we term *superconsciousness* is gained through methods of the chakra Kundalini system, which I believe to be a process where thought affects energy. The methods employed by the adept heighten the state of awareness of this quantum world internally. Due to the very nature of the process, the mystic comes back with visions that are both archetypal and unusual. The images are archetypal, because they are almost always consistent. The visions are unusual in the fact that the ordinary mind cannot comprehend what the nonordinary mind has seen. What the mystic (whether Hindu, Muslim, Sufi, Christian Gnostic, or Alchemist) is revealing is the human interpretation of the theoretical quantum world of the unconscious. This experience is what has been called *the real self*.

But there are issues with the brain to which we must resolve before we proceed on our journey. These issues have been used by those among us who reason away the enlightenment experience as a purely hormonal or emotional reaction. In order to discuss these issues we must understand the term *consciousness*. This definition has been taken from a paper titled "The Neurophysiology of the Brain: Its Relationship to Altered States of Consciousness (with emphasis on the Mysical Experience)" by Dr. Peter Fenwick:

> Consciousness arises because of a series of complex actions taking part in the normally functioning brain. By consciousness, I mean the appearance within me of an experiencing self that is able not only to know itself but also is able to differentiate a group of experiences which clearly are not part of itself or part of the body to which it belongs, in fact they come from the outside world. Wigner (1964), in his article "Two Kinds of Reality" summed this up when he said "There are two kinds of reality of existence; the existence of my consciousness and the reality of everything else. The latter reality is not absolute, but only relative"…excepting immediate sensations and, more generally, the content of my consciousness, everything is a construct, but some constructs are closer, some farther from the direct sensations…. Thus we have a primary

reality, which is the domain of the experiencing self and we have secondary reality, which is the interpretation of the outside world by the complex functioning of the nervous system. This is the external reality and it is secondary to the primary reality of the self.

Consciousness is not as clear as we may have believed. There are, according to psychiatrists, two kinds of consciousness. On the one hand, we experience our *self*. And on the other, we interpret the *outside world*—but we do this according to our *self*—so one element of consciousness (*self*) affects the other (*the outside*). In this way our experience of the outside world should differ between cultures, due to localized influences. This gives rise to differences of opinion on many subjects, causing conflict between individuals and cultures. However (and most importantly) the reality of the inner self—the experience of our own *self-consciousness*—remains a universal constant, just as the ancients believed.

We can see this in the test results of *altered states of consciousness* experiments that scientists have been doing for the last few decades. The world we see (or perceive) is not seen objectively. It is a construct of our own mind, and therefore it is subjective. The world we perceive depends on our own upbringing, cultural boundaries, and memories—in short, it is seen through the unique state of our own brain function. There is more than one world; there are 6 billion of them, all being seen through each individual human mind. If the world that surrounds us is so difficult to perceive objectively, how much more so is the inner world? Because this is a genetic (or evolved) universal archetype, the inner world is a lot easier to understand. Add to this the hypothesis I have put forward for the collective superconscious quantum mind, and all inner realities are a reflection of the greater mind. This would, of course, be the *Inner Self*, not the self that has been infected with influences locally.

THE REAL YOU?

Outer Reality

This is the Personality. It is built up over the course of our lifetime from peer pressure and other influences upon us. It is not the true reality, and is called by Buddhists the external phenomena.

Inner Reality

This is the Individual as opposed to the Personality. This has been US from the moment we were born and is the real self or Being. It is this element of ourselves that the ancients believed would continue after death, and the personality would die.

The Inner Reality is the home of enlightenment. It is the "Shining" reality that resides within each one of us according to the ancient traditions. In order to access this reality we must first realise the suffering and pain the Outer Reality causes and eradicate the desires and other elements of the ego that cause this suffering. Only then can the Inner Reality of purity, often called *Divinity*, be released.

Now that we understand a little more about consciousness, we must move on to the scientific issues with the mystical experience and the attempts to reduce it down to biological, chemical, or genetic levels. In *The Wonder of the Brain*, Gopi Krishna writes about the mystical experience:

> However brief it might be, the transcendental flight of the soul must be reflected in the cerebral matter in some way. Conversely, it can happen that as a result of a reaction caused in the brain by intense concentration, constant worship, prayer, extreme longing for the beatific vision or consuming love of God, continued for long periods of time, a process of transformation would start in the organ conducive to the extraordinary experiences of the mystical type.

In 1979, Gopi Krishna claimed to have achieved full and true enlightenment, and therefore wished to spread the word of this amazing part of human evolution. I have to agree with his statement that, if this is a natural human reaction, then it must be mirrored in the matter of our brain structure. Science should be able to pick out these effects in the various elements that make up our mind, be they electromagnetic frequencies or chemical and biological actions.

Mankind may be able to consciously alter the material brain over several generations to help further our spiritual evolution. Through our yearning for spiritual fulfilment, we may have developed a biological, chemical, and electrical method of accessing a quantum dimension. Again, Gopi Krishna writes:

> In light of the fact that the human organism is a chemical laboratory of the most elaborate kind, the possibility of a biochemical synthetic process in the neuronic material to

create a different pattern of consciousness, as happens in the case of certain drugs, cannot be ruled out. In fact, there is a growing apperception of the fact that mental disorder can be the immediate result of organic imbalances in the brain.[1]

There are many instances where animals and plants have coevolved together, where their evolution has depended on one another. This aid to evolution, between plant and animal, is perfectly natural and has been proved in thousands of studies. The pilot fish, for instance, depends on the shark for the scraps of food left in the wake of the larger predator. Many animals rely on bacteriological agents for the digestion of food. It is not a greater step to say that, in some way, the evolution of mankind's mind has and will be aided by chemical and biological reactions. The difference with humans is that we are conscious (at least many of us are) of this fact, and so we can affect our own evolution. This can be seen throughout the course of human history.

As Christopher Altman says in his paper titled "Neuropharmacology of the Mystical State: Entheogenic traditions and the mystical experience": "Many traditions throughout history have employed the use of plant sacraments to achieve a level of intense spiritual awareness, the mystical experience." These plants, and even the venom of the snake, have become sacred to man in his religious teachings. Some of these are known today as the soma of Hinduism, manna of Judaism, peyote of Shamanism, and even to the extent that venom and blood eventually became the Eucharist of Christianity. Altman continues:

> The most prominent example of entheogen use today is the Native American church's use of the peyote cactus. The dried heads, whose chief active is mescaline, are taken in ceremonies by Indians holding membership in the

church. The peyote cactus is central to the religious ceremony, and the Indians who use it say it is a gift from God. Mescaline use goes back as far as the Aztecs. The morning glory vine, in which lysergic acid amines can be found, and the psilocybin mushroom (teonanacatl, or flesh of the gods), whose active compounds are psilocybin and psilocin, were utilised in divinatory ceremonies by the Aztecs, and are still put to use today by many tribes in Mexico. The amanta muscaria mushroom was used in India and known as the Vedic Soma—its primary active compound is muscarine. Siberian tribesmen still ingest this mushroom today.

The truth is that the shaman who used to lead this process were finding ways to higher consciousness—to be closer to the gods. They all—without fail—claimed that these compounds aided the process and brought them information that they would not otherwise know. This knowledge was passed on to the tribe through visual arts and in practical healing techniques. This, in turn, aided the evolution of the tribe and affected the course of human history. But if we are to believe the purely scientific outlook to this process, then all we shall see is that these drugs were simply hallucinogens, and therefore any knowledge gained came purely from within the brain and whatever it had already learned. Science would have us believe that all the things man has seen through this process have been nothing more than an illusion created within the brain. But this theory neglects the quantum side to existence—that all things are connected, that all is *One*, and that everything depends on everything else. Just as the pilot fish depends upon the shark, so too may our mind depend on the Universal Mind. This explains how the shaman would intrinsically know the needs of the tribe and be able to find a suitable answer—even if he himself did not know it.

Man has striven to achieve this sense through several means. This may be part of our own evolutionary desires—we subconsciously know that there is more to life, and we strive for it. These other methods are now ingrained elements of our religions. Meditation, prayer, fasting, and even dervish (spinning) are all processes developed by man to attain a heightened state of awareness or closeness to God. These are all physical methods of entering a metaphysical realm—a biological and chemical way for man to improve his own conscious state.

There are various psychological elements to the process of enlightenment as described by many subjects in scientific laboratory tests. These accounts are extremely interesting, and I have provided a brief outline of their common themes:

- *The transcendence of time and space.* This is the feeling that time has either stood still or moved faster than normal. All references to time and place have become blurred. What is commonly described is the concept that time and space are at one point, where the edges between our perception of space and time become irrelevant as we suddenly see reality differently. If what I believe is true—that human minds actually enter a quantum existence—then this would be feeling of time and space are completely true. It is a reality, albeit a very different one from our ordinary experiences.

- *Oneness.* The feeling that all time and space exists at one single point is supported by another unique feeling of unity. As Christopher Altman says, "There is a feeling of oneness with the universe and a loss of ego boundaries. Self is experienced as pure awareness." This loss of ego and experience of the self is exactly what the alchemists, occultists, and gnostics speak of as the means to obtain true enlightenment.

- *A sense of the divine and sacredness.* Subjects often feel that they are at peace with existence and that they are in tune with the Divine. Yet again, this is paralleled with the experiences described by our ancient philosophers.

- *Mood.* Most subjects feel a positive mood, and their emotions express wonder and joy. Emotions are elevated to such an extent that nothing in our typical experience can compare.

- *Knowledge.* Subjects feel that they have gained insight into nature that they simply cannot express, but they believe this knowledge to be ultimate and authentic. The process gives them a strong sense of paradox, that they could not explain their own emotions or experience to others and that their experiences were contradictory. Giving voice to the inexplicable has always been the problem of the mystics, and I can personally vouch for the feeling of *knowing* that is expressed by these subjects. There are often moments of sheer illumination, which give one a sense of superconsciousness, however fleeting the feeling lasts. I have too often felt unable to express the feeling that I have intense knowledge of *why* and *how*, and yet have been unable to explain this knowledge to others.

- *Persistence.* The experience often remains with the subjects on an emotional level. They take the emotional experience with them into their own lives and it aids them, providing a more balanced outlook.

Whichever way we look at these experiences brought on by medication, meditation, prayer, fasting, or dervish, we must conclude that it is a universal human phenomenon. Although all philosophers, gnostics, religious exponents, and scientists explain the cause of the experience in different ways, it is my goal to come to a balance—to explain the process through truth. I am neither a scientist, nor a mystic. I am simply a seeker of truth.

There can be no doubt that the various chemicals bring on a process known to the mystics as *enlightenment*. There can also be no doubt that these processes can also be brought on through physical and mental actions, creating neuron transmissions that affect our thoughts and release chemical hormones. But all of this is simply reducing the process down to a scientifically physical, biological, and chemical reaction. The question is not *how* the experience is brought on, but rather *what truth is there to it?* Is this process a basic truth of human evolution? Is this process being caused by the union of our inner selves with the collective superconscious state or Universal Mind? Are we creating or assisting in our own evolution in a quantum universe?

Christopher Altman writes that science often uses this clause as a safety net:

> Though the scientific method has its bounds, enlightenment for the mystic lies not in explanation, but in direct experience. Mysticism is about potentials of human experience, and the mystical journey is a lifelong path, which culminates in direct encounter with the unknown. Irrespective of verification, mystical experiences remain the zenith of human endeavour into the hidden regions of the mind, opening doorways to the core of conscious experience itself.

Mystics usually concur with this statement, having no interest in the scientific realm. Therefore, we almost never find a balance. We do, however, want to get to the bottom of the enlightenment process, and I wish to find a balance between hard rationalistic science and true human experience, if that is possible.

Religious belief and experience are usually regarded as beyond scientific explanation, yet neurologists at the University of California, San Diego, have located an area in the temporal lobe of the brain that appears to produce intense feelings of spiritual transcendence, combined with a sense of some mystical presence. Canadian neuroscientist Michael Persinger, of Laurentian University, has even managed to reproduce such feelings in otherwise unreligious people by stimulating this area.

Typically people report a presence...[another] individual experienced God visiting her. Afterwards we looked at her EEG and there was this classical spike and slow-wave seizure over the temporal lobe at the precise time of the experience—the other parts of the brain were normal.[2]

In his book *The Real Nature of Mystical Experience*, Gopi Krishna writes:

The fact that we seem to have a religious spot wired into our brains does not necessarily prove that the spiritual dimension is merely the product of electrical activity. After all, if God exists, it figures that He must have created us with some biological mechanism with which to apprehend Him.

Here again, Gopi Krishna shows the belief that although the physical attributes of the experience can be seen scientifically, the understanding of the affect can still be seen as mystical. Where does this process originate? Is it God that gives us this element within our brain? Or is it our evolutionary connection with the Universal Mind—the collective superconscious state? Can this Universal Mind be perceived by the subjects that scientists have tested? And if so, does this give us evidence for the quantum connection? Are they able to become conscious of the all-pervading presence of this superconscious state, just as the ancient shaman, gnostics, and others have expressed? In an article called "Phantoms of the Brain" V.S. Ramachandran and Sandra Blakesless write:

> If religious beliefs are merely the combined result of wishful thinking and a longing for immortality, how do you explain the flights of fancy of intense religious ecstasy experienced by patients with temporal lobe seizures, or their claim that God speaks directly to them? Many a patient has told me of a "divine light that illuminates all things" or of an "ultimate truth that lies completely beyond the reach of ordinary minds...." Of course, they might simply be suffering from hallucinations and delusions of the kind that a schizophrenic might experience, but if that's the case, why do such hallucinations occur mainly when the temporal lobes are involved? Even more puzzling, why do they take this particular form? Why don't these patients hallucinate pigs or donkeys?

And:

> Now came a period of rapture so intense that the universe stood still as if amazed at the unutterable majesty of the spectacle! Only one in all the infinite universe. The All-caring, the Perfect One, the Perfect Wisdom, truth, love, and purity! And with the rapture came insight. In that same wonderful moment of what might be called supernal bliss, came illumination. I saw with intense inward vision the atoms or molecules of which seemingly the universe is composed—I know not whether material or spiritual—rearranging themselves as the cosmos passed from order to order. What joy I saw when there was no break in the chain—not a link left out—everything in its place and time. Worlds, systems all blended in one harmonious whole Universe synonymous with Universal Love.

What the scientific evidence shows is that subjects experience a great light or shining, just as the ancients have stated on numerous occasions. We know this to be a part of the enlightenment experience. Subjects also report a feeling of being connected to the Divine, and often experience a puzzling and archetypal effect, whereby the experiences are universal and not different in each culture or ethnic background. This is either the result of a basic human genetic makeup, or a connection through the quantum brain to a quantum state. The experience cannot be the result of man's searching for eternal life, as each culture would experience different results. This must be a result of human evolution, whether by the simple biological, genetic, and universal process of evolution, or through a co-evolved nature with the very existence of another quantum dimension. This would explain the serpent image, which has been seen both as the double-helix of DNA and as energy waves. Either way, the wavy line— physically manifested on this level of existence as the snake—is a universal image underlying the very basic levels of existence.

The fact remains that the enlightenment experience happens to humans around the world, and has been occurring for a very long time. It has given rise to the religions and beliefs to which most people adhere today. This Otherworld, envisaged by the ancients and by mystics worldwide, has been physically manifested over time for all to see and for modern science to research. These physical manifestations can be seen in structures such as the mandala, and in texts such as the Bible.

In the mandala, we can see the similarity between the outer physical world, the inner atomic structure, and an esoteric belief system. This must come from some kind of intuition, as the sun or nucleus at the center and the moon and planets (or electrons) orbiting around it match the mandala perfectly. This is not a new concept, as even the ancients saw the macrocosmic solar system as a manifestation of the three-dimensional creations of consciousness. We know the ancients believed that their minds created existence, and this matches the concept we are now coming to—that the evolution of mankind (and possibly other sentient beings) is part and parcel of the greater mind that is affecting us, just as we are affecting it on a subconscious level.

The Power of Gravity

I have already said that we must create balance internally; this is something that all the various world wisdom texts tell us. The atom—with its negative and positive polarities—has an *Eye of the Storm* or *Eye of Ra* at the center. This, I believe, can be explained in scientific terms as *gravity*, which is evident in the greater or macrocosmic universe, and should therefore also be evident in the microcosmic or miniature.

By looking closely, I have found that the age-old symbol of the dot in the center of a circle illustrates the concept of gravity perfectly—as gravity is a universal force pulling things inwards, as we are pulled in to the center of the earth. All things are pulled in that do not have sufficient force or energy to escape—similar to the electron that must be energized to escape the atom. Remember that all energy is information, and so the electron has information that it takes with it. Not all things can coalesce at the center, so physicists came up with the term *black hole*—they assumed that all energy–information disappears into this black hole. This assumption poses the question: Where does the black hole lead to? To answer this we must look at the life cycles of birth, life, and death. The energy is born from the void, it lives, and is then sucked into the black hole. The black hole is the conduit through which the cycles pass.

The fact that energy–information is constantly going in and coming out of this black hole is what makes it secure and stable, and ensures that it does not implode or explode. It is a continuum of cycles; the universe must have them to continue. Whether science continues with the term *black hole* or the theory of their existence, the evidence suggests that the universe needs to keep balance. These black holes are mirrored within our very atom, which are like the black holes in that energy is absorbed and then escapes.

The process of enlightenment is similar to that of the Kundalini, but consists of more than mental attitudes—although the mental attitude is the controlling feature. This process is more than an ancient mystical experience that has been excused away by those who have never experienced it. This process is a universal constant—one of the creative and universal truths. We have the answers to the *whole* in ourselves. We are—when entering the enlightenment process—experiencing the same process as experienced by the black hole or the cycles of an atom. The mandala—as an image of this process—is everywhere, especially in the natural world that surrounds us.

Modern physicists have discovered that subatomic particles (such as electrons) somehow know what other particles are doing, regardless of where the other particle is located. The entangled particles communicate. Both particles seem to communicate with each other across space simultaneously—meaning that they communicate instantly—faster than the speed of light, as if both particles are one item—a concept known by the term *superposition*. This implies that each subatomic particle in an entire ocean of particles behaves as if it knows what an infinite number of others are doing. If scientists are prepared to say that one particle knows what another entangled particle is doing, then how much further is it to say that—once conscious of this level of reality—we too could know what other entangled particles are doing? We are conscious of our biological and chemical reality, so why can't we also be conscious of our quantum level? These other particles to which we are entangled could be part of the Universal Mind!

The trouble is, our modern minds create the illusion of division between things, whether it be the sky and the sea or the nucleus and the electron. In fact, the theoretical physics and the Eastern concepts show us that all things are united at an amazingly minute level, and that our minds can connect with this Oneness or Universal Mind. We are not separate from anything; we are part of a greater *whole*, and as a part of this whole we can communicate and act within it.

The experience of the *shining* or *enlightenment*, seen through the power of the pranic or serpent energy—which is manifested in reality as thought and electromagnetic energy—awakens us to realize a greater part of ourselves, so that we can find our own way to it by sustaining our awareness at the fusion point of our energy. It helps us to *see* in a way nothing else can, but only conscious efforts of internal balance will help us to keep the moment.

We are told by ancient philosophers not to concentrate on this world of illusion (the physical and manifest world) but to become conscious of the Otherworld where reality truly exists. In essence, with the physically manifest world being the illusion of the human mind and seen differently by each individual, the true reality can only be in the *Oneness* spoken of in the ancient wisdom texts.

When we concentrate on the Kundalini process, we create an electromagnetic energy which is both a wave and a particle. Particles of light energy, for instance, are produced at the point in the process when and where the energy retracts back, and we perceive these points of energy all around us in our reality as subatomic particles. Only when we are in the superconscious state can we perceive the particles of thought. This is the shining, illumination, or the light part of enlightenment.

From these same points, and as the energy retracts back, waves of light energy extend outwards around these points, pulsating in all directions. Psychics and others sometimes claim to see these as auras, which are also picked up by Kirlian photography. This would, of course, be possible in a unified world where everything is interconnected and where we are capable of being conscious of this energy.

However difficult it may be to understand these statements, confusion only arises due to a certain paradox. This paradox is solved once it is realized that one of our perceptions is an illusion: Our perception and experience of everything is divided and separated in time and space. But to understand how this reality of space and time is an illusion, we first have to consider the premise that this one point of energy is pure consciousness—and that all energy is consciousness—even the illusion of matter.

We must also be careful what we claim for the Kundalini, because for many (including the Sufi mystic Gurdjieff) the Kundalini is imagination, and imagination in mankind can be a dangerous thing. But Gurdjieff and others forget that the ancients constantly talk about balance. This balances the imagination with the rational, the left with the right, the female with the male. To be purely rational leaves us with nothing but a dry, stale world, which itself is lead by the religion of science. I personally have problems with the scientific traditions we follow today, because all too often we are told one thing, only to have it being disproved soon after. One only has to think of how respectable scientists have been vilified for stating their beliefs, which have then eventually been proven to be correct, to see how this so-called rational world can also be in error, just like the imaginative world, which dreams of unreality.

The process of the Kundalini, when seen in the context of being just one term for a worldwide serpentine philosophy of *divinity in the self* and how to access it, is truly something that is on the road to enlightenment or awakening.

When you come to this remarkable understanding that both modern science and ancient imaginative philosophy can be balanced, then you will finally have the answers given to us by the ancients—that we should not search for the Divine in the clouds or in the laboratory, but in balance and within the *self*. The balances we are talking about are constant—there are balances within every level of life, in both the outer and the inner world. There are balances within the atom, in the world around us, and in our everyday lives. Only through this understanding can we perceive the knowledge of the ancients.

Chapter 5

THE HIDDEN BIBLE

Just as Moses lifted up the flaming serpent in the desert, so must the Son of Man be lifted up, that all who believe may have eternal life in Him.

—John 3:14–15

We have seen how the Kundalini energy of the Hindu prana and zero point energy have been described as Serpent Fire. In this verse from the Gospel of John, the Brazen Serpent of Moses is portrayed as the flaming serpent, and Jesus is equated to this serpent. The Brazen Serpent of Moses is the power of the healing Kundalini as seen through Hindu tradition.

> The Lord said to Moses, "Make a fiery serpent, and set it on a pole; and it shall be that everyone who is bitten, when he looks at it, shall live." So Moses made a bronze serpent, and put it on a pole; and so it was, if a serpent had bitten anyone, when he looked at the bronze serpent, he lived.

> Numbers 21: 8–9

As we can see in this verse from the Old Testament, the serpent was very much alive and well. This imagery is similar to the infamous Caduceus Staff or Rod of Aaron. It is also similar to the Kundalini. This is a belief, spanning the period between the Old and New Testament, in the healing serpent energy rising up a pole or spine.

The Book of Genesis

Angel, Eve, and serpent. Winchester, England.

"When I find learned men believing Genesis literally, which the ancients with all their failings had too much sense to receive except allegorically, I am tempted to doubt the reality of the improvement of the human mind." So said Godfrey Higgins, quoted in the book *Comte de Gabalis* by Abbe N. de Montfaucon de Villars. Let us take this theory (that Genesis should not be read literally) and try to discover instead an allegorical and gnostic truth:

> The Lord God planted a garden eastward in Eden, and there He put the man who He had formed. And out of the ground the Lord God made every tree to grow that is pleasant to the sight and good for food. The tree of life was also in the midst of the garden, and the tree of the knowledge of good and evil.
>
> Now a river went out of Eden to water the garden, and from there it parted and became four riverheads. The name of the first is Pishon; it is the one which skirts the whole land of Havilah, where there is gold. And the gold of that land is good. Bdellium and the onyx stone are there.
>
> —Genesis 2: 8–13

This biblical verse contains a set of extremely interesting clues. In many of the wisdom traditions we are told that the Inner Reality of ourselves—the true Divinity—is the creator of our manifest body; we are what we have faith in, or what we believe and what we think. Here, in Genesis, we see that the Lord God (or our own Inner Divinity) placed man in the garden facing eastward, which is obviously towards the rising sun. This could be the Inner Sun rather than the physical sun we see in the sky; although to our ancestors all things were interlinked and interdependent. In this way, the Inner Sun could not exist without the outer sun, and vice versa.

On the seventh day our Inner Divinity rested, as if by reaching the seventh level we had somehow created perfection in which our new life could live. This is remarkably similar to the seven chakra levels of the Kundalini awakening. Here we have an ancient text telling us that to create perfection we must look towards the sun, the light, the illumination, or the enlightenment. We must form ourselves by rising up from the most base of things to the perfection of man and godhead through a process that takes six periods, with the seventh reserved for rest.

Within this garden (which is within us and is a state of being rather than an actual place) there is a Tree of Life and Knowledge. Although some believe that there is only one tree, many have said that there are two separate trees; if this is the case then they are surely interdependent. These trees were in the middle of the garden, which is where we find the spine. The whole Kundalini concept suddenly appears to be growing in Genesis.

Out of Eden flowed a river, which was then divided into four, which are the four cardinal points or elements. This description gives us an indication of something much deeper. Most scholarly books will reveal that the cross is a symbol of the four cardinal points or directions of a compass. This may well be true, and in that case it also points to a fifth place. This fifth element is always the hidden aspect; it is in fact the center of the cross, to which all the directions point. It is the only location that all directions—east, west, north, and south—can agree on. Therefore, it is the most sacred. This center is the true self—we are the fifth element.

Taking this symbolism further, we discover that in Mesopotamia the great god of the shining aspect was Anu. His name literally means *sky* or *shining*, and he was recognized as the highest god in Mesopotamia. In fact, he owed his dominance to the role that the sky played in the universe, as the earth (which was the source of the life giving waters) had a male consort (Enki), as well as the maternal function (Ninkhursag). Anu was the god higher than the male and female principles—he was the internal sun or enlightened state, which can be brought about by union between our opposite sides. This was what scholars called the *Babylonian Triad*, and it was Anu who brought cosmic order out of chaos. Amazingly, it was Anu (similar to the Christian drama) who held the bread and water of immortal life. It was also Anu who gave divine authority to the rulers of Earth. In this way the kings, pharaohs, emperors, and high priests through time have had to show in some symbolic or literal way that they have received this divine spark from the greatest of deities—which is in fact their own inner divine self-realization and balance.

The pharaohs revealed this inner wisdom, knowledge, and illumination in the most fantastic ways ever seen by man, especially through the *uraeus serpent*. But this does not mean that we cannot discover the symbols that were utilized by less-dramatic rulers. In the symbol of Anu we have the symbol of the hidden fifth element and the upright axis of the earth—the cross. In many representations, these crosses are seen with wings and are looked upon as winged Shining Ones. In most representations that I have seen, the cross looks remarkably similar to the later *Maltese cross* or popular *Templar cross*.

Getting back to the story of Genesis though, and with the understanding that Eden is truly at the center of the illumination, we must follow the river to see where it takes us. One of the rivers was called Pishon, and it skirted the land of Havilah, where there was gold. Leaving aside the fact that there were four rivers, let's concentrate on where this particular river flowed—skirting Havilah. So what exactly is this Havilah? It means *Land of Serpents*, and is in fact India, where we find the origins of Kundalini and the Naga. This is the land where there is gold—symbolic of the height of the sun, the highest level our consciousness can achieve.

So what do we have? We have a flow of a river that is fertilizing the land in the garden in Eden. The river can be no other than the life of the mind, which is in balance with the Tree of Knowledge and uses the land of the serpents—the energy—to maintain its fertile mind, bringing knowledge or gold back from the Otherworld. The gold symbolizes the good nature and knowledge of those in the place of the serpent.

As for bdellium, unfortunately nobody is entirely sure what this is, although it is thought that it could be a kind of crystal, which would make sense when we consider the properties of quartz as a magnification aid to mental frequencies and the fact that onyx, which was also mentioned, is a kind of quartz.

> And the Lord God caused a deep sleep to fall on Adam, and he slept; and He took one of his ribs, and closed up the flesh in its place. Then the rib which the Lord God had taken from man He made into a woman, and He brought her to the man.... And they were both naked, the man and his wife, and they were not ashamed.
> —Genesis 2: 21–25

In this verse we see that original being was split, so that a duality arose of male and female, causing the two sides to have to reunite to be fertile. From this new duality a Son of Man could be created, which will be the result of this perfect balance, completing the circle of repeating patterns or cycles.

These are many esoteric ways of explaining the inner workings of the most ancient philosophical minds. Man has taken these stories literally for far too long, and only now are the stories being revealed as nonsense by the theories of Darwinian evolution. What these stories reveal are the collective thoughts about the most profound psychology of the human mind. They reveal the alchemy of the Bible.

We have now set the scene. We have a perfect garden, wherein lays the perfect duality of balance between man and woman. What we do not yet have is the knowledge required to create the spark of life. We have to remember that the stories of Genesis have changed, so it now reads that Eve was tempted by the snake, and it was her original sin that brought down mankind. None of this is true. The original stories emerge from Sumeria and are completely different. In fact, the serpent is the one who brings good fortune, and is the creator god.

> Now the serpent was more cunning beast of the field which the Lord God had made.
>
> —Genesis 3:1

> And the woman said to the serpent, "We may eat the fruit of the trees of the garden; but of the fruit of the tree which is in the midst of the garden, God has said, 'You shall not eat it, nor shall you touch it, lest you die.'" Then the serpent said to the woman, "You will not surely die. For God knows that in the day you eat of it your eyes will be opened and you will be like God, knowing good and evil."
>
> —Genesis 3: 2–4

Eating the fruits of the tree that is in the midst of the garden, which can only be the Tree of Knowledge of good and evil or the Tree of Life, will make you similar to God. That is, it will aid you to realize your own true potential, to release the god within, to find the Inner Divinity. This is because you will be eating something that is inside yourself! You will be taking in, digesting, and feeling the benefit of a part of yourself that the world (in this case it was God) is denying you! The world denies you this element of yourself. Your own desires and greedy nature denies you *yourself*. The ancients tell us in good faith to eradicate those desires, deny the world its power over you, and find out what lays within. We have either been mislead or have forgotten how to read the truth. In fact, if anybody truly had read Genesis in this way over the past 2,000 years and revealed the stark but simple truth of it (as I am doing here) then he or she would most likely have been burned at the stake as a heretic.

Adam, Eve, and serpent below Christ.

Getting back to Genesis, we find that this is all coming from the serpent that resides entwined about the tree. It is the power or energy of the Kundalini—it is the prana, and therefore also the Holy Spirit. This is in stark contrast to the popular Christian perception that the serpent was Satan. Incidentally, to say that there was knowledge of evil (Satan as the snake) prior to the original sin of Eve is a paradox in itself, and so throws the whole Christian perception into chaos.

The original Eve did not appear as a woman, instead showing her true nature as the serpent itself. The name Eve was spelled *havah*, which means *mother of all living*, but also means *female serpent*, being related to the name *Havilah* in India. She is mother of all, the female part of the creative process, which is both a physical truth and a psychological truth. It's no wonder that the female line of descent (the matriarchal relationship) is so important to Judaism. Even in Arabic, the words for *snake*, *life*, and *teaching* are closely related to the name *Eve*.

Early Gnostic texts regarded Eve as a serpent herself, guarding the secrets of divine immortality and wisdom. The texts taught that the Hebrews had regarded Eve with jealousy and stole the creation of mankind from the serpent and attributed it to Yahweh—how right they were—and yet they were called heretics for their statements and often murdered.

At other points in tradition, the Eve-myth takes on a masculine edge when she is married to Ophion, Helios, or the Agathodaemon—all great serpent deities and all showing that the story of Genesis is based on the serpent cult and the union of the serpentine energies. There are also texts contemporary to the biblical texts that were not included in the standard Bible that reveal the hidden wisdom of the serpent and its duality psychology. One book in particular—now lost to us—was used or written by the *Gnostic Ebionites*, sometimes referred to as the *Essene*. Incidentally,

Essene means *One Essence* or *One Light Shining*. They were a Jewish sect, probably as large as the Pharisees and Saducees. The name comes from the historical *Hasidim* or *Pious Ones* who marched out of Jerusalem because of perceived Hellenization. Suddenly two camps were created: the Maccabees, who set up their own priest and king; and the Hasidim, now known as Essene, who began to manipulate their own dynastic order. The Essene were renowned for their asceticism and communistic way of life. It was these zealous individuals who were responsible for the famous *Dead Sea Scrolls* discovered at Qumran.

The text of these Essene is called the *Book of Elchasai*, which means *Hidden Power* from a sect who were sometimes known as *pure of the mind*.[1] Although we no longer have this book, extracts and elements of it appear in later Christian texts, and from these sources it is possible to discover that it "borrowed much from Oriental sources the idea of a Syzygy or sexual duality in the emanations from the supreme Deity." This sexual duality is the way of explaining the unity required between the male and female principles within us—the sexual duality of Adam and Eve coming from the supreme Deity. Often this sexual union was seen literally, and modern-day cults owe a lot to this false interpretation.

We can see from this extra-biblical example that the dual nature of man must reunite in order to be one with the deity. Eve must unite with Adam. In old Akkadian, *Ad* signifies *father*, and according to the Victorian writer and researcher C. Staniland Wake in *The Origin of Serpent Worship*, Adam was closely associated in legend with Seth, Saturn, Thoth, or Taautus, who were all represented as serpents.

> In the old Akkad tongue Ad signifies "a father" and the mythical personages with whom Adam is most allied, such as Seth or Saturn, Taaut, or Thoth, and others, were serpent deities. Such would seem to have been the case

also with the deities whose names show a close formal resemblance to that of Adam. Thus the original name of Hercules was Sandan or Adanos, and Hercules, like the allied god Mars, was undoubtedly often closely associated with the serpent. This notion is confirmed by the identification of Adonis and Osiris as Azar or Adar.... The abaddon of St. John, the old dragon Satan, was probably intended for the same serpent-god.

Adam and Eve are symbolic serpents of energy within man that must unite in order to bring about the true Son of Man (which is Christ) to the surface. This is why the Bible tells us that "Christ is all and in all."

It is no wonder that Abel, the son of Adam and Eve, means *serpent shining*, and that Cain was thought to be of serpent descent. Wake writes that "It is curious that, according to rabbinical tradition, Cain was the son, not of Adam, but of the serpent-spirit Asmodeus, who is the same as the Persian Ahriman, 'the great serpent with two feet.'" Whether Cain was the son of the serpent Adam or the serpent Asmodeus, he was the son of serpents, as was his brother Abel. *Ab* means *serpent*, while *el* means *god* or *shining*. Again, these were not real, literal people; they are elements of the human mind. They are greed, hatred, anger, loathing, lust, and so on. Although union has been created between the male and female principles inside ourselves, this does not always mean that we will remain balanced. There are always temptations, and we must guard against such evil. This is the beginning of a repeating cycle.

There are, of course, different attributes to the male and female elements, and these are more often than not the same across the religious spectrum. The Mother is earthly and the divine mediator between your consciousness and the Father aspect. This explains why the concept of the female shaman would be the one who enters the Otherworld on our behalf. Again and again it is the female from the earliest times who goes into the

Otherworld, or who at least is the controlling factor. In reality, this is the female element or principle that communicates within us. The mother is also the one who nurtures and cares for us. She suckles the Son of Man until He is fully grown. Our true Inner Reality needs parental guidance, just like any child. We now understand why the Shekinah, Holy Spirit, or Matronit of the Hebrews and Christians was feminine. She was the passive element of the duality—not confrontational or forceful. She is the guide, caring for us. She is the element inside our mind that reasons with wisdom, and therefore she became Sophia, seen today in Islam. She is Magdalene to Christ, Isis to Osiris, Eve to Adam, Marion to Robin Hood, and Guinevere to Arthur.

Today there is much imbalance as we strive for the truth behind the bloodline grail myth that has been so prevalent ever since the early 1980s, and the publication of Baigent, Leigh, and Lincoln's book *The Holy Blood and the Holy Grail*, which has now been given new impetus with Dan Brown's book *The Da Vinci Code*. Of course this rush to discover the bloodline of Mary Magdalene is nonsense, as Christ and his disciples, including Mary, never existed as real people. They are symbols of a greater secret; they are metaphorical elements of a gnostic truth that awaits each one of us. Mary Magdalene is the feminine aspect—the *Matronit*—which must unite with the Christ in order to bring about the next level of enlightenment. The unification process is ongoing, bringing constant rebirth. This is true gnosis; that we must understand that we are sinners, and therefore must eradicate this sin from our body and mind. This is similar to the Buddhist idea of reducing our own suffering by getting rid of those things which make us suffer—namely our desires for things we cannot have, such as cravings, greed, and power. The desires that we posses are the very things that cause us to suffer. We cause suffering to one another through our own desires.

If we can eradicate these desires, then we shall be without suffering, and the true self shall rise. But we must have our serpent guardian at the Tree of Life and the Tree of Knowledge. This serpent guardian must be both a guide, gentle and mild, but also intolerant of stupidity and strong in denying a return to the old self. These are the two elements we see again and again in the myths of serpents and dragons. The guardian dragons are often seated at the foot of the tree in Arthurian tales. The dragon also protects the Golden Fleece, hung from the sacred tree. The dragon protects the Nagas, who have hidden great treasure beneath the waters. These are the symbols used across the world for the same basic tenet of humanity. It is not surprising that these symbols should also appear in the Bible.

Both the male and female principles seem to come from the godhead, both being different aspects of it. In the secret book of John we find confirmation of this, and the fact that we need to cleanse our mind:

> …when all sins and all uncleanesses are gone from your body, your blood shall become as pure as our Earthly Mother's blood and as pure as the river's foam sporting in the sunlight. And your breath shall become as pure as the breath of odorous flowers; your flesh as pure as flesh of fresh fruits reddening upon the leaves of trees; the light of your eye as clear and bright as the brightness of the sun shining upon the blue sky. And now shall all the angels of the Earthly Mother serve you and your breath, your blood, your flesh shall be one with the breath, the blood and the flesh of the Earthly Mother, that your spirit also become one with the Spirit of your Heavenly Father. For truly no-one can reach the Heavenly Father unless through the Heavenly Mother. Even as the newborn babe cannot understand the teaching of his father until his

mother has suckled him, bathed him, nursed him, put him to sleep and nurtured him.

And again:

> She is the first power. She preceded everything, and came forth from the Father's mind as forethought of all. Her light resembles the Father's light; as the perfect power. She is the image of the perfect and invisible Virgin Spirit. She is the first power, the glory, Barbello, the perfect glory among the worlds; the emerging glory, She glorified and praised the Virgin Spirit for she had to come forth through the Spirit.

This is similar to medieval alchemy, where the soul/spirit of the adept must go through a series of processes, here called *nurturing*, in order to achieve the final goal. Christianity, or Gnostic Christianity, developed this ancient system until the concept of the Holy Trinity was finally written down. This is the Father (which is the male principle), the Mother (the female principle), and the Son of Man (the ultimate result of a perfect union). This is why Jesus is God and also the Son of God, because he is the result of the reuniting of the elements of division of the one God. The later myth and tradition of a union between Jesus and Magdalene is yet another element of this repeating pattern. They must unite, as Adam and Eve did, to produce the shining, which has been seen as the Holy Grail, or the bloodline. The truth is that this cycle is perpetual motion—it is a repeating teaching pattern.

Various elements have been used to explain the nurturing of the Son and the union of the Father and Mother, but in the end they all resolve back to the same basic premise of internal balance, eradication of sinful thoughts, and nurtured growth of the new you.

The *Book of Secrets* from the Dead Sea Scrolls tells us what will happen if we can get rid of the evils we harbor:

> This shall be the sign that this shall come to pass: when the sources of evil are shut up and wickedness is banished in the presence of righteousness, as darkness in the presence of light, or as smoke vanishes and is no more, in the same way wickedness will vanish forever and righteousness will be manifest like the sun. The world will be made firm and all the adherents of the secrets of sin shall be no more. True knowledge shall fill the world and there will never be any more folly. This is all ready to happen, it is a true oracle, and by this it shall be known to you that it cannot be averted.

We are told by the ancients from Qumran that we must shut up the sources of evil to allow righteousness to manifest like the sun, which of course is the *Solar Force*. This needs both fire and water, and is the reason these two elements are utilized throughout the world of the esoteric.

> When the Day of the Pentecost had fully come, they were all with one accord in one place. And suddenly there came a sound from heaven, as of a rushing mighty wind, and it filled the whole house where they were sitting. Then there appeared to them divided tongues, as of fire, and one sat upon each of them. And they were filled with the Holy Spirit....
>
> —Acts 2: 1–4.

As we can see in this verse from the book of Acts in the New Testament, the Holy Spirit came upon the apostles as a tongue of flame only once they were as one accord in one place. This, to the gnostic and the adept, is the simple statement that the 12 elements of the nurturing process outlined in the Bible, taken directly from much older astrotheological cults, must come together to achieve illumination. Gifts of language, healing, and miracles came upon the apostles once they unified their skills. If the 12 are really constellations, then this image is of divine alignment.

There is not space in this book to go through the 12 unique aspects of each apostle, but it is a study well worth the effort and I recommend it, remembering that each one is an aspect of our selves. The Holy Spirit is the Solar Force or Serpent Fire of the later alchemists, and the coiled serpent of the Kundalini. In the Dead Sea Scrolls we have the book of Hymns, which outlines this nicely:

> I have reached the inner vision and through Thy Spirit in me I have heard Thy wondrous secret, through Thy mystic insight Thou hast caused a spring of knowledge to well up within me, a fountain of power, pouring forth living waters, a flood of love and of all embracing wisdom, like the splendour of eternal light.

In this passage there is so much symbolism. Living waters, fountains of power, and springs of knowledge can all be found in other traditions and all relate to the Kundalini awakening. The process is aimed at bringing about our own rebirth. It is the process, as we have seen, of killing off the part of us that causes suffering—what Christians would call the old self—and then giving birth to the *Inner Reality* known under so many names. In the apocryphal *Gospel of Philip* from the Dead Sea Scrolls we see this quite clearly:

> The Tree of Life is in the centre of Paradise, as is the oil tree from which the Chrisma comes. The Chrism is the source of resurrection.

This chrism and the Christ are no different; they are the Serpent Fire, the Solar Force, the ultimate goal and source of resurrection. The oil from the tree of the chrism is used to anoint the new Christ or Messiah—which is you. This is the truth of any messiah we may see—that they are anointed from the oil of the tree at the center, just as Buddha was enlightened beneath the bo tree.

Enlightened Buddha. Portmeirion, Wales.

There are other people in the Bible who are also symbols of this power within, and who also never existed in reality. Take Samson for instance. His name means *Sun*, and he was a Nazirite. He was a symbol of the Divine within us. Let's have a look at the scripture and see how we can know this. The following are extracts, beginning with Judges 13:1:

> Again the children of Israel did evil in the sight of the Lord.

This can now be translated to mean that, in the sight of our inner self, we neglected to keep at bay all those elements that cause suffering. Notice the term *again*, reiterating the repetitive cycle.

> Now there was a certain man from Zorah.

That is, there was a male principle, which dwelt in the place that Samson—the Solar Force—was buried. His name was *Manoah* and his wife—the female principle—was barren, infertile because of sin. She could have no children, which is a metaphor for the lack of mental growth we have been discussing. However, an angel of the Lord, a message from the Inner Divinity, came to her, and said that she would conceive.

> Now therefore, please be careful not to drink wine or similar drink, and not to eat anything unclean.

The reason for this is that alcohol and other unclean substances could be obstacles on our path to enlightenment, and cause the birth to be negative rather than positive.

> For behold, you shall conceive and bear a son. And no razor shall come upon his head, for the child shall be a Nazirite to God from the womb.

We are not to take anything away from the pure brilliance of our emergent son/sun. The hair on the head and the beard were symbolic of illumination and wisdom, and we were not to take this away. The Nazirites, of course, would later become the Essene, and it was these people who wrote the *Dead Sea Scrolls* I have quoted from above. They can also be connected to the Naga of India, as I show in *The Serpent Grail*. Indeed, the Nazaria group that was contemporary to Christ taught mystical spirituality that was not dissimilar to Eastern traditions. I would posit that Nazaria or Nazirite may in fact emerge from the Nazar of the Hindu. We can see this when we discover that the Nazarenes, also called *Mendaeans* or *Sabaens*, were a sect of the Essene around the time of Christ. They left Galilee and settled in Syria near Mount Lebanon. They actually call themselves Galileans, even though they said that Christ was a false messiah. They followed the life of John the Baptist instead, who they called the *Great Nazar*. We should not forget that Christ was called the *Nazarean*.

In eastern traditions, the *Nazar* is a Yogic term for the point between the eyebrows and just above the nose. It is the Third Eye, and is the ultimate home of the coiled serpent, seen in Egypt as the emergent uraeus serpent on the brow of the pharaoh. Is not the serpent the thread, which runs through the whole story? Is this not the power of the serpent, the Solar Force or Serpent Fire, and also Samson or Christ, Moses, and many more? They are all the same.

It seems the Bible is one long repetition of the same story. The Israelites do evil in the sight of the Lord, and then he sends a savior to bring them back to the fold. In this case he sends Samson, who then goes and ruins it all by being led astray! This is a warning to us all not to be guided by fools. We must maintain our vigilance if we are not to have the bond between our outer body and our inner spirit destroyed. Do not let the vices of the world detract us from the light of the son/sun.

We must end our trip through the Biblical story of the Kundalini with a look at the final book—Revelation. James Pryse, in his book *The Apocalypse Unsealed*, writes:

> Now in plain words, what does this very occult book, the Apocalypse [Revelation] contain? It gives the esoteric interpretation of the Christos-myth; it tells what Iesous the Christos really is; it explains the nature of the 'old serpent who is the Devil and Satan'; it repudiates the profane conception of an anthropomorphic God; and with sublime imagery it points out the true and only path to Life Eternal. It gives the key to that divine Gnosis which is the same in all ages, and superior to all faiths and philosophies—that secret science which is in reality secret only because it is hidden and locked in the inner nature of every man, however ignorant and humble, and none but himself can turn the key.

We begin Revelation by discovering that John is sending the message of the Christ to the *seven* churches in Asia:

> Grace to you and peace from Him who is and who was and who is to come, and from the seven Spirits who are before His throne, and from Jesus Christ, the faithful witness, the firstborn from the dead and the ruler over the kings of the earth.

> —Revelation 1:4–5

In this verse we see that there are seven spirits before the throne. The throne is obviously where the master or king is seated. It is therefore the bindu of the chakra system, the source of all creativity and illumination. In the Hebrew kabbalah it would be the kether or crown on the Sephiroth tree. This is where the true Christ is situated, at the very head before the seven spirits. He is the faithful witness—because he is the true self—not a part of us that lies. He is the first born from the dead. The kings of the earth are those things that would take you away from the true path to Gnosis.

The whole book goes on in language that has been fought over for 2,000 years, but in the end, regardless of the layers built into the text, it is all about the process which goes on inside of man. It is a call to mankind to seal the fate of himself and his brothers by taking hold of and rectifying his sinful nature.

> Now the wall of the city had twelve foundations, and on them were the names of the twelve apostles of the Lamb. And he who talked with me had a gold reed to measure the city, its gates and its wall. The city is laid out as a square; its length is as great as its breadth. And he measured the city with the reed: twelve thousand furlongs. Its length, its breadth, and height are equal. Then he measured its wall: one hundred and forty-four cubits, according to the measure of a man, that is, of an angel…. But I saw no temple in it, for the Lord God Almighty and the Lamb is its temple. The city had no need of the sun or the moon to shine in it, for the glory of God illuminated it. The Lamb is its light.
>
> Revelation 21: 14–23

Here we have an indication of the secret of the Temple of Solomon, and a truth about ourselves. Upon the foundations we have built—following our eradication of the cause of suffering—we can build a great city. We can measure this city and it will be equal. It will be perfectly balanced, and the measure of man, but it will be no ordinary human structure. Instead it will be the angelic part of ourselves, the true inner reality. This city is a perfect cube, just like the Holy of Holies and the Kings Chamber in the Great Pyramid. In this city will shine light and we will need no other, such as the physical sun or moon, to light our path, as we shall be like God, as the serpent in the Garden in Eden told Eve.

The Bible is a repeating pattern of initiation into the mysteries of the human mind. It is a tool to teach us about ourselves and is, according to most scholarly sources, an accumulation of other wisdom and religious literature from Mesopotamia, Egypt, Persia, and elsewhere.

Chapter 6

ANCIENT RELIGIOUS TEXTS

The scribes.

The Bible is a repeating pattern of ancient psychological teachings about ourselves. The gnosis of man is coming together; it is a simple secret, but one that has been hidden from our eyes. This is the genius of gnosis and gnostic literature—hiding the simple beneath the simpler.

A saint from Maharashtra was born in A.D. 1275 and was named Gyaneshwara. He left behind several texts for us to ponder. In the sixth chapter of his work, the *Gyaneshwari*, he writes:

> Kundalini is one of the greatest energies. The whole body of the seeker starts glowing because of the rising of the Kundalini. Because of that, unwanted impurities in the body disappear. The body of the seeker suddenly looks very proportionate and the eyes look bright and attractive and the eyeballs glow.

This small piece of text reveals a number of secrets. It reveals the element of the Shining Ones that gave impetus to their name—the bright eyes and glowing eyeballs—and are part and parcel of their origin. The ancient Sumerian serpent deities were said to have such eyes, and this description is found in several places in the Bible. These were not real shining eyes, they were simply revealing the esoteric light within. We also see that through this shining, the individual gets rid of the unwanted impurities that are the causes of suffering, and that their bodies are proportionate, meaning that they are perfectly balanced individuals.

The truth of the Kundalini can also be found in the greatest of Eastern avatars, Buddha. Supposedly living around 563–483 B.C., Siddhartha Guatama, or Buddha—the enlightened one—was born the son of a rajah of the Sakya tribe that lived north of Benares. When he reached the age of 30, he left behind the luxuries of courtly life and his beautiful wife and looked instead for happiness elsewhere. The wife, the riches, and the prestige are all symbols of those causes of suffering that hold us back from achieving true enlightenment. They cause us suffering because they are never enough, and we constantly desire more. To break this pattern, and to understand that we are slaves to it, is probably the hardest part of the journey.

Buddha sat under a bo tree one day after many years of searching, and finally achieved his goal. The tree was the symbolic World Tree or Tree of Knowledge or Life, where we find the serpent in the Garden of Eden.

Author at Southwell Minster.

There is no real evidence that Buddha existed, just as there is none that Jesus or any other biblical character walked the earth. However, this does not mean that his life holds no truth. Not surprisingly, the serpent was an emblem of Buddha as the messiah or savior of the people. According to Hindu oral tradition and legend (and documented in John Bathurst Deane's *The Worship of the Serpent*), Gautama "himself had a serpent lineage." And also not surprisingly, trees are sacred to Buddhists, as Gautama was enlightened beneath the bo tree.

In his book *Ophiolatreia*, serpent mythology expert Hargrave Jennings quotes a certain amateur archaeologist, named Captain Chapman, who was one of the first to see the ruins of Anarajapura in India. "At this time the only remaining traces of the city consist of nine temples...groups of pillars...still held in great reverence by the Buddhists. They consist first of an enclosure, in which are the sacred trees called Bogaha" or *Trees of Buddha*.

The basis of the Tibetan healing arts comes from the *Bhaisajya-guru* or the *Lapis Lazuli Radiance Buddha*—the master of healing. The begging bowl is made of the stone lapis lazuli, and contains the very *Elixir of Life*. Clues to this are found in a story related about the Buddha when he passes the night at the hermitage of Uruvela. The leader, Kashyapa, warned Buddha that there was only one hut available, and that a malevolent Naga (serpent) occupied it. Buddha was not concerned and went to the hut. However, a terrific struggle ensued, culminating in the hut bursting into flames. The onlookers drenched the flames, but they had to wait until morning to find out if Buddha had survived. Buddha emerged with his begging bowl in his arms, and inside was a peaceful, coiled snake. Buddha had slain the dragon of its fiery notions and emerged with a beneficial result—he had taken control. In essence, Buddha was revealing his power over the fiery snake, as balance is all-important. The healing of this begging bowl with coiled snake is an indication of the benefits to be gained from mastering the internal fire with the water of wisdom. Today, locals invoke the healing power of the snake by calling on the Medicine Buddha. The serpent and Buddha are also associated in symbolism, because he turned himself into a Naga in order to heal. Buddha epitomizes the perfectly balanced individual who can master his own self.

In the seventh and eighth centuries, a holy man by the name of Adi Sankaracharya revealed the power of the serpentine energy, when he is believed to have said: "Having filled the pathway of the Nadis with the streaming shower of nectar flowing from the Lotus feet, having resumed thine own position from out of the resplendent Lunar regions and Thyself assuming the form of a serpent of three-and-a-half coils, sleepest thou, in the hollow of Kula Kunda [the hollow of the Sacrum bone]."

In another enlightening saying, Adi Sankaracharya said that "Thou art residing in secrecy with Thy Lord in the thousand-petalled Lotus, having pierced through the Earth situated in 'Mooladhara' [the Sacrum], the Water in Manipura, the Fire abiding in the Svadhisthana, the Air in the Heart, the Ether above and Manas between the eyebrows and thus broken through the entire Kula Path."

In both sayings we see the aspect of the serpent running through the various chakras and out between the eyebrows—the Nazar, just like the uraeus serpent of the Egyptians and the phylactery of the Jews. We already know about this uraeus serpent, but what is the phylactery? And can it link the knowledge we are building directly into the Bible, and therefore also to Solomon's Temple? In Matthew 23:5, we find the writer pouring scorn on the priests for wearing their phylacteries broad, as if showing off to the world how holy they are. In truth, phylactery means *amulet*, and the Hebrews saw them as prayer carriers. An amulet was:

> Something worn, usually around the neck, as a preventative charm. The word was formally connected with the Arabic himalah, the name given to the cord that secured the Koran [word of al'Lah] to the person. The early Christians used to wear an amulet called an icthus.[1]

Amulets are magical physical manifestations of a belief. The amulet used the power of symbolism for real purposes. In the case of the Christians, the icthus or fish symbol was believed to invoke the power of the Christ (the perfect man within). Often amulets were created to ward off the Evil Eye, which is the power of others projecting evil thoughts. The idea of this Evil Eye is, not surprisingly, universal. In Germany it was the *boser blick*, in Italy it was the *malocchio*, and in French the *mauvai oeil*. The Latin version was *fascinum*, meaning to bind somebody or thing with fascination. This is an allusion to the original beliefs regarding the Evil Eye, that it was our own fascination with things which bound us, rather than another's fascination with us. The *Eye of Horus* in Egyptian times was a similar amulet, worn in association with regeneration of the self, health, and prosperity. Horus was called *Horus who rules with two eyes*, and this was an indication of the balance Horus gained from his left (sun) and right (moon) eyes. Horus, of course, shares many similarities with the Christ figure portrayed in the Bible. Therefore, to be protected by the internal balance—here manifested as the Eye of Horus—was a perfect symbol, the meaning of which is commonly misunderstood today.

The phylactery of the Jewish priests were small leather cases worn on the brow, as if the prayers held inside were somehow closer to God when in this position. If the uraeus serpent is emerging from the brow due to this being the location of the head chakra or the kabbalistic kether, then surely the location of the phylactery has a similar purpose, but as a prayer box situated to communicate with this Inner Divinity. Its seems that such a show was made of these phylacteries (to reveal to the masses how holy the priests were) that Jesus himself rebuked the priests.

All this relates to the *Sephiroth* or *Sefirot*. These are probably the most widely known terms for the *axis mundi* or *Tree of Life*. Today it has become many things, having been used and abused by writers such as Blavatsky and Crowley. The Sefirot tree is at the core of the kabbalah, and is a multilayered symbolic device. In the singular, Sefirot is *Sefirah*, which is a term used to denote 10 of the 32 principles or paths by which God created the universe—this being an allusion to the creation of the true self from the chaos of our normal lives. The sefirot is described mainly in the *Sefer Yetzirah* or the *Book of Creation*, which has been taken as a literal text by many. In truth, I believe it to be a work exploring the origin and nature of the universe as a whole, and this includes the self. The intricate system of 32 paths matches the 22 letters and the 10 numbers of the Hebrew alphabet, and this makes sense when one considers that God used words for creation. Therefore, follow the path of the letters and numbers and one has everything one needs for self-realization—we have the words and numbers of God. In reality, kabbalists believe that everything is interrelated, that nothing can be split out from the whole, that our own self-realization is part of the whole creative process.

The Sefirot is originally the Babylonian Tree of Life, with the sacred fruit only to be eaten by the gods, and which became the Tree of Life in the Garden of Eden and the *Asherah* trees of the Temple of Jerusalem. Eventually it was taken over by the kabbalah and became a method of initiation much like the chakra system of Hinduism. The term *Sefirot* comes from the Hebrew word for *sappir* or *sapphire*, and loosely means the *radiance of god* or the *shining one*, and is an allusion to the enlightenment one must achieve to gain mastery over the self.[2]

According to *Kabbalah: The Way of the Jewish Mystic* by Perle Epstein, the true element of the Sefirot is *Da'ath*, "the secret sphere of knowledge on the cosmic tree." This is the knowledge believed to be obtainable when in the Otherworld. It is "the omniscient or universal consciousness of God which, properly speaking, is not a Sefirah, but a cognitive presence of the One in each of them."

According to esoteric writer Dion Fortune in his book *The Mystical Qabalah*, "When working with the tree either to call down the greater knowledge of the superhuman universe and its infinite organisation, or to bring our self up the tree from the lower sephirah for spiritual upliftment and higher perspective, all energy must pass through Da'ath on its way into matter or disintegration into the hypertext of the universe."

This all sounds remarkably similar to the Kundalini—the words have just been altered slightly and the process has become more complicated. The bringing down of knowledge or gnosis from the superhuman universe is no different than our concept of the Universal Mind, the state of superconsciousness, and interrelationship with the quantum world.

Most (if not all) kabbalistic speculation and doctrine is concerned with this realm of divine emanations known as the Sefirot. Over many years, the kabbalists devised ways to explain their mystical experiences, and yet the Sefirot remains their chief method. Kabbalists claim that it remains because it is the principal content of their visions, a universal structure seen by all mystics. This would make sense, as many images of the Sefirot tree show entwined serpents rising upwards. They claim that in so far as God reveals himself, he does so only through the creative power of the Sefirot. This kabbalistic world of the Sefirot encompasses what philosophers and theologians term *the world of divine attributes*. These are elements of the Divine self, brought to the surface through the tree. To the mystics, this was the Divine life itself; it was the hidden dynamic of the Creator, so hidden in fact that it is ineffable and is termed the *en-sof*, or *the infinite*. The emanations from this infinite Divine life and the Divine life itself are one, and this is a prime belief of the kabbalah, that all is one, that we are interdependent bodies in a greater whole, and this is understood through visions and mystical experiences. In fact, it is believed by some that this is the only way the experience can be understood.

Similar beliefs are reflected in the sacred Jewish Torah, the priestly code found in the Pentateuch. It was often said to be the whole Pentateuch, and is a term used to describe their Divine nature. There also emerges the concept of the oral Torah, seen to be of equal importance to many. God was said to be the Torah, both written and oral, and the Torah was God. The written Torah is said to have passed through the oral Torah first, emerging from the darkness. Some say that the whole Torah is an interpretation of the Divine, and therefore there can be only one kind of Torah, whether written or oral. This Torah is embodied in the sphere of the Sefirot that only the prophets can gain access to. They simply have to raise their states of consciousness to be able to grasp the unity of the whole, to be able to perceive the One Torah, or the Universal Mind.

Kabbalists of the 13th century wrote down their understanding of this Inner Divine in a book we know as the *Zohar*. The word means *radiance*; this is due to the Divine light, which is the Torah reflected in the mysteries of the *Zohar*. The meanings of the text in the *Zohar* has kept scholars working ever since it was written. The literal meaning in the *Zohar* is the darkness. Only by seeing the hidden mystical interpretation will the truth of the *Zohar* emerge. Let's take a look at a section from the *Zohar* taken from Gershom Scholem's book *On the Kabbalah* and see if we can shed new light on old texts:

> Rabbi Simeon said: Alas for the man who regards the Torah as a book of mere tales and profane matters. If this were so, we might even today write a Torah dealing in such matters and still more excellent. In regard to earthly things, the kings and princes of this world possess more valuable materials. We could use them as a model for composing a Torah of this kind. But in reality the words of the Torah are higher words and higher mysteries.

When even the angels come down into the world they don the garments of this world, and if they did not, they could not survive in this world and the world could not endure them. And if this is true even of the angels, how much truer it is of the Torah, with which He created them and all the worlds and through which they all subsist. When she descends into the world, how could the world endure it if she did not don earthly garments? The tales of the Torah are only her outward garments. If anyone should suppose that the Torah herself is this outward garment and nothing else, let him give up the ghost. Such a man will have no share in the world to come. That is why David said: "Open thou mine eyes, that I may behold wondrous things out of thy Torah," namely, that which is beneath the garment of the Torah. Come and behold: there are garments that everyone sees, and when fools see a man in a garment that seems beautiful to them, they do not look more closely. But more important than the garment is the body, and more important than the body is the soul. So likewise the Torah has a body, which consists of the commandments and ordinances of the Torah, which are called gufe torah, "bodies of the Torah." This body is cloaked in garments, which consist of worldly stories. Fools see only the garment, which is the narrative part of the Torah; they know no more and fail to see what is under the garment. Those who know more see not only the garment but also the body that is under the garment. But the truly wise, the servants of the Supreme King, those who stood at the foot of Mount Sinai, look only upon the soul, which is the true foundation of the entire Torah, and one day indeed it will be given them to behold the innermost soul of the Torah.

Of course, we always return to the elements of our life that cause suffering, and here in the kabbalah we find that the belief is current—"if man had not succumbed to sin, the Shekinah might have dispensed with such a covering."

The *Shekinah* is the feminine principle, the Holy Spirit, and more. It is the route to the Divine knowledge or gnosis, and if she covers herself in the garments, we basically have to learn to undress her, as Solomon's Song so beautifully relates. It is the tree, once again, that is used symbolically to explain how we can be at one with the Shekinah. The tree produces fruit through the water that God provides. God's water is called *hokmah*, which means *wisdom*. It is *Sophia* (or wisdom) that will enable the tree to bear fruit, which is the soul of a righteous man. Shekinah will only dwell with the righteous, and only through *hieros gamos* or Holy Union of the male and female principles is this possible.

The Koran

Now I want to just touch briefly on the Koran, the sacred book of Islam attributed to the prophet Muhammed. In Sura 18, The Cave, taken from the Everyman's Library Edition, we find the following story about seven sleepers locked up in a cave:

> Hast thou reflected that the Inmates of The Cave and of al Rakim were one of our wondrous signs?
>
> When the youths betook them to the cave they said, "O our Lord! Grant us mercy from before thee, and order for us our affair aright."
>
> Then struck we upon their ears with deafness in the cave for many a year:

Then we awakened them that we might know which of the two parties could best reckon the space of their abiding.

We will relate to thee their tale with truth. They were youths who had believed in their Lord, and in guidance had we increased them;

And we had made them stout of heart, when they stood up and said, "Our Lord is Lord of the Heavens and of the Earth: we will call on no other God than Him; for in that case we had said a thing outrageous."

These our people have taken other gods beside Him, though they bring no clear proof for them; but, who more iniquitous than he who forgeth a lie of God?

So when ye shall have separated you from them and from that which they worship beside God, then betake you to the cave: "Your Lord will unfold His mercy to you, and will order your affairs for you the best."

And thou mightest have seen the sun when it arose, pass on the right of their cave, and when it set, leave them on their left, while they were in the spacious chamber. This is one of the signs of God. Guided indeed is he whom God guideth; but for him whom He misleadeth, thou shalt by no means find a patron, director.

And thou wouldst have deemed them awake, though they were sleeping: and we turned them to the right and to the left. And in the entire lay their dog with paws outstretched. Hadst thou come suddenly upon them, thou wouldst surely have turned thy back on them in flight, and have been filled with fear at them.

So we awakened them that they might question one another. Said one of them, "How long have ye tarried here?" They said, "We have tarried a day or part of a day." They said, "Your Lord knoweth best how long ye have tarried: Send now one of you with this your coin into the city, and let him mark who therein hath purest food, and from him let him bring you a supply: and let him be courteous, and not discover you to anyone. For they, if they find you out, will stone you or turn you back to their faith, and in that case it will fare ill with you forever."

And thus made we their adventure known to their fellow citizens, that they might learn that the promise of God is true, and that as to "the Hour" there is no doubt of its coming. When they disputed among themselves concerning what had befallen them, some said, "Build a building over them; their Lord knoweth best about them." Those who prevailed in the matter said, "A place of worship will we surely raise over them."

Some say, "They were three; their dog the fourth," others say, "Five; their dog the sixth," guessing at the secret: others say, "Seven; and their dog the eight." Say: My Lord best knoweth the number: none, save a few, shall know them.

Therefore be clear in thy discussions about them....

And when thou hast forgotten, call thy Lord to mind; and say, "Haply my Lord will guide me, that I may come near to the truth of this story with correctness."

We must be aware that this text is a revelation text. It is created to be a training text for the initiated—a second level of teaching. It is mystical in structure and content, and yet somehow we know there is a great teaching within it. We know that it is for initiation, as cave symbolism is always used as such. The cave exists in a state of darkness, away from the light of the sun, and is therefore solitary, away from the world. It is the internal reality of our own mind; it is the inside of the skull; or even the womb where we must find rebirth. It is the recess of man's own inner nature and symbolises the dormant lower nature of man.

First, we have a simple clue. The Seven Sleepers are nothing other than the seven chakra locations. Second, the title of the dog that accompanies the seven sleepers is *al Rakim*. We know that shaman always seem to have a companion dog with them, and this could be related to that in some way. However, the letters of *Rakim* have significant and mystical meaning. *R* is the letter for *external manifestation*; *A* is the *Divine Self*; *K* is *turning*; *I* is extension, and *M* is *evolution* or *amplification*. Putting this key together, we find that the dog (or the Shamanic familiar) is the extended manifestation of the Divine Self, and is therefore a very powerful being. Man's best friend is really his own true self.

In one commentary on the Koran, *Rakim* is altered to read *Katmir*, the same letters but with the addition of a *T*. This adds into the meaning of the name two distinct features: (1) that there is now a secret within the name, and (2) that the Divine Self has continuance—it goes on forever!

During the movement of the sun, we see it rising in the east and setting in the west, passing through the 12 zodiacal signs. These signs are the same as the 12 apostles in the Bible and the constellations in the sky; they are stage posts on the road to enlightenment. In the next sentence of the Koranic verse we see the sleepers being turned to the east and then the west. They are still asleep and therefore not fully superconscious, being moved in the way of the Solar Force of the sun, through the various staging posts, similar to the Kundalini.

Roman tombs in Cypru. Note the sun rising between pyramid hills on the horizon. This is the Gateway, on the in-between state.

Next, the two parties are awakened, and yet we only knew of one set of seven. These two parties are the divided nature in man, the lower and higher natures, and they are tested to reveal the enlightened aspect. The sleepers reveal their enlightened state by knowing that the Lord is both Lord over Heaven and Earth. They have discovered this through the power of the Solar Force and their newfound duality.

Next, we discover that Allah has a duality, in that he can guide us well or mislead us, and if Allah or El is truly the Inner Reality or Divinity of balance within us, then it is us—our self—who is the guide. "And thou wouldst have deemed them awake, though they were sleeping." This is an obvious allusion to the fact that, although we would see these people with physical eyes open, in truth their metaphysical eyes had been tightly closed.

"So we awakened them." This simply means that the servants of the Divine Self—the thought processes—have opened the eyes of the chakra levels. One by one the eyes of the Inner Man have been opened. In simple everyday terms, we will slowly learn and gather knowledge, and this will help our inner mind, the part of us that thinks things through, to open up new ways of seeing the universe. Eventually we will be consumed by this enlightenment and we will feel warm, emboldened, and powerful. We will be, as the serpent told Eve, as God. There will no longer be little sparks. There will instead be one light shining—a free flow of thought.

There are, of course, those who see the mystical side of Islam. These are the Sufi, the unsung heroes of the true path inspired by the mystic Muhammad. Yes, Muhammad is seen by many as a mystic. It is also understood by John Baldock in *The Essence of Sufism* that where the *House* or *Temple* is discussed in this mystical context, we are really discussing the Inner world.

> ...those who interpret the "House" spiritually—that is the Sufis—say that it refers to our inner world, which we ask God to cleanse of worldly desires and temptations so that it provides a sanctuary where we can commune with Him in peace and security.

Baldock reveals the plain fact that the House of God is the place where the causes of suffering must be cleansed to provide a psychological sanctuary to commune with Him. This God we must commune with is, of course, ourselves—the side of ourselves that is the Superconscious state and not the egocentric self. Baldock quotes from the Sufi mystic Jalaluddin Rumi:

> Make yourself free from self at one stroke,
>
> Become pure from all attributes of self,
>
> That you may see your own bright essence,
>
> Yea, see in your own heart the knowledge of the Prophet,
>
> Without book, without tutor, without preceptor.

Notice here the subtlety of the language used. We must "become pure from all the attributes of self" and yet "see in your own heart the knowledge of the Prophet." It is, to those who do not understand the true gnosis, a paradox. We must understand the difference between what is called *self* and the truth and knowledge that we have. This truth and knowledge is no different to that of the Prophet, who was a mystic and, therefore, had the ability to see beyond the worldly and illusionary self. We have one self, which is tied to the outer world of desires, and we have a true inner self, wherein lies the knowledge we are seeking.

This is a revealed mystery of the Koran and the mystical element or esoteric side of Islam. Yet again, the hidden truth is within the true self, and yet again it is as simple as the petals of a flower. It just takes a few rays of sunlight to reveal them.

Chapter 7

THE GODDESS IN THE TEMPLE

We have seen that the serpent of wisdom, of energy, of movement, and of our internal Divinity is the same the world over. We have learned that it all relates to the internal process of self-illumination known in the Hindu tradition as the Kundalini. I chose the Kundalini because it is a modern concept that is understood by most people. If I had chosen the Sefirot of the kabbalists, then I would have struggled in getting a great number of people to understand. If I had chosen the Mesopotamian *Sacred Tree*, then I would have had to explain an awful lot of the ancient belief system surrounding it.

We have seen how this serpentine wisdom tradition is implicated strongly within the pages of the Bible and Koran, and also how Buddha gained enlightenment through the hidden and simple mysteries clouded in chaotic language. We have also seen how this serpentine and dual energy uses the tree as a metaphor for its rising aspect. This tree has also been called a metaphor for man's spine—thereby swapping one metaphor for another. In truth, the tree, axis, spine, or whatever we wish to call it, is simply a ladder.

Jacob's ladder to heaven, seen at the Kykkoss Monastery in Cyprus.

In each case—whether kabbalah or Kundalini, the Tree of Knowledge or the Oak of the Druids—what we have is a process of growing that is linked with rising. This is the self—the internal self—which must grow and rise towards the light of the internal sun in order to reveal its true nature. We must grow or climb, repeating the process again and again, to learn and gain more knowledge. As the tree increases its own strength year after year, so we must increase our own strength, through our own energy, which is willpower and knowledge.

Three Secrets

In the introduction to this book I explained that, during the course of my research, I was invited to join a secret society. During this process I have learned many things. One of these is a supposed secret wisdom that lies at the heart of being able to grow as the tree does. It is an extremely simple internal process that can and has aided many people over the course of time. I have taught the three basic principles in lectures across the United Kingdom, and each time it is a joy to see the faces of those individuals who really grasp this gnosis. Others, probably what the mystics call *the blind* and what Jesus called *fools*, miss the whole point and say things like *so what?* If cynicism is the result of the knowledge of these three points, then the individual has completely missed the point.

I will give an extract from one of the great mystics and Catholic magician, Eliphas Levi, in his book *The Great Secret of Occultism Unveiled*, to express this principle:

> Progress is a possibility for the animal: it can be broken in, tamed and trained: but it is not a possibility for the fool, because the fool thinks he has nothing to learn… this then, at the outset, is a potent secret which is inaccessible to the majority of people—a secret which they will never guess and which it would be useless to tell them: the secret of their own stupidity.

I will now reveal the three secrets. You may have already picked up on some of these points from the preceding chapters, and will hopefully be more prepared for them. I also said that I will take you, the reader, along a path similar to the initiated of the mysteries of old. It is now time for the next stage.

The first point we must look at is the word *will*; remembering at all times that not one of these words taken in isolation will make the individual a fully realized person. All three words or points must be understood to gain illumination.

Baptism in the Grail, Cyprus.

Will

Try to understand this word in as full a way as possible. What does the dictionary tell us? It tells us that various aspects of the wisdom of this word can be found in other words. Most dictionaries use the following ideas to explain *will*:

Determination. Simply having a mind of ones own will not help us succeed, but adding determination to our own mind will help. *Will* is to determine by choice, our choice, not anothers. We cannot have the *will* of someone else. Again, even this word relates back to our own true self.

Purpose. The determination of our own self must also have a purpose to be fully compliant with the word *will*. No purpose in life eradicates our desire and reduces the *will*. The *will* is the faculty that determines whether or not we do something. If there is no purpose, then there is no *will*, and therefore no determination.

Strength

The second of the points is the word *strength*. Again, it is a word we must understand fully and in relation to the other words to be able to gain mystical illumination.

Strength is a force of energy. A weak force of energy is not strong. In the same respect, to be too strong when a situation calls for calm can also be a weakness. It is not being overly strong all the time; it is having strength in balance. *Strength* in our business life could be related to having sufficient funds to carry out a specific marketing campaign or the authority to see through a business plan. In our personal life, it could be the strength of the sufficient funds to achieve a personal goal. In each case, we must also have the *will* to use the *strength*. *Strength* can also be gained from our spiritual lives and is backed by a word that is often quoted by the mystics—*faith*. Many times we will read that the alchemist says his art is nothing without faith. This faith, if true, will empower the individual and give him internal *strength*. Without the *strength*, the *will* is useless, for determination will be weak and half-hearted.

Knowledge

The final chapter in our search for complete balance is *knowledge*. This is obviously the title of this book, but true gnosis is *knowledge* in union with *will* and *strength*. We may have plenty of *will* and *strength*, known as willpower, but if we are completely stupid, then all this will-power will do is get us into trouble. The *will* and the *strength* must be balanced by *knowledge*. In the same respect, having all the *knowledge* in the world will not give us the *will* or the *strength* we are looking for. For instance, I may work for a large business, and each night of my life after work, I read every encyclopedia I can get my hands on. I eventually have lots of *knowledge*. But when I get to work, my boss hates me because he is stupid and, therefore, he neither gives me money nor authority (*strength*) to carry out my knowledgeable proposals. Eventually I lose my *will*. In our personal lives, we may spend spare time alone in our room reading and gaining huge amounts of *knowledge*, but we may be weak and lack determination, and therefore never put our *knowledge* to good use. Or we may have lots of *will* and *knowledge*, but cannot get the *strength* to power them along.

Union of opposites.

The truth of the mysteries is that these three aspects, which can be used at every level in our lives, is hidden in the arcane texts for the initiate to discover. The process is slowly released until the mind fully realizes the wholeness of the concept. We are suddenly enlightened to a new and invigorating aspect of our own lives. We are fully realized. This is the true self.

Now this may seem strange, but it is time to move on to *Asherah*, the goddess in Solomon's Temple. We must try and understand how this wisdom literature and ancient knowledge relates to the Goddess in the Temple. In truth, these three secrets are the three aspects of wisdom, and the Goddess in the Temple (of Man) is Sophia.

The Goddess in the Temple of Wisdom

The ancient Goddess Sophia, who gave her name to the great mosque of Istanbul, is the aspect of *wisdom*. Most readers will also be aware that the female principle to which we often refer is seen on many levels as that of wisdom and is often symbolized with water. This is the reason that Mary is often seen on a boat or as a boat, because she is the mistress of wisdom. The boat, as in the symbol of the city of Paris, is also seen with an upright pole, balanced upon the crescent moon-shaped boat. This is the moon aspect of the Goddess (the negative or feminine principle), and the pole is originally the Tree of Asherah. To understand Asherah, we must take a brief look at the deities of the Canaanite-Phoenician and Mesopotamian religions and deity structure. What we will find is a repeating pattern, which matches our own internal process.

The god *El* or *Il* is the consort of Asherah. In one title (*ilu mabbuke naharemi*) he is called *the head of the source of two rivers*. The meaning of this is, of course, now obvious. *El* means *god*, but it also means *to shine*. The two rivers are the energies of the Kundalini, and the shining is the enlightenment found at the true source or center. The same symbolism is found in another of his titles (*ilu qirba 'apige tihamatemi*) or *he who is in the midst of the springs of the two oceans*.

The Goddess Diana in Rome.

He is also the *father of years or time (mailk 'abi shanima/shunemi)*, the *ageless one (dordoru dykeninu)* because the wisdom of the enlightenment—the internal reality of mankind—passes on from generation to generation. In the Bible, El is found as the *eternal father ('abi 'ad)*, the *Shining Ones* (Elohim), and the *ancient of days (attiq yomin)*. Initially, *El* or *Il* simply meant *the One*, an indication of the wholeness and unity of mind. As the Creator (*baniyu banawati*), all things flow from him. He is the One who must give birth to the duality.

In most references, El is seen as a bearded figure, copied over time by the priests of the period and through to the biblical references to wisdom (Samson and the Nazirites) to the Essene, and even the Knights Templar. The beard as a symbol of wisdom reflects its association with enlightenment.

Kings were referred to as *Sons of El* for the distinct reason that they gained their authority from the wisdom of the enlightenment, and were therefore seen as being deities—above the ordinary noninitiated person. This is why Alexander the Great and the pharaohs of Egypt would travel from place to place, showing the people just how enlightened they were.

El is said to epitomise strength, wisdom, and knowledge, and to inspire *will*—thus all things can be created. But he was often fairly inactive, needing his consort Asherah. Like the female shaman who goes into the Otherworld on our behalf, Asherah is not too shy to approach El on our behalf, and offerings are often made to Asherah for this purpose.

Asherah is known by many names. She is known as *she who treads on water or the sea* (*rabatu 'athiratu yammi*) and *the Holy One* (*qdsh*).[1] With El, she helped create the gods (*qynt ilm*). In Sumeria, Asherah is found as Ashratum, the bride of that other Shining One, Anu (who is the same God as El), who was depicted as the cross and center of the four cardinal points, the sky, and the fifth element. Eventually she became the consort of the Israelite god Yahweh and was known as *Shekinah*, revealing her true identity as the wisdom energy within us all. Not surprisingly, we see the truth of this in the title of Asherah in Phoenicia and North Africa—Tanith, meaning *serpent lady*. She is also known as *Dat ba'thani* or *Lady of the Serpent*.

In the first millennium B.C. Asherah was called *Chawat*, which is basically *Hawah* in Hebrew and *Eve* in English. Eve is, therefore, a remaking of Asherah, the Queen of Heaven and Serpent Lady. I should note that Eve came from Adam, and therefore Adam is El.

Asherah is often represented by bronze serpents. Examples of this have been found in the Levant. It is debated among scholars whether this is in fact the *Nehushtan* or *Brazen Serpent* of Moses—especially as it is spoken of in the same sentence in the Bible. If it is (and in all likelihood it is) then this proves the worship of the serpent as the mother goddess in

Adam, Eve, and the serpent from Lincoln Cathedral.

union with a male deity. It shows that Asherah is the serpentine and feminine aspect of one of the original versions of the Kundalini.

Asherah is a feminine singular noun; the plural (just as *El* becomes *Elohim*) is *Ashtaroth*, although the Hebrew version *Ashtoreth* is made to imply shame from *bosheth*, thus showing the rewriting of the original concepts by the patriarchal Jews. She appears 40 times and in nine books in the Old Testament. *Asherim*, which also appears in the Bible, are manufactured wooden poles made to mimic the *Asherah* trees, although in this name it now has a masculine ending.

The Asherah trees were probably not real trees, as we have evidence that they were made like the *Asherim*, if indeed the two are not the same.

For instance, in Kings 1:14–15 "The Lord will strike Israel...because they have made the sacred poles," and verse 23: "For they built for themselves high places, pillars and sacred poles on every high hill and under every green tree." In both instances, sacred poles are Asherah poles.

Indeed, in Kings 2:23–7, the women actually weave cloth for the *Asherah*, indicating that there is some kind of form to the pillar. In Kings 2:18–19 there is reference to the 400 prophets of Asherah who dine at Jezebel's table, indicating a large religious following.

One of Asherah's symbols in her serpentine aspect is almost exactly that of the Caduceus. It is two entwined serpents upon the *Asherah pole* or *Tree of Life*. Obvious fertility influences are seen on images of her holding aloft a cornucopia and pomegranate. On her shoulder is often seen a bunch of grapes. Asherah, quite simply, is the female energy on the Tree of Life. She is the goddess of life, bearing fruit in the arid desert, sustaining life.

Asherah was symbolized as a sacred tree and worshipped in groves. "Praise Qadashu, Lady of the Stars of Heaven, Mistress of All the Gods, May She grant life, welfare, prosperity, and health. Mayest thou grant that I behold thy beauty daily." (A prayer to Asherah found in Egypt from a Levantine burial).[2]

Asherah is also seen with curly hair holding serpents. Often she is depicted as a lioness or riding a lion (a symbol of bloody sacrifice, but also a symbol of our lower nature—the bloody sacrifice of which is required by Asherah), while holding serpents. In Phoenicia she became known as *Astarte*.

Asherah really needs balance. It cannot be El or Anu, as he is the ultimate Shining or enlightenment at the source of the two rivers. We need another river, and if Asherah is the Goddess of Peace and is associated so strongly with water or the sea, then this balance must be strong and powerful. We have the exact match in Baal. Baal is the *Most High Prince* (*al'iyanu ba'lu*), indicating his position below El. He is the *Conqueror of*

Isis, Astarte, Ishtar with crescent moon.

Warriors (*al'ilyu qarradima*) showing his fiery spirit. As *Pidar* he is bright or shining, and as *Rimmon* he is the *Thunderer*.

Baal was most actively worshipped in Canaan and Phoenicia as the storm god, and is considered a possible origin of the fertile Green Man— who is needed for fertility and is frightening in many respects. Baal is a dynamic force; he is the strength to the wisdom and peace of Asherah. Through a complex series of stories it turns out that Baal is not the son of

El, but of Dagan (Odakon the fish god), and in order to approach El, he must enlist the aid of Asherah.[3]

Baal is often also associated with Amon, the Egyptian ram-headed god of fertility and the breath of life, whose name strangely means *hidden*. This may relate to the fact that Baal is also known as *the one hidden in the clouds*. This is an interesting point to note, that this aspect of the inner duality is hidden from us by the clouds, and that its name is Amon. The Egyptians tended to see Set as their version of Baal, the brother of Osiris. It may actually be that the Egyptians simply split up the two aspects of the fiery serpent or positive energy element of the Kundalini into both Osiris and Set. It is obvious that Asherah and Baal were together in both religious symbolism and reality. In this verse from Judges 6:25, we have Gideon being told what to do:

> Now it came to pass the same night that the Lord said to him, "Take down your father's young bull, the second bull of seven years old, and tear down the altar of Baal that your father has, and cut down the wooden image [Asherah pole] that is beside it."

Needless to say, Gideon did exactly as he was told, and even sacrificed the bull that was seven years old with the fire from the wood of the Asherah pole. Whatever the truth of this story, it illustrates that Baal and Asherah were seen together as something highly important—so important that the Jews had to eradicate their existence. This, of course, is the world of the causes of suffering, which tears down our defences and make us repeat the cleansing process so that we can constantly attain higher wisdom.

> But the high places were not taken away; the people still sacrificed and burned incense on the high places.
>
> —2 Kings 12:3

However the high places were not taken away, and the people still sacrificed and burned incense on the high places.

—2 Kings 14:4

And he sacrificed and burned incense on the high places, on the hills, and under every green tree.

—2 Kings 16:4

This is a small indication of the repeated sin of this worship, spoken of again and again in the Bible. It seems that, for thousands of years, Judaism (and possibly even the Catholic Church) has strived to wipe out this balanced female/male relationship to replace it with their patriarchal and authoritarian rule. This may have backfired on them—seen in the previous Bible verses and in the veneration of the Cathars and Templars in the 12th century, the Marian and heavily loaded feminine bloodline Grail theories, and the 21st century *Da Vinci Code* myth, to name but a few. No wonder that this worship of the Divine Inner Reality has been ruthlessly stamped out across time, as it undermined the very power base of established Orthodox and masculine religion.

In one of the very same books of the Bible, which tells us about the Temple of Solomon, we find a distinct example of this worship being stamped out:

In the twentieth year of Jeroboam king of Israel, Asa became king over Judah. And he reigned forty-one years in Jerusalem. His grandmother's name was Maachah the granddaughter of Abishalom. Asa did what was right in the eyes of the Lord, as did his father David. And he banished the perverted persons from the land and removed all the idols that his fathers had made. Also he removed

Maachah his grandmother from being Queen, because she had made an obscene image of Asherah.

—1 Kings 15:9-13

So the granddaughter of Abishalom (the serpent of peace) was removed from her throne by her own grandson (and religious opponent) for the simple act of worshipping Asherah.

Moving slowly towards Solomon's Temple then, we have to look at whether Asherah as the female principle was seen as consort to Yahweh, and whether this explains her presence. In 1967, excavations at Khirbet el-Qom discovered two grave complexes with some intriguing inscriptions. One from the seventh or eighth century B.C. reads as follow:

Uriah... his inscription Blessed is Uriah by Yahweh—from his enemies he delivered him by his asherah. By Oniah.

This is a pretty cryptic clue, but one that never the less raises a question: Is Asherah seen here in union with Yahweh to eradicate Uriah's enemies, namely those things that gave him suffering?

Scholars argue persistently whether *his Asherah* signifies a simple wooden object used to save Uriah, or whether Asherah is a possession of Yahweh. The truth is that scholars are looking in the wrong place. They look for literal interpretations and ignore the wisdom literature, because their eyes cannot see the truth. These inscriptions are upon graves, not on some great ceremonial wall. These are very personal inscriptions, speaking about how this ancient man managed to see off his personal enemies. In this way, the truth is seen clearly, that Yahweh used Asherah (wisdom, compassion, and so on) to great effect (by the power of Yawheh in union with knowledge).

Similar inscriptions of the union of Yahweh and Asherah have been found elsewhere, such as Kuntillet Arjud in the Sinai Desert. In 1975, a large building (called by some a sanctuary for traders enroute through the desert) was discovered in the area from around the ninth century B.C. On the white plaster that covered the walls, several inscriptions were found. One of them speaks of blessings by Yahweh and his Asherah. Also two storage jars were found, and upon one of them the inscription "I bless you by Yahweh of Teman and by his Asherah" and the other "I have blessed you by Yahweh smrn [sic] and by his Asherah."

Regardless of what the scholars debate for the next 300 or 400 years, the fact remains that Asherah was Shekinah, and that Shekinah was also Matronit, the consort of the Jewish god. There can be no denying that the duality of the female and male principles are important to Jewish religion, whether the scholars or the Orthodox priesthood agree or not.

We know that, across the world and throughout all religions, the duality between the twin serpents is required. From Adam and Eve to Baal and Asherah, we have the repeating pattern of the power, wisdom, and balance of the serpent. Our true past is in the secret wisdom literature of our ancestors, and if we decide that we can alter our internal belief system sufficiently, then we will be able see this as truth and begin the real alchemical work.

The Goddess in the Temple, in our minds, and our body, is therefore the element of wisdom within us. It is balance, and this balance is aided by such wise concepts as *will*, *strength*, and *knowledge*. This concept was part and parcel of the Temple of Solomon. It was in the very precincts of that holy place, and the religious authorities have tried to wipe out its existence.

Chapter 8

The Temple and the Templars

Remember the concept of repeating patterns we have been discussing throughout the book? Well be ready for some more because the Temple of Solomon has been built, destroyed, built, destroyed, and the Jewish and Christian faiths (not to mention the Freemasons) want it rebuilt yet again.

Author in Rome.

There are many theories about the Temple, and we should just consider a few of them. Probably the most interesting theory in the current climate of the bloodline hysteria is the concept that those medieval warrior monks, the Knights Templar, dug beneath the Temple and discovered a great and tremendous secret. This secret, as you might know, is claimed to have been either the Ark of the Covenant or the Holy Grail, or maybe it was a secret text, or perhaps it was even the head of Christ.[1]

Whatever you choose to believe about these myths, you have to understand that there is almost never smoke without fire. The Knights Templar went to Jerusalem from the Languedoc region of southern France. Most people believe them to have developed in the Middle Ages, although I have seen evidence of a much older lineage.[2] As most of the world seems to have gone mad about the Knights Templar, and as they seem to be intricately involved in the whole story of the Temple itself, we should spend a few moments considering their role in history.

Originally, the Templars were a group of nine knights taken from the ruling nobility in the region of France known as Champagne. They gathered in Jerusalem under the guidance of Hugh de Payens around A.D. 1118 and formed the Knights Templar. All of this followed the huge success of the First Crusade and the establishment of *Outremer*, meaning *overseas*.[3] To the north of Jerusalem was the city of Antioch, ruled by Bohemond of Taranto. To the east was Edessa, ruled by Baldwin of Boulogne. In the south we find Tripoli, ruled initially by Raymond of Saint-Gilles, and in the midst of them all stood the Kingdom of Jerusalem, ruled by Godfrey of Bouillon.

These men pledged to commit their lives to a strict code of rules, namely those of Augustine of Hippo. On the face of it, they were charged with ensuring the safe passage of pilgrims to the Holy Land. The knights, originally known as *The Poor Fellow-Soldiers of Jesus Christ*, requested this task of the first King Baldwin of Jerusalem, who refused. Not surprisingly (and to the joy of conspiracy theorists the world over), Baldwin soon died under mysterious circumstances. He was replaced by Baldwin II, who almost immediately granted the Knights Templar the privileges they requested, as well as prime real estate in part of the al-Aqsa Mosque on the southern edge of the Temple Mount. This area was known universally as *Templum Salomnis*, or the Temple of Solomon.

Now I want to explore a brief tangent and consider some numerological evidence surrounding the Temple and other buildings arising from it.

The Temple of Jerusalem

In the tenth century B.C., King Solomon the Wise supposedly founded the Temple of Jerusalem, also known as Solomon's Temple. This was not, as is widely perceived, a Jewish temple. Instead, it was a church dedicated to pagan idols. (*Pagan* is the term given to pre-Christian religion, and really means *people of the earth*.) Solomon, according to tradition, had hundreds of wives and hundreds of concubines, all of whom came from across the Middle East, and all of whom worshipped different gods. All these gods were represented in this great center of Middle Eastern religion. (Unfortunately, there is no evidence from surrounding nations or cultures that any of this really happened.) However, the story goes that, by 587 B.C., the armies of Babylon managed to destroy the Temple, leaving the task of rebuilding to those Jews who would return from Babylonian captivity. We would, of course, do well to remember that the city of Babylon was often used as an allegory for sin. Therefore, this story could be interpreted that sin brought the Temple down, and those who escaped sin would one day rebuilt it.

This second Temple was built by Herod, who (according to some) built it even bigger than before. He began construction in the period just prior to the birth of Christ. However, just as this magnificent building was coming to completion (in around A.D. 70) the Romans destroyed it as part of their reprisals against the *Jesus Bar-Kochba* uprising. Nothing remained but the *Wailing Wall*, thought to be part of the original Temple. It seems that nobody is entirely sure of the exact location of the original Temple, and the conclusions of this book will highlight exactly why this is the case.[4]

Inside Saint Peter's Cathedral.

Solomon's Temple has been intricately linked with the Knights Templar. Indeed, it is the reason for their name. But what was it that the Templars saw in the Temple of Jerusalem that inspired them? In the years following the return of the Templars from the Middle East, we see a surge in Gothic architecture. Before this period, churches were mainly small and often constructed of wood. Suddenly, with the inspiration gathered from the Middle East, Europe was awash with building fever. More than 80 cathedrals were built between A.D. 1128 and 1228 in France. Most of these projects were led by the Templar-linked Cistercians monks. All of these buildings have or had gnostic influence, with hidden symbolism rife within the stonework. Some of these churches gave rise to the Freemasons. It is an accepted fact among scholars that the Templars were instigators in the rise of these Masons, and it is the Masons who hid profound wisdom within the stone. Another amazing coincidence is that, suddenly at this time, Europe saw a rise in alchemical, astronomical, medical, and philosophical texts and interest—all of which run parallel to the Temple.

The question still remains, however: What did the Templars find in Jerusalem? According to John Michell in *The Temple at Jerusalem: A Revelation*:

> Legends of the Temple describe it as the instrument of a mystical, priestly science, a form of alchemy by which oppositely charged elements in the earth and atmosphere were brought together and ritually married. The product of their union was a spirit that blessed and sanctified the people of Israel. In the Holy of Holies dwelt the Shekinah, the native goddess of the land of Israel. It was her marriage chamber, entered at certain seasons by the bridegroom.

Michell is defining something that can be proven from the mythology and tradition of the Jews. He tells us of the traditions revealing the *Goddess in the Temple* (or Shekinah) and the unity of the ritual marriage. It is a profound statement that gives us insight into the amazing truth of what the Templars were looking for—a link to the enlightenment experience of the shining ones. As I have pointed out, the Temple initially was not made for just the one God, but for many gods. This was a place of union, a joining of the opposites seen in the Kundalini experience where the male and female (positive and negative) are joined to bring about true illumination. It was this mystical experience that was at the heart of the attempted revival by the Templars. Many alchemical texts of the time speak of the hidden symbolism of the European churches and cathedrals— especially those similar to the Scottish chapel at Rosslyn.

This same mystical and hidden symbolism can be seen in the numerology implied by the Templars and Solomon's Temple. It is well known that the Templars were initially nine in number and were later *divided* into 72 ($72 = 7 + 2 = 9$) heads or chapters. Why would this be?

To answer this question, we have to look at the symbolism of the number 9. It is probably the most important number in mystical numerology, as its mathematical structure makes it a perfect number. For instance, 9 always reverts back to nine: $9 + 9$ is 18, $1 + 8 = 9$; $9 \times 9 = 81$, $8 + 1 = 9$, $99 + 99 = 198$, $1 + 9 + 8 = 18$ and $1 + 8 = 9$. This scenario repeats itself in many variations. The number 9 is also composed of the all-powerful 3×3, or the *triple triad*. It is the end number, the fulfilment, and therefore the completion of all prophecy—the perfect number. It is the number of the angels or watchers, also known as the *Shining Ones*. It is also linked geometrically as the number of the circumference of a circle: 360 degrees $= 3 + 6 + 0 = 9$. The four quarters of a circle are all made up of 90 degrees. Symbolically, it is seen as a triangle inverted within an upright triangle, and hence also as the infamous *Eye of God* within the pyramid. The Templar cross is a hidden symbol of the number, with eight points and the center point making nine. The Celts saw this number as significant of their own trinity—the triple goddess who was three times great (similar to the *Thrice Great Hermes* or *Hermes Trismegistus*).

In China, the number 9 was the most auspicious of numbers and is seen remarkably in Feng Shui with the eight exterior squares for the cultivation of the land and a central or ninth square, which is called *God's Acre*. This concept of the number 9 being paramount to Feng Shui also links it to architecture, as Feng Shui involves the best place to locate a building. This building is, of course, the lower body or nature of man and its place on earth. The number 9 or *God's Acre* is therefore the other dimension or spiritual side of man. For Feng Shui, the number 9 implies a heavenly power or higher human consciousness in the place that is built. This is also telling in the positioning of the Temple of Solomon.

In Hinduism, the shining god (Agni) is seen as the number nine. In the kabbalah it signifies the foundation (stone). In Scandinavian mythology, Odin or Wotan is crucified on *yggdrasil* (the world tree) for nine days, to win the secrets of immortality and wisdom. In fact, I could name hundreds of instances from across the ancient and modern world where the number 9 is used in the spirituality of man and sacred architecture, but the fact remains that it is a deeply important number all over the world. It is linked auspiciously with building and the enlightenment process because of its perfect geometrical nature. We must not confuse the number 9 with the number 7, as 7 is the process we as individuals must go through to gain enlightenment.

The exact position of the Temple is hotly debated, although in gnostic truth, there is no need for the debate. But there are a few known facts that do relate and have a bearing on why the Temple was supposed to be built to specific measurements.

An ancient temple in Rome.

There is an axis running through the Temple complex called the *Messianic Axis*. People of Jewish faith believe that this line is the path that the coming Messiah will take. Christians believe it was the line that Jesus walked when he appeared. This line begins on the Mount of Olives, which is where Jesus is said to have ascended; it then enters the Temple Mount through the Golden Gate, and crosses the Dome of the Tablets and a rock (which is thought to have been the Holy Rock within the Holy of Holies in the Temple). The axis then continues westward straight to Golgotha, where Jesus was supposedly crucified. Amazingly, similar to the *Ley Lines* or *Dragons Paths* in the rest of the world, this straight line links extremely holy spots together. All these sights are important to the illuminative aspect of the enlightenment experience. Souls are thought to pass along this holy line to their reward in the *Holy Sepulchre* or *Paradise* (meaning the place of enlightenment). Indeed, the Jews believed that when the Temple was destroyed, the holy Shekinah fled, following this line. This relates to the traditions of the other energy lines seen around the globe (and to modern science) as it is believed that the positive (male) and negative (female) lines of wave (serpent) energy cross certain points called nodes along distinct lines. These nodes are where important buildings are placed, and this is one of the ideas of Feng Shui. Amazingly, the distance covered by this line is just more than half a mile—the precise distance from the center of the Earth to the surface, and is therefore an extremely holy location, as the two rocks that make up this distance are natural (864 cubits [8 + 6 + 4 = 18; 1 + 8 =9] of 1.728 feet [1 = 7 = 2 = 8 = 18; 1 + 8 = 9], multiply this by 14,000 to get the radius of the Earth, and we get 12,096,000 cubits [1 + 2 + 9 + 6 = 18; 1 + 8 = 9] or 20,901,888 feet [2 + 9 + 1 + 8 + 8 + 8 = 36; 3 + 6 = 9]). The profundity of this mathematical enigma is beyond the scope of this book. Suffice it to say that many religious, mystic, gnostic, and philosophical people around the globe have been drawn to the number 9's mathematical perfection.

The number 864 cubits is prominent in the measurements of the Michell Temple. This is interesting, as it also resolves back 9. According to the language of numerical symbolism, 864 is the center of radiant energy and is symbolic of the sun and the shining experience. The Earth is 864,000 cubits in diameter; the moon is 2,160 cubits (2 + 1 + 6 = 9). This language has been included in buildings as far back as the Egyptian empire. This is indicative of the hidden language of the Shining Ones across the world, and is also seen in the infamous megalithic yard. [5] It is an indication of the knowledge of astronomy seen from Sumerian times onwards. Even the name for Jerusalem equals 9 when using the Greek letters and the language of numerical symbolism. (Iota, epsilon, rho, omicron, upsilon, sigma, alpha, lamda, eta, and mu = 864 = 9.)

I know from my work in *The Serpent Grail* that water is seen in many representations of the Serpent Divinity (which is linked with the female Shekinah). It was no surprise to find a *Serpent Pool* beneath the Temple Mount. Amazingly, we also find that there is a fault line running near the Mount that is being used by Christian and Jewish fundamentalists as a sign that the Bible is correct when it says that the Mount will be split in two. (This is really a symbolic device for splitting the positive and negative fields—as Adam was split to create Eve.) These fault lines have been shown to be in many places around the world, and have been linked to ancient and sacred sites. Some people believe that tectonic plate movement has charged the underground rocks. These same rocks have been shown to improve growth in plants and are linked to quantum entanglement effects. This charged energy is, in part, the serpent energy spoken of by the ancients, and is utilized in a deep meditative state to bring on the enlightenment process—merging the human electro magnetism with the earth or universal electromagnetism at subatomic particle levels.

The line taken in all instances is from the east—and thus the rising sun or shining one. An indication of the enlightenment process is shown by the writers of Psalm 24:9–10:

> Lift up your heads, O ye gates; even lift them up, ye everlasting doors; and the King of glory shall come in.

This reference to gates and doors is simply the opening up of the mind to the illumination process by lifting up the head. Who is the King of Glory? He is none other than the Lord of Hosts, the Lord of the Shining Ones.

So the Temple was theoretically built in an auspicious location with all the symbolism of the duality of energies believed in by the ancients of the world. But I want to get back to the number 9 for a moment, which is so relevant to the Knights Templar. For this purpose I turn to John Michell and his book *The Temple of Jerusalem: a Revelation*.

Author at the Coluseum in Rome.

In A.D. 135 the Roman Augers designed the new city of Jerusalem after it was crushed during the Bar-Kochba revolt. These Roman Augers were mystics of the highest order, and their history can be traced back to Sumeria and the original Shining Ones, and forward to the Freemasons, as the infamous Masonic historian Albert Pike and others have attempted to prove. They had a ritual code of town planning, which they claimed to have inherited from the serpent-worshipping Etruscans. According to John Michell, the idea was just like Feng Shui, and was to "bring order and good fortune to cities and settlements."

In the first instance, the Augers put down their standard north-south axis called the *cardo maximus* or, as more commonly known, the *axis mundi*—the *world axis* or *universal axis*—a symbol also utilized in the Kundalini. The *via dolorosa* (the *way of sorrows*) taken by millions of pilgrims through Rome runs parallel to the *cardo maximus*. Marking the terminus of the *cardo*, the Augers placed a tall pillar forming an angle of 36 degrees. (Remember, 3 + 6 = 9; 36 degrees is the measurement of each corner in a pentagram; it is also the symbol of the perfect man as illustrated by Leonardo da Vinci.)

The Roman Augers followed the messianic axis from Mount Olives to Golgotha. "Parallel to it, 360 cubits to the south, is the extended axis line through the temple identified by Tuvia Sagiv. It is also the line of the Roman Decumanus. It runs between the northern edge of Absalom's pillar and the corner of the tower of David's citadel at the Jaffa gate...."[6]

Note the use 360 cubits (an ancient measurement) which resolves into the number 9. Even streets, which do not match the new axis or the *corda* meet this device. The streets that run away from the column of Hadrian run away at 36-degree intervals, similar to the center of the pentagram. This center of the pentagram is located on the messianic axis, with each side measuring 720 cubits (7 + 2 + 0 = 9). The Messiah is, therefore, represented by the pentagram, which is the symbol of the perfect man.

According to John Michell, there is also an amazing rectangle created by the Temple, that measures 720 × 1728 cubits (both numbers revert back to 9) and when measured in the *cubit and a handsbreath* system is 2.0736 feet (which also reverts to 9). This rectangle was envisaged by the builders as a framework through which the messianic axis runs, and upon which is placed the pentagram/pentacle—the four sides of the rectangle adding to the 5 sides/points of the pentagram/pentacle, equalling 9 yet again.

The pentagram is also linked in etymology, as *pen* means *head*. This head is seen at the top of the messianic axis, as Christ is seen at the top of the crucifix. It's no wonder, therefore, that the pentagram or pentacle is always linked with the illumination experience, as it means both *head* and *9*. It is also a symbol seen as a star across the ancient world, and means Shining One in glyph form. Michell found that the reciprocal pentacle conjoined with the first and on a common axis, and the messianic axis actually reduced down—one inside the other—to a point that pinpointed Golgotha, the place of the head or skull.

Pentagram from Silves.

I wonder whether this architectural symbolism was something that the Knights Templar (among others) had discovered. Was this one of the divine secrets they had brought back from Jerusalem? Did this give rise to the building surge seen during the 12th century? I decided to do a little detective work of my own.

Choosing Chartres Cathedral in France, I first found a ground plan and noted the position of the labyrinth between the nine sets of columns on either side. Taking an idea I had previously discovered (that the labyrinth was also symbolic of the head/mind, as well as the path of the serpent energy) I centered a pentacle within the labyrinth. The head of the pentacle met up with the West Door, while the feet at the other end met a row of columns running from north to south. When I mirrored this image so that the head was facing east, the center of the new pentacle was centered on the choir. I then drew a circle around both pentacles and found that they crossed at the center of the cathedral to form a perfect *vesica piscis*—which is the *Ru Gateway*, or entrance into higher consciousness. Symbols of gnostic beliefs have definitely been built into the architectural designs.

Considering this architectural message, I decided to look at other cathedrals built around the same time period and with the original ground plans. Every single plan matched this sacred geometry. I also found within each one a representation of the life of man or 72 years, which is a processional year and equals 9.

We now understand a little more of the scope of numerology, and we know that its underlying aspects revolve around the enlightenment or illumination of the mind. We have also discovered that this very understanding was brought to Europe, where it was physically manifested in the great cathedrals and churches.

As time passed, the Knights changed their title several times, including: *The Poor Fellow-Soldiers of Jesus Christ and the Temple of Solomon*,

The Knights of the Temple of Solomon, *The Knights of the Temple*, *The Templars*, or even just *The Temple* itself. This title, *The Temple*, is a true indication of the real meaning of the *Temple of Solomon*, for this is how they saw themselves.[7]

Author at a Templar Castle in Portugal.

For nine years the Knights Templar excavated beneath the Temple of Solomon in complete secrecy. The Grand Master returned to Europe, supposedly with secrets that have been hidden for hundreds of years. Very quickly, the knights achieved a special dispensation from the Pope to allow them to charge interest on loans—indicating their swift path to wealth and their underlying importance. Soon the great period of cathedral building began across Europe, using the new architectural secrets discovered by the crusaders. It appears almost as if this knowledge needed to be placed across all of Europe.

This knowledge may have come from some of the discoveries made by the Templars, especially when we consider that the man responsible for the building program was none other than Saint Bernard. (This is the same Bernard who gave the Order of the Knights Templar their rules, and who was related by blood to various members.) In all likelihood, the new building influence came about through the fresh and invigorating contact with Islamic and Middle Eastern architecture and the Islamic mathematical advances, which were far superior to anything Europe possessed.

The Templars grew in wealth and power, supposedly using their new-found wisdom. Their land-holding and banking system made them one of the most powerful and feared groups in all of Europe. No one could match their international strength.

According to George F. Tull in *Traces of the Templars*, they were also "well placed to obtain relics" as they held the respect of nobility and had many strategically placed premises across the Holy Land. Near Loughton-on-Sea in England there are several Templar-connected sites. The Temple here was "well provided with liturgical books, plate and vessels of silver, silver gilt, ivory and crystal, vestments, frontals and altar cloths. Among the relics kept there were two crosses containing fragments of the True Cross and a relic of the Holy Blood." Tull also tells how some of these relics entered Britain: "Sometimes the ships returned with more specialised cargo, as when in 1247 Br. William de Sonnac, Master of the Temple in Jerusalem, sent a distinguished Knight Templar to bring to England and present to King Henry III 'a portion of the Blood of our Lord, which He shed on the Cross for the salvation of the world, enclosed in a handsome crystalline vessel.' The relic was authenticated under seal by the Patriarch of Jerusalem, the bishops, abbots and nobles of the Holy Land."

In Surrey, the Templars held land known then as Temple Elfold, with 192 acres of arable land. In 1308, there was mention of a grail and a chalice at this location. It is obvious that part of the wealth of the Templars came from the propaganda tools of the medieval relic business, proving their astute business acumen. They were also incidental in spreading the cult of Saint George, which is especially interesting when we consider that they knew of his shrine in Lydda, not to mention being incidental in the medieval marketing of King Arthur and the Holy Grail myths. But in the early 14th century, all this was to end as King Philip of France organized their downfall, and the supposed secrets and wealth of the Knights Templar disappeared.

At their trials, the Templars were not only accused of worshipping the sacred head (known today as Baphomet) but also the veneration of the serpent. As Andrew Sinclair points out in *The Secret Scroll*, another Templar emblem was the foliated staff of Moses, the very same staff that turned into a serpent and was itself emblematic of the serpent religious cult and Kundalini awakening.

The *Rosslyn Missal*, written by Irish monks in the twelfth century, shows Templar crosses with great dragons and sun discs. Upon the Secret Scroll is the symbol of the 12 tribes of Israel—the breastplate of Aaron (who's serpent staff is said to be in the Ark), with 12 squares signifying the 12 tribes, surmounted by a serpent. The serpent, ruling the tribes as a symbol of dominance over the 12 human aspects, is also depicted. Many people believe that quite a few of the Templars (along with their secrets) escaped to Scotland, and the dawning of Freemasonry emerged soon thereafter. Some people believe that the Freemasons are directly related to the Templars.

The Masons of Lichfield Cathedral erecting the superstructure of a Gateway to the Otherworld.

In the year 1314, King Edward of England invaded Scotland, hoping to bring an end to the border battles. Meeting the Scottish army at Bannock Burn, he was surprised by a force of well-trained men fighting for the Scots. The tide of battle turned and Scotland achieved independence, although only for three years. The standard history has it that these well-trained men who turned the tide against the English army were no more than camp followers and servants. But many believe that these were the famous Knights Templar, who had taken root in Scotland to hide from Catholic tyranny. Strangely, immediately after the battle at Bannock Burn, Robert the Bruce (the new Scottish King) rewarded the Templar-linked Sinclair family with lands near Edinburgh and Pentland. The very same lands are now associated with hundreds of Templar graves, sites, symbols, and more.

An indication of the historical popularity of the Templars is shown in the peasant's revolt, led by Wylam Tyler in A.D. 1381 when a mob marched in protest of oppressive taxes. Strangely, they did not harm the old Templar buildings, but instead turned their attentions to the Catholic Church. In one instance, the mob carried things out of a Templar Church in London to burn the Catholic items in the street, rather than damage the Templar building. It may be that this uprising was a coincidental incident, or it may be that it was inspired by the actions of a hidden and now secret society of the Templars—hidden because of Catholic hatred. If it is the case that the Templars inspired this revolt, then even though they were not successful, they tried again a hundred years later and began the Reformation. It was around this time (the 15th century) that the first records of Scottish and York Masonic meetings begin to appear.

I wondered whether the Templars gained insight into the ancient wisdom we have been discussing, and whether they included more of the symbolism of that wisdom within their own works. (And also whether this had grown so large and popular that it was just too dangerous for the Catholic authorities to accept.) It would, of course, have been absolute heresy to claim that Jesus was a symbol of the divinity within, and that certain key Catholic doctrines were spuriously literal.

There are, I believe, links between Sumerian iconography and Templar symbolism that need to be explored. The worship of the serpent can be traced back into Sumeria, as I have discussed in *The Serpent Grail*. The most obvious Templar image is that of the two poor knights seated upon a horse, which is very similar to the idea and concept of two riders commonly seen in ancient Sumeria. It is believed by orthodox historians (who obviously have little or no knowledge of the esoteric traditions) that this was purely a tactical device in warfare, but it could also be seen as symbolic of duality and balance. This is the lower nature and higher conscious nature of man in union and balanced. It is the balance of the inner world with the outer world, which is the hidden or esoteric tradition of the Sufis—the mystical element within Islam, and a tradition that the Templars simply must have come into contact with.

The Templar cross is also seen in many Sumerian images. It is normally associated with an upturned crescent moon. This cross is a symbol of Anu, the great Shining One, and the upturned crescent moon is a symbol of the goddess Asherah. This is a symbol of the Divine union. By using this symbolism, the Templars may be indicating their own inner balance. We discovered in *The Serpent Grail* that the colors of red and white are symbolic of this union, and a red cross on a white background (commonly used by the Templars) is indicative of the serpent.

Grand Master's Armour, Knight of Malta.

Another symbol seen in various forms from Sumeria to France is the *abraxus*. A figure with snakes for legs is a symbol used for gods such as *Oannes* (the father of Baal), which later became the symbol of the Grand Master of the Templar Order. What could this mean? Did the head of the Order of the Templars see himself as the chief of the serpents?

The Templars also used the serpent symbol of eternity and immortality: the snake eating its own tail. Thus we have a serpent secret being held by the very highest of Christian organizations. The *abraxus* reveals a man/deity who is empowered by his balancing of the twin serpents. These are symbols of mystical knowledge. The Templars are revealing, through symbolism, just what ancient wisdom they uncovered at the Temple of Solomon.

The cross of Lorraine, the symbol used by the Templars before their Maltese cross, is also seen in Sumeria as a symbol for kingship, which we know was only bestowed on those who possessed shining enlightenment. These influences must have been picked up while the Templars were in the Middle East. We know that they used these symbols, because, during the trials of the early 14th century, Templar prisoners etched these symbols onto their cell walls.

The cross of Lorraine was the emblem of heraldry for Rene d'Anjou, said by researcher Charles Peguy to represent the arms of both Christ and Satan and the blood of both, from an article by Boyd Rice titled "The Cross of Lorraine: Emblem of the Royal Secret." Is this representative of balance on the cross? The cross of Lorraine is also said to incorporate the symbol *phi* or the *Golden Ratio of Sacred Geometry*—so very important to the Masons and symbolic of the perfected man. Rene d'Anjou was keenly aware and interested in many things occult, himself leading a search for ancient Hermetic texts. The cross of Lorraine was therefore taken on by Rene, and subsequently by Marie de Guise (the wife of James Stuart V, and the parents of Mary Queen of Scots) because of its occult symbolism. It symbolised poison. Proof of this meaning comes from the fact that it became a symbol used by chemists on the bottles of poisonous substances. The idea is hidden in duality. Why would monarchs and Templars use a sign for poison, if the poison did not have an opposite? The Templars were the antidote.

In the early twentieth century, Aleister Crowley, the arch Magus (creator of the Order of the Oriental Templars) and self-proclaimed alchemist, would assign this very same symbol as the *Sigil of Baphomet*. The cross of Lorraine is also thought to be a sign of secrets. It is a sign of the *angelic race*, which supposedly came down and imparted wisdom and the secrets of immortality to the royal bloodline. But who is this angelic race if not the Shining Ones? It is the symbol of those who gained enlightenment. According to Boyd Rice it is "a sigil of that Royal Secret, the doctrine of the Forgotten Ones." For this reason it seems peculiar that, in the 1940s, Charles de Gaulle should make it the official symbol of the French Resistance. But the cross of Lorraine is not the only symbol that holds a deeper wisdom.

I was playing with the standard Maltese Templar cross one day, wondering why and how the design had evolved. I knew that it had eight points and all that this entailed, but then I remembered that Fulcanelli believed that Gothic architecture was a three-dimensional esoteric message. Due to the fact that the Templar mysteries emerged from many places (including Arabic or Muslim influences, Judaic kabbalistic beliefs, and even Egyptian sacred rites), I was sure that there had to be another message enclosed within this simple shape. Working from the assumption of the three-dimensional aspect, and wondering if there were any links to one of the greatest mysteries in the world, I wondered what would happen if you cut out the cross from a piece of paper and lay it flat to create a two-dimensional image. If you then take hold of the cross in the very center and lift it up, you end up with a perfect pyramid—a symbol of Egyptian wisdom and immortality. But on some Templar crosses the edges are angled inwards to create eight points. I thought that the pyramid of Giza had straight walls, until I looked deeper. The Great Pyramid at Giza holds a secret architecture—its walls bow inwards. This is the only pyramid that does so!

Could it be, I wondered, that the Templars included this hidden symbolism in the Great Pyramid? It was fashioned to incorporate the three-dimensional geometry spoken of by Fulcanelli and said to have been brought into Europe by the Templars and their allies the Cistercians. That these mysterious brothers in gnosticism understood the meaning behind the symbolism of the pyramids—that it was symbolic, in all aspects, of the immortality of the serpent.

hiram and the Temple

Hiram was the son of a Jewish mother and a Phoenician father, and is credited with the decoration of the Temple of Solomon. He was said to have been the "son of a widow of the tribe of Naphtali…. He cast two bronze pillars" 1 Kings 7:13–15. We must also note something of interest mentioned in 1 Kings 16:

> Then he made two capitals of cast bronze, to set on top of the pillars. The height of one capital was 5 cubits; and the height of the other capital was five cubits. He made a lattice network, with wreaths of chainwork, for the capitals which were on top of the pillars: seven chains for one capital and seven for the other capital.

These pillars became known as *Jachin*, meaning *he establishes*, and *Boaz*, which means *in him is strength*. These pillars are now familiar to most modern Freemasons as central to their own Lodge or Temple. Copies of these can be clearly seen at Rosslyn Chapel.

What is interesting here is the original text about these pillars. First, bronze is used for the capitals, just as bronze is used for the *Brazen Serpent* of Moses and is indicative of the fiery aspect of the serpent. The height of the pillars was 5 cubits, matching the five hooded cobras seen across India and atop many pillars (although the Bible calls them lilies, which are a symbol of balance). Leading up to these capitals then were *wreaths of chainwork*, seven on each pillar. Strangely, these chains were for the capitals, which points to the head! Does this mean that these chains were meant to lead up to this important brass capital—the head? Like a snake on the Brazen Serpent? In any case, it is interesting and probably no coincidence that seven specific chains were chosen, just like the branches of the Mesopotamian Sacred Tree and the Kundalini.

There are real links between Hiram and the serpent. For instance, we noted above that he was of the Tribe of Naphtali. The standard of the Tribe of Naphtali, according to Jewish tradition, is a serpent or basilisk. This could have Egyptian origins, as Jewish tradition states that Naphtali was the brother of Joseph, who was chosen to represent the family to Pharaoh.

> And now I have sent a skillful man, endowed with understanding, Huram [Hiram] my master [father] craftsman, (the son of a woman of the daughters of Dan, and his father was a man of Tyre), skilled to work in gold and silver, bronze and iron, stone and wood, purple

and blue, fine linen and crimson, and to make any engraving and to accomplish any plan which may be given to him, with your skilful men and with the skilful men of my lord David your father.

—2 Chronicles 2:13–14

In this verse, Hiram is said to be a son of the Tribe of Dan, which had an emblem of the serpent, this time with a horse. Incredibly, there is also a hidden truth and repetitive pattern in this verse about the real skills of this literary character. Follow this pattern: Hiram is skilled in (1) gold and silver; (2) bronze and iron; (3) stone and wood; (4) purple and blue; (5) fine linen and crimson; (6) to make any engraving; and (7) and to accomplish any plan that may be given to him. Note that there are seven balanced elements to the skill of the man who will build the Temple! This is a real clue to the Temple's secret indeed.

According to this book of chronicles, Hiram was a cunning man, accomplished in understanding, and skilled in the work of gold, silver, brass, stone, and timber. But he was also credited with certain tools that could pierce stone. Stone is symbolic of wisdom and foundation. Hiram's tool, therefore, pierced the veil of wisdom.

According to the book of Kings, the Temple was built of stone (built of wisdom) before it was brought to the site. It was similar to a ready-made or prefabricated building. It is said by tradition that neither hammer nor axe, nor any tool of iron was used in the building. So how was it built? This in itself is a paradox, which can only be answered by revealing the true secret of the Temple.

In Exodus, Moses is told to build an altar to the Lord without tools, lest he should pollute it.

> And if you make Me an altar of stone, you shall not build
> it of hewn stone; for if you use your tool on it, you have
> profaned it.
>
> —Exodus 20:25–26

It seems the same symbolism was utilized in the building of the Temple.

According to rabbinical teaching, the prefabrication of the Temple was performed by the Shamir, a giant worm or serpent that could cut stones. (Incidentally, worm means serpent.) This is similar to Nordic and Celtic beliefs, where Valhalla and Camelot were built with the fire of the dragon; and in China, where building was aided by the serpent energy.

According to Rashi and Maimonides, the Shamir was a living creature. But this is hardly likely in the strict sense of the meaning. What is more likely is that the idea of the wisdom of the worm or snake Shamir was used in the construction of the Temple. This is a universal concept, as can be seen in India, where it was the the Naga of fable who escaped their country and took architectural wisdom abroad. The architect gods, such as Thoth of Egypt are linked strongly with the serpent wisdom, because they are linked with the building of Temples of Wisdom inside ourselves. Other references also link the Shamir to the snake, such as the *Testament of Solomon*, which calls it a green stone, such as the *Emerald Tablet*.[8] According to one legend which has been recorded by William Bacher and Ludwig Blau in *Shamir*, the Shamir had been placed in the hands of the Prince of the Sea, which of course is symbolic of the Prince of Wisdom. In essence, what we really have is the Temple of Wisdom being built by the serpent. That serpent is none other than the internal Kundalini.

Strangely, the name Hir-Am actually means *exalted head of the people* (*Hir = head* or *exalted*; *Am = people*) and is closely related to Abraham (*Ab Hir Am*). Of course, this is a subtle clue as to the reality of Solomon's

Temple. The exalted head is surely the only element that can make the real Temple. It is only the head raised above all others, that has the wisdom to achieve such an amazing feat.

However, we also have another and more telling meaning of Hiram. *Ahi-Ram* actually means *exalted snake*. So, in either meaning, Hiram was the exalted head or snake; both meanings are paramount to the discovery of the thread of the snake cult and religious underlying beliefs. Both the exalted head (as having wisdom above all others) and the exalted snake (as being the height of the Kundalini) are telling etymological devices.

According to David Wood in his book *Genesis*, Hiram was also believed to be descended from Cain through Tubal-Cain, who was said to be the only survivor of the *superior race* after the flood. The race is supposed to be called *Elohim* (people of the fiery snake) or the Shining Ones, also known as the serpent people. This tale is derived from a text known as *E* or *Elohim* from around 750 B.C., and also gives rise to the stories of the *Dionysiac Architects*, who are said to be one of the progenitors of the Freemasons. It's no wonder that the pillars of Hiram should be closely related to the worship of the snake.

Rosslyn Chapel, which I mentioned earlier, is in Scotland, not far from Edinburgh, and is incredibly important to the Freemasons. This is due to its mock Temple pillars, which are entwined with the symbolism of snakes. These were not built with a direct relation to the Norse myths of yggdrasil and its relationship to the Sinclair family, who built the place in the 15th century, but ultimately as symbols of the religious power of the gnostic serpent.

On the *Secret Scroll* we mentioned earlier (discovered by Andrew Sinclair) one of the most important images is the sight of a large coiled serpent beneath the Temple steps with a crown, a pick, and a shovel, as if pointing towards the excavation of the Temple itself.

There is a legend that may support Andrew Sinclair's findings. This oriental legend tells that the Queen of Sheba was attracted to Hiram and that King Solomon became jealous. He was so jealous that he plotted the death of Hiram. Molten metal used in the casting of a brazen sea was going to be used to kill Hiram, but he was saved by the spirit of Tubal-Cain, his ancestor who was linked with serpent worship. He was, therefore, saved by the serpent of death; he was warned from the other side.

Hiram threw his jewel down a deep well (meaning hidden wisdom), but was then killed by Solomon's assassins with a blow to the head. It was said that three masters later found the body and venerated it. The jewel was found and placed on a triangular altar (which Solomon had erected) in a secret vault beneath the Temple.[9]

What was the jewel of this builder? Why did it cause so much veneration? Whatever it was, later crusader knights under the guise of the Knights Templar were to dig furiously beneath the Temple to discover the truth. Of course, the Templars may have dug for other items as well, such as the Ark of the Covenant, but I believe this is symbolic language and that the true jewel was that of gnosis.

Following these supposed excavations, both the Templars and the Cistercians under Saint Bernard grew wealthy. It is true that Templar remains have been found in and around tunnels at the Temple site, but these could easily have been for defensive purposes, as such tunnelling was common practice at the time.

Great buildings were contructed across Europe, all hiding secret symbolism of the snake, and all using the architectural skills discovered by the Templars while they were in the Middle East. The hollow *Brazen Pillars of Hiram* became the twin pillars of the later Masons, who, similar to Moses—the emergent serpent—emerged from the Templars. These pillars were said to be hollow and to contain secret manuscripts, which remind us of the supposed discovery of the manuscripts from Rennes Le Château, also thought to have been found inside a pillar.

Of course, during the period of the Crusades, there was not one depiction of the crucifixion on any of the buildings erected, backing up the claim that the Templars denied the crucifixion. It is thought that the Templars and Cistercians found a wealth of ancient manuscripts containing secrets, giving them insight into the truth behind Christianity. One thing that did emerge was the cult of *Baphomet and Sophia*, the elements of serpent wisdom. If the Templars had discovered the Holy Grail, as many have said, then the secrets of the Grail were what they truly discovered. And it was these secrets that they spirited away from Montsegur, the Cathar stronghold taken by the Catholic Albigensian Crusade.

But I digress. Our true course does not lay with the Cathar or the Templar. These are but incidental players on a much bigger stage. The truth of Solomon's Temple spawned these enigmatic groups; it also spawned the world's largest modern secret society. We have also seen that inside this Temple was Asherah, the entwined serpent goddess worshipped across the known world. We have also seen that a mystical serpent helped in the creation of this Temple, and that it was a secret discovered by the Knights Templar.

Chapter 9

Solomon's Secrets

The Journey to Enlightenment

We believe that the writings of Moses, the Prophets, and all earlier Teachers are not to be taken literally but figuratively, and as containing a secret sense hid under the mere letter. These writings are to be compared to a beautiful woman who hides her charms under a veil and expects her admirers to take the trouble of lifting it; which is also the case with the word of God being hidden under the veil of a figurative sense, which cannot be lifted even with the highest human ingenuity and greatest degree of wisdom without the assistance of divine grace. In other words the things spoken of in the Torah (Word of God) must not be taken literally according to the mere phraseology, but we must pray for the Teaching of the Divine Spirit to be enabled to discern the kernel which lies under the mere shell or husk of the letter.[1]

The Divine Spirit that is said to help us understand those things that some people fail to comprehend is nothing more than the inner strength discovered while on the road to inner wisdom. The true Temple will be discovered on this same journey. But more than that, the journey consists of the destruction of the Temple we had previously imagined and the building of a new Temple. To destroy the Temple we have in our minds, we must come to an understanding of what the true Temple really is. Only then can we rebuild it for our own Inner Divinity. Our new Temple, which has been built by us, is a collection of our experiences, influences, and causes of suffering. But what about the physical Temple of Solomon? Did it ever exist?

During the period traditionally ascribed to that of King Solomon (namely 1000–900 B.C.), the rest of Europe was in the middle of the Iron Age. According to Professor James Pritchard in *Solomon and Sheba*:

> …the so-called cities of Megiddo, Gezer and Hazor, and Jerusalem itself were in reality more like villages. Within were relatively small public buildings and poorly constructed dwellings with clay floors. The objects reveal a material culture which, even by the standards of the ancient Near East, could not be judged sophisticated or luxurious.. The "magnificence" of the age of Solomon is parochial and decidedly lackluster, but the first book of Kings implies exactly the opposite.

For there to have been a Temple of the magnitude that we are led to believe, we need an archaeological miracle. We need to uncover a massive edifice with all the surrounding magnificence that is implied. Unfortunately, archaeological excavations reveal simple villages and poorly constructed dwellings. It's no wonder that the exact position of the Temple is hotly debated—it simply cannot be found. In *A Test of Time: The Bible from Myth to History*, author David Rohl claims a similar finding:

> Byblos is rich in fine stone buildings from the Bronze Age. However, when it comes to the Iron Age (which is purportedly the time of Solomon and his ally, Hiram of Tyre) there are no stone buildings at Byblos. How then did Solomon acquire building expertise from Phoenicia if the Phoenicians did not have the skill or resources to build stone structures for themselves?

Mnadjra, Malta. A portal or gateway into the very feminine temple.

John Allegro, in his book *The Sacred Mushroom and the Cross*, believes that the Temple was a symbol of the womb of rebirth:

> The temple was designed with a large measure of uniformity over the whole of the Near East now recognisable as a microcosm of the womb. It was divided into three parts; the Porch, representing the lower end of the vagina up to the hymen, or Veil, the Hall, or vagina itself; and the inner sanctum, or Holy of Holies, the uterus. The priest, dressed as a penis, anointed with various saps and resins as representing the divine semen, enters through the doors of the Porch, the "labia" of the womb, past the Veil or "hymen" and so into the Hall.

Of course, if the Temple simply was not there, then this element was symbolic of the regeneration of the self, required under gnostic beliefs. The symbolic element of the female attributes would relate entirely to Asherah's presence as the *Goddess in the Temple*, the Asherah pole being the male phallus, signifying the unity of the male and female inside the true Temple. This would explain the switch from the feminine word *Asherah* to the male version of *Asherim*. Even the Gospel of Philip tells us that the Temple signifies unity: "The Holy of Holies is the bridal chamber." But what does the Bible say?

> The foundation of the temple of the Lord was laid in the fourth year, in the month of Ziv. In the eleventh year in the month of Bul, the eighth month, the temple was finished in all its details according to its specifications. He had spent seven years building it.
>
> —1 Kings 6:37–38

Here we have an indication of the truth. The period of *seven* was utilized for the building of the Temple. There are seven chakra wheels of life before we achieve true enlightenment, and this is at the root of the truth behind the Temple of Solomon.

There is more evidence to show that the Temple was purely a metaphor and never existed in reality. The Temple of Solomon has been called *Templi omnium hominum pacis abhas*, meaning the *God of the Temple of Peace among men*. Shortened, this reverts to *Tem Oph Ab*. When written backwards, this spells *Baphomet*. Baphomet, of course, is the head the Knights Templar were accused of worshipping. *Baphe* means *immersion* (as in *baptism*) and *metis* means *wisdom*. Therefore, Baphomet is truly the immersion of oneself into wisdom. It is the true Temple.

The Templars were accused of worshipping their own head, like the exalted head of Hiram, for instance, which was nothing more than immersion into inner wisdom. This was heresy, but one that was for some reason allowed to develop. It almost appears as though organized religion was giving the Templars sufficient rope with which to hang themselves.

This is the great secret of the Templars. The truth of Solomon's Temple is that the Templars discovered something just after the First Crusade that could very well have been found back Europe—the Templars found *themselves*. We now need to investigate two main players who supposedly walked the grand corridors of power in the 10th century B.C.: Solomon and Sheba.

Solomon

The Greek name *Solomon* derives from the Hebrew *Sh'lomoh*, which means *peaceable*, and gives us the Arabic names *Soliman* or *Suleyman*. There are many others who claim that *Sol Om On* are three different titles for the sun god. This would make complete sense—the solar divinity is within each and every one of us, and is where we find true wisdom. This inner sun is enlightenment, illumination, and shining. The word could also derive from *Salim*, meaning *whole* (seen in the phrase *Jeru Salim*). This would also make complete sense, as we have seen that unity and oneness is of paramount importance to achieve enlightenment.

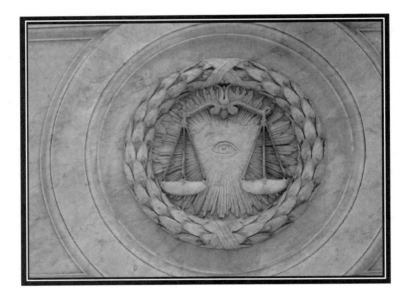

The eye of God in balance and shining, hence illumination and wholeness.

Historically, Solomon was the third king of Israel and David's chosen heir. He is said to be the wisest man who ever lived and authored Ecclesiastes and the Song of Solomon, as well as many proverbs and psalms. Solomon supposedly grew up in a polygamous household with David's 18 wives. His own mother was Bathsheba. This is another example of repetition in the Bible: *Bath* means *house of*; *Sheba* means

Saba, the Kingdom of the Sabaeans. So King David married or was in union with the House of Sheba. Solomon was the wise result, the shining, or illumination, seen in his name, which means *sun*.

David took Bathsheba from Uriah and created the savior King Solomon. In the tales of Arthur, much the same is done when Uther Pendragon takes Igraine from her husband to produce the savior king Arthur. Arthur then goes on to marry the Queen of Serpents, Guinevere, just as Solomon goes on to marry Sheba, the Queen of the Land of Serpents. It is this repetitive process that teaches.

Of course, there is no evidence that any of these people actually walked the earth other than in biblical and religious texts. There is no archaeological or historical evidence for Solomon's existence. We must therefore, take all that is said about King Solomon as if it were *purely symbolic*. In this way, his story shall become clear.

We can see this in the tale of how Solomon came to learn of Sheba's existence. The story goes that he invited all the birds of the world to sing for his invited guests one evening. However, one bird was missing—the hoopoe, or lapwing. According to Harold Bayley in *The Lost Language of Symbolism*, *hoop* means *shining eye*. Solomon was angry with the absence and ordered a search for the bird. Eventually the bird was found and rebuked for his absence. But the bird explained that it was quite the opposite. He had been away, searching the land to find somebody who did not know of the wonder of Solomon's reign. Finally he found the land known as Sheba (Saba), ruled by a beautiful and wise woman called Queen Balkys (Belqis). This land did not know of Solomon's existence. The inhabitants of the land did not know of war, and peace reigned in the land (showing the peaceful side of Sheba as opposed to Solomon's fiery anger).

The king wrote a letter to the queen and tied it to the hoopoe bird, inviting her to come and pay tribute. If she did so, the land would remain hers. If she did not, then he would take it by force. The queen's counselors were against the visit, but the queen wrote back to Solomon, saying that although the journey would take seven years, she would endeavour to be there in three. When she arrived, she was received with great honor and went straight to the throne room to stand next to the king.

Dissecting this little folklore is fairly simple. The hoopoe bird is our spirit or conscience. It is conversing between the sides of our mind. One side is fiery and powerful; the other peaceful, strong, and wise. The two sides need to be in union to have full knowledge of each other (as Sheba had no knowledge of Solomon, and Solomon had no knowledge of Sheba until the spirit conversed between them). The hoopoe bird is our consciousness—a realization of the duality within our minds. Unless we know that we have split personalities or dual aspects, we cannot attempt to find balance. This process takes a period of seven years. Instead, because both sides are coming into balance together, Sheba accomplished her journey in three years. This reflects the seven aspects or levels of the Kundalini—in balance. It is a teaching system of our own internal balance. We must all recognize that we are out of balance, but to do this we must have knowledge of the other side. If we do not have the knowledge of either side, then how can we bring about balance? We must converse internally to discover this knowledge, and then we must go through a period of travel or journey to discover this union of opposites and become a perfect being.

Sheba

The legendary Queen of Sheba has spawned hundreds of films and thousands of books. She is the equal only of the great Egyptian Queen

Cleopatra, who died with the aid of a serpent. There are few females in history who have captured mankind's imagination in such a way. And yet, just like King Solomon, Sheba never really existed. Her story has been repeated many times and in many contexts, but there isn't a scrap of evidence for her existence, apart from the religious writings of the Bible, Koran, the Kebra Nagast, and a few others. Like Solomon, Sheba's real name is an enigma.

Let's just have a look at the life and times of Sheba and Solomon, as seen through the fables of popular orthodox religion. The biblical story goes that:

> ...when the Queen of Sheba heard of the fame of Solomon, she came to Jerusalem to test Solomon with hard questions, having a very great retinue, camels that bore spices, gold in abundance, and precious stones: and when she came to Solomon, she spoke with him about all that was in her heart.

> —2 Chronicles 9:1

Here we see that Sheba is portrayed as an equal to Solomon, even though in other tales the patriarchal authorities tend to reduce her position. This equality is the balance of wisdom to Solomon's harsh and powerful behavior. Solomon has been playing the male positive energy element of the duality process. Sheba, the female passive counterpart, is sent in to question and bring gifts of wisdom (spices, gold, and especially jewels). Sheba, being a Queen of the Land of Peace, speaks nothing but peace to Solomon (all that is in her heart), and they are balanced. We should also note that she brings with her gold and jewels—both symbols of divinity and wisdom.

The story continues that Sheba sees that Solomon's wisdom is good and worthy and that they are truly equal. This equality is played out with mutual gifts. To see deeper into why the Queen of Sheba was chosen as a symbolic element of this wisdom literature, we need to look towards her homeland, a place we know today as Ethiopia, and was once known as Cush.

The Cuthites

Cuthites are simply *the people from Cush (Kush)*, which is modern Ethiopia. Hargrave Jennings, in his tremendous work *Ophiolatreia*, points out that these were called the *sons of Vulcan*. Vulcan is the Egyptian father god Ptah, who is equated with the Mesopotamian Enki (the serpent god,

Masonic Lodge at Llanfairfechan, Wales.

who gives acquaintance to the first couple and tells Utnapishtim to build an ark to prepare for the coming deluge). Ptah's son is the Egyptian healer Imhotep, or the Greek Aesculapius, both being the serpent deity and healer. Imhotep is also the first builder and architect; he is implicated in the Masonic guilds.

The Cuthites, or People of Cush, were sons of Vulcan (*can* means *serpent*, while *volo* means *will*) and therefore serpent worshippers similar to Imhotep or Aesculapius. They were descended from Enki, the one who gave gnosis to Adam and Eve, and who told Noah to build his ark. These Cuthites are said to have moved to Egypt, then Syria, then near the Euphrates, and also to Greece, spreading serpent worship among the great civilizations. The Cuthites can be linked tentatively with the Babylonian priests and the Nergals of Cutha, where the city Opis (which means *serpent*) was situated on the Tigris River.

The Ethiopians appear to have been great worshippers of the serpent and to have been originators of serpent worship in other lands, such as Egypt, Syria, and Greece. But there is an element here other than the serpent that also seems to draw a thread through them all—the ark. Now, this *ark* or *Solar B'arque* is both the ark of Noah, carrying the hopes of mankind, and the Ark of the Covenant.

In the Egyptian legend, the Solar B'arque is seen to pass through the Duat or underworld:

> The Otherworld, known as the Duat, is divided into twelve sections or countries, each section having its own name and being divided from the next by a gate which is guarded by a warden. The sections correspond with the twelve hours of the night. The boat of the sun [b'arque] is filled with deities who are there to protect the god from all the

dangers of the Night, and is piloted through each section by the goddess of that hour, who alone knows the password for the gate at the far end of her domain; without that password even Re would not be allowed to go through. The Sun dies at sunset, and it is only his corpse that passes into the Realm of Night. Two great events occur during the Journey. The first is the ever-recurring attempt of the terrible and awe-inspiring serpent, Apophis (Aa-pep), to destroy the Sun, an attempt which is always frustrated by the guardian deities; the other is that Khepri, in the form of a scarab, awaits the coming of the dead Sun, then the soul of Khepri and the soul of Re are united. Khepri means existence, hence Life. The soul of Re is thus revivified, and he passes on alive to the sunrise, his dead body being cast out of the Boat before he rises on the land of Egypt.[2]

I would like to note that Apophis, the serpent of the Otherworld, is seen as an aggressor, and yet the serpents of the Otherworld are sometimes protective and sometimes hostile, revealing their dual purpose. For instance, the serpent Mehen is seen to cover the b'arque with its coils to protect it from the attacks of Apophis—the aggressive serpent. If the b'arque has emerged as an idea from Africa, and the serpent with it, then this is a revelation of the dual nature of man. In other stories, especially those related to the *Kingdom of Sokar*, the b'arque is actually turned into a serpent and Osiris (Sokar) is said to voyage through the belly of the serpent. Whatever the real meaning of all this, the serpent is intricately involved in the b'arque.

The b'arque is filled with deities to protect us on our spiritual voyage. The journey is a repetitive process, not just because the sun repeats a cycle each day, but because we must also repeat a cycle in order to better ourselves. This is not dissimilar to the Hindu and Buddhist versions of escape from *samsara* (the wheel of life or cycle) to *nirvana* (a kind of heaven or escape from cycles). This includes an idea of reincarnation—all these serpentine origins are from the same root, after all. Even Christianity began with the concept of reincarnation.

> Another theory of the Hereafter, one which has received little attention from Egyptologists, is the theory of reincarnation. Herodotus is very definite on the subject; "The Egyptians were the first who asserted that the soul of man is immortal, and that when the body perishes it enters into some other animal, constantly springing into existence; and when it has passed through the different kinds of terrestrial, marine, and aerial beings, it again enters into the body of a man that is born; and that this revolution is made in three thousand years. Some of the Greeks have adopted this opinion, some earlier, others later, as if it were their own; but although I knew their names I do not mention them." This statement by Herodotus is fully borne out by the Egyptian evidence. As is usual in all aspects of the religion of Egypt, the faculty of reincarnation was originally inherent in the Pharaoh alone. The ka-names of the first two kings of the xii-th dynasty shows this clearly; Amonemhat I's name was "He who repeats births", and Senusert I's name was "He whose births live."[3]

Even in Egypt, reincarnation and the ever-existing element of the soul is known. This relates to other serpent-worshipping areas, such as India.

Ark from Lincoln Cathedral. Note the priest has horns, hence illumination.

Getting back to the ark or b'arque, which carried the gods and protectors through the Otherworld. The b'arque carried them on a journey that balanced the protective and destructive serpent towards rebirth. In the first place, we have the ark of Noah, a story we know goes back to Sumeria and Enki, the serpent Lord. This boat is no different, symbolically, to that of Egypt, whereby the Lord chooses a good man to journey for a specific period through a fabulous and dangerous journey on an ark. The story of the ark changes though, as we discover the Ark of the Covenant. This doesn't seem to relate to the b'arque at all! But it does. The Ark of the Covenant is given to the people of Israel to protect them on their journey. It is the device used to connect them to their God and is placed at the head of the tabernacle or mobile temple—later to be found in the stone Temple itself in the Holy of Holies.

In Isaiah 37:14–16, there is a peculiar mention that Hezekiah worshipped the "God of Israel, that dwellest between the cherubim." Of course, these dual cherubim were placed to protect the Ark, and therefore what lay between them was the Ark itself. This is peculiar, because what "dwellest" in the Ark was the *Rod of Aaron*, which had turned miraculously into a snake (and was itself a symbol of serpent worship) at the very time Moses erected the Brazen Serpent in the wilderness. This is enlightening, as God was said to only be where the Ark was; he dwells there. It is, strangely, after this time of Hezekiah that the Ark is lost to history, never to be seen again. The serpent worship is obviously being sent underground in favor of monotheism.

I would just like to sidestep the Ark a moment to look at the cherubim mentioned in relation to the Ark. In Genesis 3:24 we have the following verse:

> So He drove out the man; and He placed cherubim at the east of the garden of Eden, and a flaming sword which turned every way, to guard the way to the tree of life.

Here are the same cherubim being used as a device to guard the Tree of Life, which is in the center of the garden. This Tree of Life is the *axis mundi* (pole or spine). It is the upright method of obtaining true life. Up this tree rises the twin serpents to enlightenment in the Kundalini tradition. The very same device is used in Persia, where innumerable attendants are protecting the *Hom* tree situated in *Heden*.

The cherubim are also the same as the Egyptian *kherufu* or *kherubs*, which hold up the sun on the horizon—they are the shining element between the balancing powers. They are also similar to the cherubs of Assyria, Babylonia, and those of the Orient, being fabulous winged beasts similar to the medieval griffin. In essence, the cherubim are the guardian serpents or dragons. They are the powers we raise up within ourselves, equated with serpent energy, and which we must use to protect ourselves from external influence that would have us wander from the path. They are seen across the world in one form or another. In India, Mount Meru is guarded by the dragon, where Meru is yet another *axis mundi* or pole symbol. To reach the summit of the world-mountain is to achieve heaven, just as we need to raise the serpents up the tree. So the Ark is equated with the Tree of Life and the world mountain as it is guarded by two Godly beasts. It is, therefore, part of us, just as the tree and mountain are. Whoever took the physical Ark then (if it ever existed) may very well have had the safety of it in mind. Secrecy would be paramount in such an undertaking.

Hezekiah's son, *Manasseh* (687–642 B.C.) went on to bring condemnation upon himself with graven images, erecting more Asherah groves and much wickedness. The graven image of the grove that 1 Kings 21:2-7 speaks of is, in fact, the image of Asherah. In 628 B.C. Josiah purged the Temple of all graven images. He had the Asherah burned in the river Kidron (2 Kings 23:6). Although Ezekiel—a century later—blames Josiah for having the walls painted in idolatrous images. In *Peake's Commentary on the Bible*, the author "sees mural paintings containing pictures of 'creeping things' and other mythological scenes…which seem to point to syncretistic practices of Egyptian provenance."

In 520 B.C., the Persians, the world's first Indo-European nation, conquered Babylon. It is said in the *Elephantine Papyri* by Bezalel Porten that "they knocked down all the temples of the gods of Egypt, but not one did any damage" to the Jewish Temple. The religious influence of this Persian/Indian invasion must have also had social influences as well, especially regarding Zoroastrianism.

Now we arrive at Sheba's country—Ethiopia. The reason we are coming here is simple. A few scholars have claimed that the Ark rests in the town of Axum, in Ethiopia. Amos, writing in the 8th century A.D., said, "Are ye not as children of the Ethiopians unto me, O children of Israel? Saith the Lord."

The word *Ethiopia*, although much debated, comes directly from the snake, as in *Aithiopians*, coming from *Ath-Opis*, the snake god they worshipped. These people were seen as the *children of the snake*. Therefore, the Lord sees the children of Israel as children of the Ethiopia, or people of the snake. Indeed, it is probable that there was a flow of Hebrew migrants across Egypt and into Axum or Abyssinia. According to the holy book and king list of Ethiopia, the *Kebra Nagast*, written in the 13th century A.D., the Ark was brought to Ethiopia by Menelik, the legendary wise son of the Queen of Sheba and Solomon.

Not surprisingly, the Ethiopians still venerate the serpent without knowing it in the *Betre Aron* service of the Ethiopian Coptic Church and the *Boku Rod* of the *Oromo Gada* procession at Axum. According to the standard religious history of Ethiopia, the serpent *Arwe Waynaba* is the only ruler mentioned for the first few centuries of recorded history. The Queen of Sheba (or as one of her other names, *Makeda*) was the daughter of a man named *Angabo*. He is said to have tried to suppress serpent worship, but it was continued secretly.

The idea of the serpent in Axum has many traditions behind it. For instance, it is said that once a serpent-king called *Arwe* or *Waynaba* (Naga), ruled over the land, taking the tribute of a young girl each year. This reflects the social memory of serpent worship in the area. Eventually Angabo, the father of the Queen of Sheba, arrived and rescued the chosen girl, killing the serpent-king at the same time. The people then elected

Angabo as king. His successors was Makeda—the Queen of Sheba. Sometimes the legends say that it was the Queen herself who was the intended sacrifice. However, the essential element of this story is the time and place: the legends all refer to the remote origins of Ethiopian history. Nathaniel Pearce, who lived in Ethiopia in the early 19th century, related how these stories were still current among the modern Ethiopians; "In the evening, while sitting with Ozoro, she told me a number of silly tales about Axum, among others a long story about a large snake which ruled the country…which sometimes resided at Temben, though Axum was the favourite residence of the two."

Pearce was later shown what seems to have been a fruit press, but which he interpreted as being "made by the ancients to prepare some kind of cement for building." His Ethiopian friend told him that this item had actually been designed as a container for the snake's food. I had to laugh at the linking of the snake food and the cement being in the same container, as these are surely both indicative of the body or mind of man. We are the food for the wise serpent, which is symbolic of so much, and we build the Temple of ourselves!

It is highly unlikely that any of the legends surrounding Axum are literal. The most likely event is that some of the legends of Solomon and Sheba are the later Christian attempts to justify Christianizing the region, whereas others are folk memories of a serpent-worshipping past. As for the serpent, he was turned into a terrible monster that ate little girls. The truth is the hidden aspect of the *Rod of Aaron* and the *Asherah*—the ancient healing symbols of the serpent. Once again, Christianity has destroyed our past.

So in Ethiopia we have a serpent-worshipping history, in myth and legend. The Queen of Sheba was seen as a sacrifice for the snake. She is a version of Asherah, and when she departs from her land to visit the passionate King Solomon, she is entering the Temple as the serpent Queen. Indeed, her worship has not died away, it has come through in the womb-like element of the Holy Grail in ways that the readers of the *Da Vinci Code* could never imagine.

The Sacro Catino

The *Sacro Catino* is a relic from the Holy Land. It is a great dish made of green glass, taken by crusaders at the sacking of Caesarea in A.D. 1101. It was said to have been brought by the Queen of Sheba to Solomon, and passed down the ages until it was used at the Last Supper. This reveals the constant belief in the aspect of the wise serpent and the duality of female serpent with male serpent counterpart in the rituals and hidden beliefs of Christianity.

Sheba came to Solomon and they were equal. She was the serpent Queen of a serpent land. She was indicative of the Asherah feminine aspect, which was inside the Temple itself. They called her *Astar*, meaning *womb*. Amazingly, Makeda (the Queen of Sheba) was also known as *Magda*, meaning *greatness*. I have often wondered whether the name *Mary Magdalene* was purposefully used as an allusion to this ancient female serpent goddess.

The Koran tells us that Solomon travelled south to meet Sheba in her capital. Although this is different than Christian tales, the difference is slight. Either way, the union is complete—male wisdom and power with female wisdom and peace. Sheba is said to have sired a child by Solomon, named *Menelek*, which is the usual symbolic result of such a union. His Arabic name is *Ibn al-Hakim*, meaning *son of a wise man*.

According to Arab tradition, Sheba (known to Muslims as *Bilqis*) ruled with the heart of a woman and the head of a man, and worshipped the sun and the moon—revealing her own perceived internal balance. She is depicted in many legends in Arabic folklore, in particular with the miraculous transfer of her court and throne to Solomon's palace, which is symbolic of the raising of the serpent to the place of peace and balance. Even the gifts of Sheba to Solomon reveal the balance. Frankincense was one of the prime products of the Sabaeans, and was an antidote for poison.

Saba (as well as Sheba and Sabaeans) means *Host of Heaven and Peace* and was a region much larger than modern-day Ethiopia. It stretched from the tip of the Red Sea, over Yemen, and through Ethiopia. Even in descriptions of the people of Saba we have a peculiar duality at play. They are described variously as woolly haired and straight haired, and to be black of face and yet illuminated by their god.

When Sheba visited Solomon, she was the peaceful side of ourselves meeting and balancing the powerful but often fiery side of our internal mind. Together, and in balance, both became strong and brought forth our true self, which is depicted as the savior son. But the process is repetitive and must be constantly recycled if it is to remain a powerful tool. In the stories, this is implied when Sheba leaves Solomon. After Sheba's departure, Solomon continues to write wise words, but Israel as a whole deteriorates, just as England loses its fertility when Arthur is split from Guinevere. The tales are the same and have the same ancient and sacred meaning—that we must work hard to maintain balance, or risk losing all. Solomon knew this and tried to recover the other side of himself by raising temples to Asherah (under many different names). But this was false, and is the element of ourselves that believes we have found balance when we truly have not.

Solomon became aggressive in his attempts to recover his lost Sheba, alienating himself from those around him, as we do ourselves when we become deterministic and self-centered. He raised taxes to pay for his temples, and forced labor on his own people. Eventually this resulted in Israel being split apart. Is this the real reason that the Ark is said to reside in Ethiopia? The traditions state that Menelek, the son of Solomon and Sheba, took the Ark and buried it in an underground chamber. The Ark, as the device for talking to God, was no longer with Solomon, as he had lost all balance. He no longer knew himself. Menelek, as the result of this union, is the true divine center of Solomon, and Menelek has hidden it from his ego-self.

The crowning glory of Solomon's symbolic and wise life was nothing other than the Temple. The fact that the story of Solomon and Sheba are stories of ancient wisdom and psychological teaching leaves us no other option than to see that the Temple itself was purely symbolic. This is the truth of the Temple—that it did not exist. It is a symbol of our own spiritual growth.

We can, however, see a little of what was meant by the stories of the Temple in the term *Shiloh*. This Hebrew word was used for the Israelite stone temples or Houses of God. In fact, it means *messiah*. In Judges 28:31 we find this use of the word, which proves this etymology:

> The sceptre shall not depart from Judah, nor a lawgiver from between his feet, until Shiloh come; and unto him shall the gathering of the people be.

Shiloh is the perfect man, the one in touch with the divinity—or as we would term today, *in touch with himself*. This person is equated with the Temple or House of God, as he is truly the House of God, for he alone can reach God, which is himself.

But there are still those who believe that the Temple may have actually existed, and currently lies hidden beneath the stones of Jerusalem. Think about this, and the truth will reveal itself to you. We saw how the Lord told his people to build his Temple without the use of tools, because their would be an affront to him. The reason for this is simple: We already know that the true divinity or Lord of Shining is the true Gnosis of the self. It is the Inner Reality, and if this Inner Reality needs a Temple building, then it is the Temple of the physical and spiritual body. No tool is needed for this work, as it would be an affront to our own intellect.

We also see that the one given the power to build the Temple was another fictional character, Hiram, who was balanced and had seven levels of skills, similar to the Kundalini method of gaining enlightenment. This man was the *exalted head/snake*, similar to the Kundalini aspect of the *Bindu point* or the *Kabbalistic Kether*.

To add to this, our Temple must have the Goddess Within, or Asherah, who is depicted in the Bible as the serpent entwined pole—again, just as the Kundalini depicted her. This *Goddess Within the Temple* is the symbolic serpent energy of ourselves. The true Temple is built by the King and the Queen in balance.

The Twin Pillars

Although we covered these pillars in the previous chapter, we must now consider them in light of this new concept—that all things related to the Temple (as well as the Temple itself) are purely symbolic.

One of the first and most important elements of the supposed physical Temple are the pillars, called *Jachin* and *Boaz*. These symbols become physical when built by Masons around the world. For instance, at Rosslyn Chapel there are two marvellous pillars that have been the center of a great deal of controversy for decades, but which truly signify the arcane secrets of the Temple. Of course, both the Grail and the head of Jesus are (symbolically) the same thing, and so, in a sense, Rosslyn contains the ultimate secret.

Apprentice pillar at Rosslyn.

The pillars in Solomon's Temple were made of bronze, just as the Brazen Serpent of Moses was. They were located at the very entrance to the Temple. This positioning is important in our interpretation. To enter the place where the connection with the Divinity or self exists, we must be balanced. This is depicted symbolically by walking between the pillars. We could also say that the pillars are legs, and we must walk between them to enter the womb of the goddess. They are something we must walk between—balanced.

The pillar on the right is called *Jachin*. Pronounced *Yakini*, the word actually means *One* and signifies unity and wholeness—something we have seen is paramount in symbolism to gaining true Gnosis. It also means *he who establishes*, and together with *Boaz* means *he provides the whole strength*.

Boaz, the pillar on the left, comes from the root word *awaz*, meaning *voice* or *Torah*, *the Word of Creation*. Both pillars make up the *vitriol* of the alchemists, the vital force of creativity. Quite simply, we cannot even think about entering the Temple until we have passed between the pillars of creation and wholeness. Of course we should remember that Solomon, as Salim, actually means *wholeness*.

The Floorplan

The floorplan of the Temple is known as the *tabnit*, giving rise to the word *tabernacle*. The word can variously be described as meaning design, structure, form, or shape, and is also used for the phrase *the form of man*. Although many assume that the Temple we are discussing in this book was of Solomon's creation, in fact it was supposedly devised by David, his father. David is said to have received the form by Divine inspiration in the same way that Moses received inspiration for the tabernacle. And in the same way that Moses was never to enter the Promised Land, King David was never to realize the Temple. This was left to Solomon, his son.

Tabnit is also related to *banah*, which basically means *to build* and is used in relation to both buildings and families. The terms are interchangeable, and so gathering what the original writers meant is difficult. All we do know is that Solomon built the Temple, while David was given the form. Of course, this linking of form and build with father and son implies that the father gave form to his son's growth. Taken inside ourselves, this means that we must give birth and form to our own true inner self in order for it to grow to fruition.

So Solomon built the Temple in place of his father, and the Lord then spoke to Solomon:

> Concerning this Temple which you are building, if you walk in My statutes, execute My judgements, keep all My commandments, and walk in them, then I will perform My word with you, which I spoke to your father David. And I will dwell among the children of Israel, and will not forsake My people Israel.
>
> —1 Kings 6:12–13

Jacob's Ladder

We can go back to Genesis with verse 28:10 to discover more insight:

> Now Jacob went out from Beersheba and went toward Haran. So he came to a certain place and stayed there all night, because the sun had set. And he took one of the stones of that place and put it at his head, and he lay down in that place to sleep. Then he dreamed, and behold, a ladder was set up on the earth, and its top reached to heaven; and there the angels of God were ascending and descending on it.
>
> —Genesis 28: 10–14

Jacob goes on to say that this place was awesome, and that surely God was in it. But more than this, he says, "This is none other than the house of God, and this is the gate of heaven." Jacob was on his way to find a wife so that he could unite with her and begin forming and building a family—the family that would become Israel. We know that this supposedly came to fruition, because Jacob's two wives were actually called builders. Again, there is no evidence that any of this is real. What we really have is the man who will become Israel. If we split the word apart into *Is Ra El*, then we have three elements that constitute the solar divinity or the illumination aspect of ourselves. *Is* means *light*, *Ra* is the *Egyptian solar divinity*, and *El* means *shining*. Of course, this may appear contrived, and the real meaning might be simply *he who struggles with God*, as is seen in Jacob's constant questioning. But etymology often works that way—having meanings on many levels.

To the kabbalist, Jacob's Ladder has come to be a powerful alchemical vision, which is another way of expressing the site of the superconscious—the vision of the subatomic elements brought on by or aided by the laying of the head upon a stone. Folklore and traditions have erupted around this stone, due to the importance many have seen in it. According to some, it was taken to Egypt or moved around by the Israelites. Some people even believe it is the stone of the *Tuatha De Danaan*. To others, it became the *Stone of Scone* or *Destiny*, upon which the kings and queens of Great Britain have been crowned. Yet again, people are looking for a real stone, where in fact it was a literary teaching device. The Lord was in that *place*, and all the other places Jacob decided, because He is within—He is Jacob, and you, and me. We all have this divinity inside of us. We can all connect to the quantum state we have termed *the void*, we just need to learn how to build this Temple.

Chapter 10

Mystics, Alchemists, and Gnostics

Every time you find in our books a tale the reality of which seems impossible, a story which is repugnant both to reason and common sense, then be sure that tale contains a profound allegory veiling a deeply mysterious truth; and the greater the absurdity of the letter the deeper the wisdom of the spirit.

—Rabbi Moses Maimonides

Now we know the secret of the Temple of Solomon—that it is simply a teaching device utilized symbolically over the years to aid us in achieving enlightenment. We know that the Temple exists within mankind. We should now be able to understand texts and puzzles that we have not been able to comprehend before. With our new understanding, we have gained sight. We can read again, where before we were blind. This chapter includes new insights from various mystics, alchemists, and other exponents of gnosis. Hopefully these new interpretations will excite and astound you.

The Freemasons

Mnadjra, work of the stone mason.

The medieval Freemasons work. Salisbury Cathedral.

First, we obviously have to tackle the Freemasons, as their entire history is based on the building of Solomon's Temple. In the end, they have kept the secrets of the Temple within their initiated few, and kept alive for us the truth of the crossover between the literal stone building and the building of our inner truth. They have kept the spirit of the truth behind this ancient wisdom literature alive within their secret degrees.

According to the authors of the *Encyclopedia of Freemasonry*: "Of all the objects which constitute the Masonic science of symbolism, the most important, the most cherished, by the Mason, and by far the most significant, is the Temple of Jerusalem. The spiritualising of the Temple is the first, the most prominent and most pervading, of all the symbols of Freemasonry."

These are not the words of a conservative fundamentalist trying to trip up the Mason; these are the words of nineteenth century Masons themselves. What can we learn from this? In the first place, we learn a very important lesson, that Masonry is the *science of symbolism*. Secondly, we learn how this symbolism applies to the Temple. We learn that the most important and most pervading symbol in Masonry is the *spiritualizing of the Temple*. This, of course, does not mean making the Temple real, or the actual physical building of the Temple. No, this means that the Temple is, was, and always will be seen by Freemasons the world over as a symbolic spiritual device. There is no Temple of Solomon and there never was. The degrees and statements of the Freemasons seem to back this up. However, the Masons do physically manifest their belief (symbolic) systems in the architecture of their lodges.

Albert Pike writes in *Morals and Dogma* that "every Masonic lodge is a temple." The Masons build and decorate their lodges in the form of the Temple, and are therefore physically and spiritually builders, in that they follow the ancient wisdom literature. They encompass the very nature of the teaching literature we have been discussing. How do we know this? How do we know that the Masons—or at least those adepts within their ranks—understand the deeper secrets and teachings surrounding the true nature of the Temple of Solomon? Statements like this prove it:

> The traditions and romance of King Solomon's Temple are of great interest to everyone who reads the Bible. They are of transcendent importance to Masons. The Temple is the outstanding symbol of Masonry, and the legendary building of the Temple is the fundamental basis of the Masonic rule and guide for conduct in life.[1]

From this statement, it is apparent that, to most people, the Temple is of great importance, which it is. But to the Masons it is *transcendent*. This word means *to excel above normal human capabilities*. That is, the Temple hides a deeper meaning for the Freemasons than for everybody else, and that meaning is greater than ordinary human reasoning. As we have discovered, the truth is that the Temple of Solomon, once built, enables the individual to talk to Divinity. (Or at least it is the language and terminology utilized for being able to discover one's self.)

"Today the Temple of Solomon is the spiritual home of every Mason."[2] This is as it should be if one were to follow the teachings of the Temple. The home of the spirit should truly be in the building one raises for one's self—the *Temple of the Solo man*. We are left in no doubt about interpretation when the infamous Mason Albert Pike writes, "To the Master Mason, the Temple of Solomon is truly the symbol of human life." Pike states quite clearly that the Temple is a symbol of human life, nothing more. "[The Temple] becomes a fit symbol of human life occupied in the search after Divine Truth, which is nowhere to be found...."

Pike reiterates the point that the Temple is about the search for truth, and states quite clearly that as such we shall not find truth anywhere but in the Temple, which is truly our selves.

> The Freemasons have, at all events, seized with avidity the idea of representing in their symbolic language the interior and spiritual man by a material temple.[3]

In *Masonry and Its Symbols in the Light of Thinking and Destiny*, Harold Waldwin Percival writes, "The lodge as a room or hall is an oblong square, which is a half of a perfect square, and which is inside or outside the lower half of a circle. Each lodge meets in the same room, alike furnished, but the lodge working in the Apprentice degree is styled the Ground Floor, the lodge working the Fellow Craft degree is called the Middle Chamber, and the lodge working the Master degree is called the Sanctum Sanctorum, all in King Solomon's Temple."

But Freemasonry has gone one step further nowadays and has found another level. From the *Encyclopedia of Freemasonry* we find this entry and the classes of degrees:

> But there is a second and higher class of the Fraternity, the Masons of the Royal Arch, by whom this temple symbolism is still further developed. This second class, leaving their early symbolism, and looking beyond this Temple of Solomon, find in Scriptural history another Temple, which years after the destruction of the first one, was erected upon its ruins; and they have selected the second Temple, the Temple of Zerubbabel, as their prominent symbol. And, as the first class of Masons find in their Temple the symbol of mortal life, limited and perishable, they, on the contrary, see in this second Temple, built upon the foundations of the first, a symbol of life eternal, where the lost truth shall be found, where

new incense shall arise from a new altar, and whose perpetuity their great Master had promised when, in the very spirit of symbolism, he exclaimed, "Destroy this temple, and in three days I will raise it up."

The writers of this piece allude to the statement by Jesus Christ about raising it up in three days. This statement goes along perfectly with what we have learned thus far. That we need to destroy the causes of suffering before we can once again build the Temple—we must raise up the serpent energy. It is also interesting to note that the higher Masons are meant to believe not just in the Temple of Solomon as a symbol of a better life now, but that they should also believe in a second Temple for the life eternal:

> And so to these two classes or Orders of Masons the symbolism of the Temple presents itself in a connected and continuous form. To the Master Mason, the Temple of Solomon is the symbol of this life; to the Royal Arch Mason, the Temple of Zerubbabel is the symbol of the future life. To the former, his Temple is the symbol of the search for truth; to the latter, his is the symbol of the discovery of truth; and thus the circle is completed and the system made perfect.[4]

Of course the lessons of the Temple of Zerubbabel must await the reader, now hopefully gifted with new insight. However, let's just have a quick look to see what we can see from a fleeting glance.

In Ezra 3:1 we find:

> And when the seventh month had come, and the children of Israel were in the cities, the people gathered together as one man to Jerusalem. The Jeshua the son of Jozadak and his brethren the priests, and Zerubbabel the son of

Shealtiel and his brethren, arose and built the altar of the God of Israel, to offer burnt offerings on it, as it is written in the Law of Moses the man of God.

The first thing I noticed in this passage was the fulfilment number of *seven*, as if this was the right number for the completion of the perfect Temple. Next, I noted how the *people gathered together as one man*, which is the wholeness or unity factor. I also noted how two distinct groups or opposites had to come together to build the altar.

In Zechariah 4:6–7 we get another insight into Zerubbabel:

This is the word of the Lord to Zerubbabel: "Not by might nor by power, but by My Spirit," says the Lord of hosts.

All-seeing eye of the Universal Mind. At the center, a Masonic device.

Again, we are being told that in order to build this Temple, we must not use might or power, but rather spirit. How can we build a physical structure with just spirit? We cannot. But we can build a spiritual structure with spirit! (Or alternatively, a psychological strength with psychology.)

Eliphas Levi

Alphonse Louis Constant, better known as Eliphas Levi or Eliphas Levi Zahed, was a master of the traditional Rosicrucian translation of the kabbalah. His alternative name is thought to be a Hebrew equivalent of his real name, used for magical purposes. He was born in 1810 in France, the son of a shoemaker, and was educated for the church of Saint Sulpice, where he was educated without charge and with a view to entering the priesthood. In addition to Greek and Latin, he also learned Hebrew. He entered as a clerical novitiate, took minor orders, and soon became a deacon. He was appointed professor at the Petit Seminaire de Paris where he was later expelled for teaching "doctrines contrary to those of the Roman Catholic Church."[5]

By 1825, Levi had begun studying the occult. He would go on to write about these arcane sciences for the next 30 years. Levi states that, beginning in 1825, he went from "suffering to knowledge," which is the path of the true initiate.

Over the past 100 years, many researchers have tried to pin Eliphas Levi down. According to some, he was an evil antichrist and was fundamentally opposed to Christianity. According to others, he was an ardent defender of the faith. All I can say is that you must read his work to discover the truth, and that only with the knowledge explored in this book will you be able to understand his works.

Why have I chosen to focus on this man when there is such debate as to his beliefs? The truth is simply that I like him. Because of the debate, I deemed it worthwhile to give him a decent hearing. Now we have knowledge of the truth, we can see what Levi was getting at, in the same way we can now see what the Bible, Koran, Upanishads, and many other ancient texts are truly saying. Let's have a look at some his writings that can be found in *The Great Secret of Occultism Unveiled*:

> …here is a common life shared by all souls; or at least a common mirror for every imagination and every memory, in which it is possible for us to gaze at one another like a crowd of people standing before a glass.

A simple enough statement, but what does it mean? We all share a common life. What is this about a common mirror for every imagination and every memory? We have to remember the science of the *Void*. Could this relate to being able to see every memory in reality? Does Levi give us any further clues?

> This reflector is the odic light…which we call the astral light, and is the great agency of life termed od, ob and aour by the Hebrews. The magnetism controlled by the will of the operator is Od; that of the passive clairvoyance is Ob: the pythonesses of antiquity were clairvoyants intoxicated with the passive astral light. This light is called the spirit of Python in our holy books, because in Greek mythology the serpent Python is its allegorical representative.

This is a place or location where we can see the astral light. Levi is saying the same things that we are giving scientific terms to today. He is also linking this magnetism to the serpent:

In its double action, it is also represented by the serpent of the caduceus: the right handed serpent is Od, the one on the left is Ob and in the middle, at the top of the hermetic staff, shines the golden globe which represents Aour, or light in equilibrium.

This is an image of the Caduceus, and contains the concept of the Kundalini. Of course, to those who have not gained enlightened knowledge, the text would be complete nonsense. But Levi goes much further and gives us the whole truth. He tells us quite simply that those who have seen this place enjoy its warmth and fertile nature. It becomes a nexus to which we need to return. It is no different from the reactions seen in those scientific test subjects of preceding chapters. He feels a oneness with this place, a wholeness that he can only see as God.

Believe me, you do not need to travel far for that: the void is in your spirit and in your heart.... True love, natural love, is the miracle of magnetism. It is the intertwining of the two serpents of the caduceus. Its generation looks fated, but it is brought into being by the supreme reason, which produces it according to natural laws. It is fabled that Tiresias incurred the wrath of Venus for separating two serpents who were copulating, and became a hermaphrodite: which neutralised his sexual potency.

As we can see, Levi is quite clear about the duality of the serpent energy. He is certain that these energies follow nature—they are perfectly natural phenomena—which is Levi's way of saying that they are scientifically explainable. This is not surprising, as in his contemporary age of magnetism and electricity all things were deemed possible. Levi is also totally sure that by splitting apart those balancing serpents we only cause disaster, just as when Sheba left Solomon or Guinevere left Arthur. We must keep our balance at all times or disaster can ensue.

But how do we gain such insight? Levi gives us the clues. As we know, the point of being conscious of the unconscious world is known as the *hypnagogic* (falling into sleep) or *hypnapompic* (waking up). It is the point of falling into asleep or waking from sleep. It is the in-between state—between the pillars if you will. Once we have managed to control this point and remain there for a while, we can begin to manipulate it. Did Levi, and perhaps other occultists, know of this state? Language sometimes hides knowledge, and it is difficult to interpret what Levi knew or did not know. But with your knowledge, read this section from Levi's *The Great Secret* and see if you can spot the hypnagogic:

> In his book on the perpetual motion of souls, the Grand Rabbi Isaac Loriah says that it is necessary to take special care in using the hour preceding sleep. In fact, the soul loses its individual life for a time during sleep to immerse itself in the universal light which, as we have said, appears as two opposite currents. The sleeping entity either yields to the embraces of the serpent of Aesculapius, the vital and regenerating serpent, or lies back in the poisoned coils of the hideous Python.... Dream life is essentially different from real life; it has its scenery, its friends and its memories; and in that life one possesses without doubt faculties belonging to other forms and other worlds. One meets again loved beings whom one has never known on this earth; those who are dead are seen alive again; one is carried along in the air; one walks on water as if the action of body weight were less; one speaks unknown languages and makes contact with creatures who are very

oddly organised. Everything there is reminiscent of so much that has nothing to do with this world; might these not be vague recollections of previous existences? Do dreams spring from the brain alone? Well, if the brain produces them, who invents them? Often they terrify and tire us. What Callot or Goya invents our nightmares?

Levi knows the psychological methods of keeping balance—*strength*, *knowledge*, and *will*.

To attain such an achievement it is necessary to KNOW what has to be done, to WILL what is required, to DARE what must be attempted.... The man-God has neither rights nor duties, he has knowledge, will and power.

In this case, and because Levi is speaking of the journey as symbolized in the Odyssey, he has simply improved on Strength with Dare, but either way, the point remains the same. In the second statement Power replaces Dare anyway. Levi also knew some of the secrets of Solomon:

Solomon is supposed to have been the sovereign pontiff of the religion of the initiates, which gave him the right to the royal prerogative of the occult priesthood, for he possessed—so it is said—universal knowledge, and in him alone was realised the promise of the great serpent: "Ye shall be as gods, knowing good and evil."

Here Levi claims that Solomon had the universal knowledge, which I would agree with, especially if we consider that Solomon did not exist and that he is the pinnacle of our own self. Levi also spells out the meaning of the dual nature:

Each one of us can feel a dual life within ourselves. The struggle of the mind against the conscience; of unmanly desire against noble feelings; in a word, of the brute against the intelligent creature; the weakness of the will so often betrayed by passion; the reproaches with which we upbraid ourselves; our self-mistrust; the dreams which haunt us in our waking hours; all this seems to demonstrate within us two persons of a different character, one of whom urges us to do good while the other tries to involve us in evil.... The strength of magnets resides in their two extreme poles and their point of balance is in the centre between these two poles.

Now we can understand the many twins found in myths around the globe. From Castor and Pollux (the Gemini twins), to the biblical brothers Jesus and Thomas, and many more—these are the symbolic devices throughout time of this struggle we all have within. But in the allusion to the magnet, Levi is telling us that the secret lies between the twins, where there is nothing but the force created by two opposites.

Our emotions have given us desire. This desire exists in each one of us to find the truth. I personally see this as an evolutionary device, enabling us to strive for greater goals, all the time becoming the fittest of the species. I see this as the most important spark of human life. Without that spark there would be no life, and without life there would be no sparks. The spark is the creative element, but where does it come from? The Universal Mind? Levi puts it this way:

The Brahmin discovers them [emotions] when lost in the contemplation of Iswara; the Israelite is possessed by them in the presence of Adonai; the devout Catholic nun sheds tears of love on the feet of her crucifix. Do not try to tell them these are illusions and lies: they would give you a pitying smile, and rightly so. Each of them has been filled with beams of light from the Eternal Thought.

In the end, Levi reveals the same truth to which we have been searching all along—that we ourselves are Divine:

> The great arcanum, the inexpressible arcanum, the dangerous arcanum, the incomprehensible arcanum may be definitively formulated thus:
> The divinity of man.
> Such is the man who has succeeded in reaching the central point of balance, and one can, without blasphemy or folly, call him the man-God.

Abbe N. de Montfaucon de Villars

Now I will move on to another favorite of mine, a book titled *Comte de Gabalis: Discourse on the Secret Sciences and Mysteries, in Accordance with the Principles of the Ancient Magi and the Wisdom of the Kabalistic Philosophers* by Abbe N. de Montfaucon de Villars. There is an opening warning:

> Warning. This book is for the student who seeks to illuminate his intelligence by the Torch of his own divinity. Let him whose quest is gratification of a selfish intellectualism beware its pages, for this is a book of hidden mystery and power. Therefore let the mind be pure that it may invite the approach of the Pilgrim Soul and come into a new realisation of God's Omnipotence and Justice.

Why is this book so close to my heart? The simple reason is that it is witty and precise. It is also one of those books known by the initiates to hold secrets of the arcane. It leads the reader on an esoteric journey. Let's have a look now at some of the text and see if de Villars agrees with Levi and if what he says agrees with my revelations about Solomon's Temple.

In the commentary on the Comte de Gabalis and his statement about the wisdom of the serpent, we find that this wisdom is thought to be a Solar Force or a Serpent Fire. The explanation is quite precise and even matches modern scientific discoveries:

> The Earth derives from the Sun not merely light and heat, but, by transformation of these, almost every form of energy manifest upon it; the energy of the growth of plants, the vital energy of animals, are only the energy received from the Sun changed in its expressions. A supreme manifestation of this vital or solar energy upon the physical plane is found in the sympathetic and cerebro spinal nervous system of man and its voltage can there be raised into the Super-Sensible Energy, the instrument which the soul of man uses to build up its deathless Solar or Spiritual Body. The unfoldment of the supersensible or spiritual nature of man is but the progressive manifestation in him of that vital energy derived from the Sun and its Divine Source, known throughout the ages as the Solar Force or Serpent and proceeding from the Creator of the Sun and Worlds, the Great Architect of the Universe.

Although it may sound a little scientifically naïve, this statement makes a great deal of sense. The energy discussed by man for thousands of years in his myth, religion, and folklore as the power of the serpent surely has to have come from somewhere. It is the power to control this energy within, which we have seen in the science chapters of this book, and which is the job of modern scientists to discover. All these ancient wisdom traditions cannot be wrong. The subjects of our contemporary scientists have adequately shown that this is a real human experience. The difference I have with some of the texts is the use of the word God. I can accept from all that I have discovered that this is a term for the Superconscious state and its direct link with what we have termed the Universal Mind through the void. In this extract, the concept is termed the Universal Architect, which of course links the whole thing to formers, builders, and the Masons.

The Comte continues to tell us that "we have only to concentrate the Fire of the World [Solar Force or Serpent Fire] in a globe of crystal, by means of concave mirrors; and this is the art which all the ancients religiously concealed, and which the divine Theophrastus discovered." The divine Theophrastus is, of course, Paracelsus, to whom we shall turn soon. But first we must analyze a strange statement that seems to make no sense. It is one of those peculiar sayings that leads the gullible to rush out and buy crystal spheres and concave mirrors. The truth of the matter is much more simple: The true globe of crystal is the *Philosopher's Egg*; it is the aura of energy or luminous mist seen by those with the eyes to see. It was believed to be the divine manifestation of the thoughts of the mind or soul. This Serpent Fire was thought to be with us during life, whether awake or asleep, and that we could control this power of thought by simply looking inwards to our true Divine Self. This is the meaning of the concave mirrors, they reflect our true self inwards, not outwards. But what evidence do we have that de Villars understood the seven-principle chakra system of the Serpent Fire or Kundalini, which we have seen appearing in many various religions and traditions?

> You must, however, consult your own heart in this matter for, as you will one day see, a Sage governs himself by the interior stars, and the stars of the exterior heaven but serve to give him a more certain knowledge of the aspects of the stars of that interior heaven which is in every creature.

Here we have a strange statement. The sage, who is a wise person of good judgement (or shall we say well-balanced) governs himself by the interior stars. There were seven stars in the heavens, which of course relates to the seven stages of the chakra. Each planet has a specific location on the body. Saturn was the sacral, Jupiter the prostatic, Mars the epigastric, Venus the cardiac, Mercury the pharyngeal, the Moon was the postnasal, and the Sun was the pineal—the Third Eye. All of this relates entirely to both the Kundalini and the Koran story of the seven sleepers. This association would make sense, as Muslims also believe that man can only be born again in spirit through the aid of heavenly powers typified by the angel Gabriel (Jibreel), who took Muhammad on his mystical night journeys. This is the same Gabriel from the book of Enoch who was "One of the Holy Angels, who is over Paradise and the Serpents and the Cherubim." In the Bible, Gabriel is the angel who explains the visions of Daniel and announces the births of both John the Baptist and Christ. He is the Vision Angel of the mystics.

The very same aspect of seven is mentioned throughout *Comte de Gabalis*. We learn of the Holy Kings, who are hierarchical beings called *Kings* as they are states of our own crown or consciousness. They governed intelligence and had authority over the seven planets. We also find a quote from Hermes Trismegistus in *Poimandres I* where the mind is equated to God, balance is paramount, and our Mind creates these seven elements:

> But the Mind, The God, being masculine-feminine, originating Life and Light, begat by Word another Mind Creator, Who being God of the Fire and the Spirit, created some Seven Administrators, encompassing in circles the sensible world.

Notice how these seven administrators encompass the world of the senses in circles. This is similar to the chakra wheels of life. The place of God, or the mind, is of course envisaged as a Divine and kingly throne, but before we can take up our seat and truly become masters of ourselves we must move through the seven levels.

> Grace be unto you, and peace, from Him which is, and which was, and which is to come; and from the seven Spirits which are before His Throne.

> —Revelation 1:4

The author of the book of Revelation reveals that he knows the purpose of the Temple and its real meaning. The Levite clan were descendants of Levi, the third son of Jacob. It is debated whether his descendants formed one of the 12 tribes, as no territory was ever allocated to them. The reason is quite simple, as they were symbolically not of the Earth or lower nature of man. This is shown because the enlightened Moses is a descendant of Levi. Instead, the Levites were placed in charge of the sanctuary. They carried the tabernacle in the wilderness. Similar to Jesus, Buddha (and any number of other avatars who represent our own enlightenment) priestly Levite came of age when he was 30 years old. There is a peculiar serpent in the Bible called the Leviathan, which is made up of two words, *Levi* and *Than* (ThN). *ThN* is the root of the word *serpent* or *dragon*, and Levi is the progenitor of the Levite clan. So the Leviathan is the serpent of Levi, the one who is in charge of the mind.

> The root [of Levi] we may suppose, describes the coils of the serpent, perhaps the metallic gleams of its scales. For Levi was the serpent tribe, bred for generations to the knowledge [Gnosis] and control of the World Serpent, Solar Force. Leviathan or the Serpent of Levi signifies the Solar Force governed and directed upward through the spine by the priest of the tribe of Levi for regeneration, the upbuilding of the deathless Solar Body [spiritual body]. Accurately speaking, Leviathan is the Solar Force manifesting in the cerebrospinal nervous system after its passage through the ganglia [chakra] of the sympathetic nervous system.[6]

So the Levites are in charge of the Temple, and their root is said to be in the coiled serpent, which is known as Kundalini. They have a Leviathan or serpent associated with them, and they seem to not be one of the 12 tribes of earth. They are the Serpent Priests who aid mankind in his search for Divinity in building the Temple.

We also find in the *Comte de Gabalis* the stark statement that Jesus and the serpent are one, and that this is a secret of the Masons and Knights Templar—the very same Knights who gained the Gnosis through the true Temple. (And not the one supposedly buried beneath Jerusalem.)

In the Gospel of St. John 3:14, we read "and just as Moses lifted high the serpent in the Desert, so must the Son of Man be lifted up in order that every one who trusts in him may have the Life of the Ages" (literally of the Solar Force). This verse intimates that the serpent and the Son of Man or Messiah are manifestations of the same Divine Force, a fact which their identity of numerical value indicates and which Masonry confirms, "In the Templar and Philosophical degrees, the serpent is an emblem of Christ."

The messiah, or anointed one, is the same as the serpent. The truth of this statement is seen in the Templar degree in the Freemasons, whereby Christ is depicted by the serpent. We must recall that the original Templar Master had the serpent *abraxus* as his symbol. Throughout time, this serpent imagery has remained. It is there because it symbolically guards the secret of our own divinity and aids us in attaining it.

But what was that about numerical value? The Brazen Serpent, which Moses lifted up high in the desert (of his mind), was numbered 358, which is the same as the word *messiah*! Even numerologically the two supposedly opposite elements are identical.

Paracelsus

It is time now to pursue others who might have knowledge of the Inner Divinity. One of those individuals who has been both vilified and glorified is known as *Paracelsus*, and we shall use the book *The Life of Paracelsus* by Dr. Franz Hartmann as our guide.

His real name was Philippus Aureolus Theophrastus, Bombast of Hohenheim, but is commonly known as Paracelsus. He was born in 1493 near a place called Maria-Einsiedeln, close to Zurich in Switzerland. He was a relative of the contemporary Grand Master of the Order of the Knights of Saint John, who were closely related to the Templars. By 1492, Paracelsus was a physician and had married the matron of a hospital under the authority of the abbey of Maria-Einsiedeln. As time passed, Paracelsus studied and practised alchemy and magic, merging both his scientific medical background with his love of the alchemical arts. He became a very successful doctor, although he never really achieved the credit for his work. He died in 1541 in a small room at the Inn of the White Horse in Salzburg, following a short illness.

Paracelsus did not have a personal liking for writing, and the few texts we do have are mainly those written by students. Only occasionally did he take pen to paper himself. Let's have a look at some of the things that Paracelsus is famous for, as depicted in *The Life of Paracelsus*, and see if they relate to the secret of Solomon's Temple.

> The Soul-essence of Man is formed by the ethereal or astral influences coming from the souls of the world and of the planets and stars, especially from the soul (or astral body) of the planet whereon he lives. As the soul of each man and of each animal has its peculiar qualities that distinguish it from others, like the 'soul' of each planet, each sun, each world has its peculiar characteristics, and sends out its beneficial or its destructive influences, pervading cosmic space, acting upon the Microcosm of man, and producing finally visible results. These astral elements are the organisers of the soul of man. They are the builders of the temple in which the spirit resides....

Paracelsus is really quite clear here. The soul of a man is built just as the Temple is built. It is influenced by other bodies, like the planets and stars from the astral plane. In short, these planets are the internal planets or wheels of life. It was by understanding this principle that Paracelsus was able to ignore the quackery of the day and to heal people from within. He also understood the quantum relationship of man to the universe, the fact that we are one, whole, and interconnected to everything else that exists.

> Man is therefore the quintessence of all the elements, and a son of the universe or a copy in miniature of its Soul, and everything that exists or takes place in the universe, exists or may take place in the constitution of man. The congeries of forces and essences making up the constitution of what we call man, is the same as the congeries of forces and powers that on an infinitely larger scale is called the Universe and everything in the Universe reflects itself in man, and may come to his consciousness; and this circumstance enables a man who knows himself, to know the Universe.

I found this an amazing statement coming to us from across the years. We are told here that, similar to modern quantum physics, everything that happens can happen in us. We are even told how we may become aware of this. By knowing our self, we can know the Universe.

> Such things are possible, and the greatest mysteries may be laid open to the perception of the spirit; and if we earnestly desire gifts, and pray with an unrelenting faith to the power of the Supreme, that rests in ourselves, to grant them to us, we may be enabled to see the Mysteria Dei, and to understand them as well as Moses, Jesaiah, and John.

Note the phrase *rests in ourselves*. This is the true gateway to the mysteries of God, which is inside of us. Also, when Paracelsus says we must have relentless faith, he means that true faith comes from knowledge, for without knowledge there can be no faith. But where does true knowledge come from?

> All knowledge comes from the stars (the Universal Mind). Men do not invent or produce ideas; the ideas exist, and men may be able to grasp them.... The inner consciousness will awaken to an understanding of the influences of the stars, and the mysteries of Nature will be revealed to his spiritual perception.

Paracelsus also tells us that the Comte de Gabilis taught these things himself, and reveals the truth of Gabalis—that he is in reality the spiritual perception of man:

> This art is taught by Gabalis (the spiritual perception of man). It is a power which may become especially active in dreams, and that which is seen in such dreams is the reflection [mirror] of the light of wisdom.

Paracelsus tells us that men who are fully awake cannot know such things. They have to be dreamers, but aware, similar to the hypnagogic state we have mentioned previously. Men, he tells us, do not know their true self and therefore cannot know the things that are in the inner world. Each man has the essence of divinity inside and all the wisdom and power he needs within. He tells us that there is an inner light in the spirit of man that illuminates everything and by which we may be able to perceive supernatural things. This is the shining.

The perfectly simple truths spoken by Paracelsus in a simple way are what have been hidden from us by esoteric, arcane, and often ridiculous language for hundreds of years. As Maimonides wrote, such truths would indeed be hidden in stories, which seem impossible to believe.

Alchemy

The central tenet of alchemy is that of unity—bringing together the lower nature of man and uniting it with the higher spiritual nature of the divinity within (the outer and inner worlds of the Sufi). If that connection can be found, the alchemists truly believed that it would be to man's benefit. The alchemists of the past may have dabbled in the world of chemistry, discovering all kinds of weird and wonderful substances, but the value of their acts can be found in the fact that they were transforming nature to understand themselves. It was a basic belief that man was part of nature, and, therefore, patterns discovered in nature would relate to man. Often there are so-called alchemists who claim to have done this or that, but the work of alchemy was truly a lifelong repetition of biblical proportions upon the self.

There was no difference between the gnostic and the alchemist. Both were searching for regeneration or rebirth of themselves through the knowledge (gnosis), which they believed could be gained by the union or Oneness of the self. Symbols of the levels of alchemy were created, but were in fact no different from the underlying truths of the Chakra and Kundalini traditions. Thousands of alchemical symbols were created, including the many devices we have found from ancient times: the twin pillars of Jachin and Boaz, the coiled or twin serpents, the star signs, and always *balance*. Metals or *prime materia* replaced or matched the planets and nothing greater than *aqua vitae,* or fire water, would be so highly esteemed, because it so perfectly exemplified the union of total opposites or the *coincidentia opposoitorum*.

Through seemingly physical processes, the alchemist would talk about dissolving or burning (or any other number of terms which were metaphors for reducing), the causes of suffering. They understood that this was a *Great Work*, and that it was ongoing.

> Analyse all the elements in yourself, dissolve all that is
> inferior in you, even though you may break in doing so;
> with the strength acquired from the preceding operation,
> congeal.[7]

The alchemists understood that their secrets were nothing new and that they were the secrets of the ancients. Their own tradition stretched back thousands of years. In *Secret Fire: An Alchemical Study*, E.J. Langford Garstin wrote that alchemists were the builders of the Temple and controllers of the Serpent Fire, which they knew to be the same as the *Paraklete* (Holy Spirit) of the Bible, the *Speirema* of the Greeks, and the Sanskrit *Kundalini*.

> This process of arousing Kundalini has to be repeated
> constantly, so that the act becomes thoroughly natural,
> when at length she returns only at the will of the Yogi.
> And this constant repetition finds its parallel in the various
> stages of the Alchemical processes, not merely in the
> purifactory, but in the multiplication.

One of the most enigmatic images of the journey to this wisdom and state of pure gnosis is the Holy Grail. It is something we cannot all attain, and will never find in the literal sense. But the original idea of the bowl or chalice is complete gnosis of the mind.

> Hermes: He filled a great bowl with nous [mind], and
> sent it down to earth, and he appointed a herald, and
> bade him make proclamation to the hearts of men:
> "Hearken, each human heart; baptise yourself in this
> bowl, if you can, recognising for what purpose you have
> been made, and believing that you shall ascend to Him
> who sent the bowl down." Now those who gave heed to
> the proclamation, and dipped themselves in the bath of
> mind, these men got a share of gnosis; they received
> mind, and so became complete men.[8]

This is a hint to the truth of the Grail nearly a thousand years before it would emerge in the image we have today. It is from the *Hermeticum*, the body of texts attributed to that illusive and nonexistent character Hermes Trismegistus. Instead, Hermes is a useful figure to associate with any wisdom literature.

The hermetica

In the book *The Hermetica: The Lost Wisdom of the Pharaohs*, Timothy Freke and Peter Gandy interpret the various texts of the Hermetica and bring them together in chapters, which are useful for those who do not have the time or privilege to go through the original texts themselves. I have chosen to leave these texts for the end, because these are some of the original places that alchemists (Paracelsus and the Abbe de Villars) would have turned to for their own works.

> My senses were suspended in mystic sleep—not a weary, full-fed drowsiness, but an alert and conscious emptiness. Released from my body, I flew with my thoughts, and while I soared, it seemed to me, a vast and boundless Being called my name: "Hermes, what are you looking for?" "Who are you?" I asked. "I am the Way-Guide, the Supreme Mind."

This, the opening line from Freke and Gandy's interpretation, is most revealing. Hermes was suspended in mystic sleep, which was not full sleep but still alert. This is without doubt the hypnagogic stage, and is the method we need to use to stay at that point in the cycle to be aware of our unconscious world. This released Hermes from his body, which is in fact his lower nature—the nature of man, which keeps him in suffering. Once released and aware of his own consciousness, Hermes met up with his own superconscious state, the *Way Guide* or *Supreme Mind*. This is what

Hermes calls the *Atum*. It is himself, and yet it is all, wholeness, oneness, and connected to everything. Without Atum, Hermes tells us, there can be nothing.

> Do you understand the secrets of this vision? I am the Light—the Mind of God, which exists before the chaotic dark waters of potentiality. My calming Word is the Son of God, the idea of beautiful order.... When he had said this, he looked into me, I to I.

Here we have the truth of the matter perfectly clear. I am the Light, the Mind of God, and I look into I. I am, therefore, God.

This Atum is the *Primal Mind*, his Being is *known through thought alone*, He is the *Whole which contains everything*, *He is One not Two*, *He is All*, *not many*. This reminded me of the terms given for al-Lah, the God of Islam. He too, is the *One god*, and so I turned briefly to a wonderful book by John Baldock titled *The Essence of Sufism*. Baldock swiftly goes about orienting us in the right direction.

> Orientation is a key word here, for it means more than simply pointing oneself physically in a particular direction. It also refers to our inner orientation, whether this is towards ourselves—that is, our ego-personality—or towards something much greater, to the Source on which we depend for our being.

Baldock makes a distinction between the self and the source, something I have not done throughout this book. This is because I have taken the liberty of deciding that the source is part and parcel of our true Divine Self—which is said by our ancestors to be connected to the source or Universal Mind. There is, of course, this ego-personality of which John speaks, but I have left this as part of the causes of suffering. Either way, what we have here is the Sufi (mystical Islam) way—that truth is within. We next get a beautiful rendition of Muhammad's Night Journey (Isra') and Ascent (Mi'raj):

> One evening Muhammad was by the Ka'ba, "in a state between sleeping and waking" when Gabriel (Jibreel) appeared to him and told him to mount a winged beast called Buraq. The animal, which was smaller than a mule and larger than an ass, had a woman's head and a peacock's tail. Muhammad's wondrous steed took him to Jerusalem, to the site of the ruined Temple of Solomon, where Abraham (Ibrahim), Moses (Musa), Jesus (Isa) and all the other Prophets were gathered. Muhammad led them in prayer, and then Buraq bore him upward to the Seventh Heaven. As they passed through each of the seven heavens he met one or another of the Prophets who had preached Oneness of God to humankind.

We have in this classic tale of the journey and ascent the perfect example of the shamanic journey. It is the hypnagogic (or hypnapompic) state that brings on the vision—the state between sleeping and waking. Muhammad goes upwards through the seven levels and speaks of the Oneness of God. How is this different from the ancient words of *The Hermetica*? *The Hermetica* also tells us about our modern discovery of quantum entanglement:

> Atum is everywhere. Mind cannot be enclosed, because everything exists within Mind. Nothing is so quick and powerful. Just look at your own experience. Imagine yourself in any foreign land, and as quick as your intention you will be there! Think of the ocean—and there you are. You have not moved as things move, but you have travelled, nevertheless. Fly up into the heavens—you won't need wings!... All things are thoughts.

We also find the seven levels of heaven or the chakra, which we know as the inner planets:

> Then the soul mounts upwards through the structures of the heavens. In the first zone it is relieved of growth and decay. In the second, evil and cunning. In the third, lust and deceiving desire. In the fourth, domineering arrogance. In the fifth, unbalanced audacity and rashness. In the sixth, greed for wealth. In the seventh, deceit and falsehood. Having been stripped of all that was put upon it by the structures of the heavens, the soul now possesses its own proper power and may ascend....

We could not have any clearer vision of the self-imposed seven levels of human suffering, which we know we must get rid of. Only then can we truly ascend to the power of our own mind in union with the quantum world of existence, and be rebirthed through the womb of wisdom.

Conclusion

Author at a cathedral in Southwell Minster, England.

D uring the writing of this book, I visited many cathedrals and churches in England, always looking for the fragments of esoteric life and gnostic influence. Normally I am accompanied by my wife and two children running around like a pair of crazy people—all to the disdain of the men in ecclesiastical robes. On one particular occasion, we visited Lincoln Cathedral. After we paid the extortionate entrance fee, we slowly looked around. The children ran off as usual looking for snakes and Templar crosses for Daddy.

After taking several photographs and being immersed in the history of the beautiful stone, my wife (looking rather glum) said, "you know, it's just going to be a rockery one day."At first I put this observation down to her usual disdain for "boring stone buildings," as I have been destroying her soul for years with trips to "rockerys" and "quarries." But then I thought, maybe she's right.

I looked around and saw the various self-important Christian clergy, all pompous and self-righteous. They were no different to a thousand other churches and places of worship I had visited over the years. In some places, however, there was life. The stones became animated, as though they were a living temple. But others were dull and had been overtaken with the desires or causes of suffering. Mankind has affected the buildings he erected, whether for good or bad. In this instance I was reminded of the time Jesus cast out the money lenders from the temple. Charging fees that poor people simply cannot afford for a self-righteous and pompous trip around a deadened religious building is something a real Christ or Christian would get angry about. This should be a place of reflection, in the true sense of the word (reflect our Inner Divinity)—not a place of finance.

The analogy swept over me that this massive edifice to a nonexistent God, high on a hillside, was no different from the human Temple. It was crumbling under its own sins. There was no longer any life in the place, except the kind of life that Jesus kicked out of the temple. It was the macrocosm and microcosm all over again. We are the Temple of Solomon—or can be—and the temple or cathedral is the form of the perfected man—or should be.

Yet again, my wife, my feminine principle, had brought something home to me. She has often astounded me with her insight. (Insights that I have regularly been too engrossed to see for myself.) Yet again, this is the wisdom of the ages, playing out in a physical three-dimensional manner, man and wife in unison and unity.

The true understanding of what has been written in this book will come when we understand, that at every level of our lives—physical and spiritual, coarse or fine, related to ourselves or others—what we must always begin with is balance. But each level must be worked on. We must understand that there are elements that cause us suffering, and these appear and reappear. We must repeat the cycle of eradication if we are to proceed to the next level and be free from the world of evil desires. Once our minds are free of all the elements that distract us, we will truly shine. Once we understand the true nature of our own interconnectedness to each other and the very Universe, then we will have that knowledge, or gnosis, of the very thing for which we aim. We will understand fully that all faiths, all religions, all myths, and all traditions all relate to one thing— the truth of our self. Once mankind has built its 6 billion Temples, then maybe there will be hope for the world.

Appendix A

THE KNOWLEDGE DICTIONARY

'abd

Sufi term meaning *servant* or *slave*. In Islamic doctrine, the individual is seen as being the servant or slave of God and not necessarily the son, as in the Judeo-Christian father/child relationship.

ablution

An alchemical term for washing a solid with a liquid. However, the real meaning is to purge oneself of those things that cause suffering, such as desire or ego.

Adam and Eve

According to the Ante-Nicene Christian Library, Clemens Alexandrius claimed that *Heviah* (the root of *Eve*) means *female serpent*. "If we pay attention to the strict sense of the Hebrew, the name Evia aspirated signifies a female, serpent." The name is connected to the same Arabic root that means both *life* and *serpent*. The Persians called the constellation Serpens the little Ava or Eve. In old Akkadian, *Ad* signifies *father*, and according to C. Staniland Wake in *The Origin of Serpent Worship*, the name *Adam* was closely associated in legend with

Seth, Saturn, Thoth, or Taautus, who are all associated strongly as serpents. *Abel*, the son of Adam and Eve, means *serpent god*. Cain was thought to be of serpent descent. Adam and Eve are names that spelled out their meaning, and yet over time we have lost that meaning. In essence, the two aspects of the serpent energy must be reunited to attain the perfect man—the Adam Kadmon of the Alchemists.

adder

The word *adder* is derived from *gnadr*, a Druidic term. The Druids traditionally stated, "I am a Druid; I am an architect; I am a prophet; I am a serpent"—linking the Druids to the *Dionysiac Architects* of Freemasonic fable. According to Christianity (and especially St. Augustine) the adder was evil and was one of the four aspects of the devil. The deaf adder depicted sinners who have closed their ears to the truth.

adept

Taken from the Latin *adeptus*, meaning *he who has obtained*. In this instance, it is wisdom that the adept has obtained. The adept is beyond the Initiate stage of enlightenment and is now either a Master Adept or on the road to becoming one.

Adytum

The Greek name for the Holy of Holies in any temple. It is the most secret and sacred of locations known to man, into which nothing profane can enter.

agartha

This Tibetan word means *the underground kingdom placed at the center of the earth, where the king of the world reigns*. It is symbolic and is used extensively to imply the true center. This is a device utilized by the followers of the enlightenment experience to describe the central aspect needed to achieve illumination.

Agathodaemon

Good serpent or *sacred serpent* of the Gnostics and Phoenicians. This good serpent is none other than the Solar Force or Serpent Energy, which aids man along the path of enlightenment. It is also the coiled serpent of the Kundalini. In the Bacchanalian rites there was, remarkably, a *Cup of the Agathodaemon*. This serpent-consecrated cup of wine was handed around and received with much shouting and joyousness. The hymn sung through the serpent to the Supreme Father was just the same as the one sung in the memory of the Python at Delphi on the seventh day of the week, mimicking the seventh chakra in the Kundalini process to Divinity. Now, thousands of years later, Christians still take the cup of Christ (called *the good serpent* by the Gnostics) and eat the consecrated bread. This modern ritual is similar to the original, but renamed *Cup of the Sacred Serpent*, which gives the body and blood of our oldest god.

Agni

Hindu god meaning *Shining One*. He illuminates the sky. In this, we can see the cross association with the physical sun and the internal sun.

ajna center/chakra

This is the Eastern Chakra point between the eyebrows that is aligned to the pituitary gland. It is the center of the personality of the individual. It is also known as the *agni chakra* or *fire/shining chakra*.

Akashic records

Records of every person's word and deed that will be found in the spiritual realm. In *Gateway to the Serpent Realm*, I posited the theory that these were to be found in a quasi-quantum vacuum field, and that mankind is capable of seeing the records in a superconscious state.

akh

Egyptian term meaning *Shining Soul*. Note the use of the term in the names of certain pharaonic names, such as *Akh-en-Aten*, the Egyptian king who is said to have worshipped only the Outer Sun.

alchemy

Al or *El* means *God* or *Shining*. *Khem* or *Chem* is from the root Greek *kimia* and means *to fuse*. Therefore, *alchemy* means to fuse with God or the Shining—to be enlightened. Basically it was a cover for the Eastern traditions, which were diametrically opposed to the Church of Rome. Alchemy was brought to Europe through the teachings of Geber (Jabir ibn Hayyan, A.D. 721–815) as well as several others. In later years, the psychoanalyst Carl Jung concluded that alchemical images he was finding emanating from his subjects' dreams and thoughts explained the archetypal roots of the modern mind and underscored the process of transformation.

Alexander the Great

Ambassadors of Alexander, after returning from a visit to Kashmir, made mention of the fact that the king had two large serpents, named Ida and Pingala. Obviously these were the two serpents of the Kundalini. According to Strabo, the King of Taxila showed him a huge serpent actually being worshipped. Alexander is well known to have made an extensive search for his own spirituality, especially among Indian culture.

alkahest

This is the alchemical term for *the power that comes from above*, and allows or makes possible alchemical transformation. Sometimes translated as *universal solvent*, it is the concept of transmuting material (or mental) elements into their purest form. It is, in essence, the concept of revealing the hidden and true nature of mankind, which is the real "gold" of arcane philosophers.

Allah

The God of Islam coming from *Ilah* or *El*, meaning *shining much*. It is the inner enlightenment. It is similar to the inner reality of our own divinity, which engulfs us in light.

anahata

The Eastern Chakra center related to the heart.

anchor

The *Foul Anchor* symbolizes the boat and mast, which is a symbol of Mary. This is significant, as it symbolizes the union of the male (mast) and the female (boat or crescent moon). In Egyptian symbolism, this union of the opposites was strengthened with the serpent coiling up the mast—similar to the Kundalini energy of Hinduism. This union of opposites was also associated with a dolphin, which has speed against the slowness of the boat—thus symbolizing the occult *hasten slowly*, another union device. This dolphin and boat symbol was also used to symbolize Christ on the cross. It is also closely associated with the ankh.

androgyny

From the Greek *andro-genika*, where *andro* means *man* and *genika* means *woman*. Otherwise known as the *hermaphrodite* (Hermes and Aphrodite joined). This philosophy supposes that once the human is free of his or her innermost darkness, he realizes that he is bisexual in spirit and mind. It is not a literal concept. Once in this state, the alchemist, magician, or Shining One represents the perfect human and is seen as connected entirely to the universe. It is a very ancient idea, and is a stepping-stone to the enlightenment experience.

anima

This is a term often used by alchemists, and is Latin for *the soul*.

anima mundi

Latin for the *soul of the world*. It is an esoteric term meaning the modern collective consciousness or the superconscious state.

ankh

The *Crux Ansata*. A simple *T-cross*, surmounted by an oval, also known as *the ru*, or *Gateway to the Otherworld*. This symbol of Egypt represents *eternal life* and is often found in the names of pharaohs, such as *Tut-ankh-amun*. The anhk has been depicted as being held by a pharaoh, giving his people life. This basically sets aside the immortals from the mortals, for anyone wearing or carrying the ankh gains immortality. It can also be worn as an amulet to sustain life. It is the loop (*the ru*) of the Ankh, that is held by the immortals to the nostrils. (This imagery reflects the biblical God breathing life into the nostrils of Adam.)

Thoth, the Egyptian deity, was said to have symbolized the four elements with a simple cross, which originated from the oldest Phoenician alphabet as the curling serpent. As recorded in *A Discourse of the Worship of Priapus* by Richard Payne Knight, Philo believes that the Phoenician alphabet is "formed by means of serpents...and adored them as the supreme gods, the rulers of the universe." Thoth, who is related to the worship of serpents, created the alphabet. According to C. Staniland Wake in *The Origin of Serpent Worship*, the 19th century writer Bunsen saidthat "the forms and movements of serpents were employed in the invention of the oldest letters, which represent gods." This symbol was altered slightly, and became the Egyptian *Taut*, the same as the Greek *Tau*, which is where we get the phrase *Tau Cross*— a simple T.

In shape, the Ankh is very similar to the Egyptian musical instrument, which is shaped like the oval *ru*—the *sistrum*. The sistrum is an Egyptian musical instrument closely associated with female gods—especially Hathor the serpent/cow goddess, and Isis—the consort of Osiris. In form, they are very much like the Ankh, with a loop at the top—also representing the egg—and three serpents striking through the loop with small square pieces of metal, which rattle. It's possible these three serpents represent the *pingala*, *ida*, and *sushumna* nerve channels of the Eastern Kundalini tradition and which converge and fuse together within the center of the brain (the thalamus)—which, in the individual, was also thought to represent the cosmic egg.

During the ascent of these serpent energies up the spine to the center of the head, the individual will hear sounds similar to the sounds of the sistrum. One will also hear sounds like a rattlesnake, and also whistles and flute-like instruments—a white noise now associated with the Otherworld. Underlying these sounds is a very low and strong rumbling sound, that fades in at first and becomes louder and louder as the process proceeds culminating in the bright, white light explosion in the center of the head. The sistrum then may have been a symbol of this experience.

The sistrum was used in pictures and carvings to show the various gods and pharaohs subduing the power of a particular god.

antahkarana

An Eastern term for the invisible channel, through which meditation bridges the area between the physical brain and the soul.

antimony

An alchemical term that symbolizes the animal nature or wild spirit in man that must be eradicated. There is a metal called antimony that was used by the alchemist Basil Valentine, and which he fed to some Benedictine monks, almost killing them in the process. A tincture of antimony is said to cure some venereal diseases.

animism

This is the belief that inanimate things, such as plants, posses souls.

anthroposophy

Founded by cult leader Rudolf Steiner, a German mystic. The term means *wisdom of man* and teaches the ancient truth that wisdom, which is truth itself, is to be found within man.

arcanum

Coming from the Latin *arcane*, meaning a secret or mystery. The term is connected to the word *ark*, as in the Ark of the Covenant, or the ark used by Noah. Both are also connected to the barges or b'arques seen in ancient Egypt, which carry the souls of the dead to the otherworld.

ascended masters

On a literal level, these are spiritual teachers of higher consciousness as proposed by Helena Blavatsky, and thought to exist across time and from the East. However, some would see them instead as inner teachers from within us.

ascension

The Ascension of Christ, although taught as a literal event (where Christ ascended to Heaven) is, in reality, the rise of the Christ consciousness within man. It is the Kundalini rising up the spine or axis mundi to full enlightenment. It is the realization that man is the Divine.

assiah

A Hebrew term for the fourth world of the Kabbalah. It means *the physical body*. The term was ranslated in the biblical Revelation of Saint John as Asia.

astral body

A projection of the inner self, or the *Haqiqah* of the Sufi. The astral body is thought to exist after death. In *Gateway to the Serpent Realm*, I showed how this can easily be related to quantum physics and the quantum entanglement of the superconscious state with the universe, thus giving rise to the Akashic records. It is related to *astral flight*, which is the travel of the soul during sleep or meditation. The common astral body is also known as the *Kama Rupa* or *Body of Desires*, whereas the true astral body is the Solar Force or Spirit as spoken by Jesus in John 3:5–6: "Except a man be born of water and of the Spirit, he cannot enter into the kingdom of God. That which is born of the flesh is flesh; and that which is born of the Spirit is spirit." Jesus is indicating the two distinct human attributes, one of flesh or body and one of spirit or astral body.

athanor

A term in alchemy for the oven, which itself symbolizes the union of the male and female principles within man—uniting opposites within. It is sometimes symbolized by a mountain or a hollow oak tree.

atman

This is the true inner reality, the Spirit or the Son of God element within each of us. Alchemists say that the atman does not die, it is without end of days, and is absolutely perfect.

aura

The glow, halo, or radiation around living or inanimate objects, thought by many to be the visual element of the soul or spirit. These auras are now photographed using Kirlian photography.

avatar

The manifestation of a higher entity for the benefit of mankind. Christ, Buddha, and Zoroaster are all seen as avatars. These are the inner reality elements of mankind being seen or envisioned by the mystic who has attuned himself to the universal truths held within. The teaching of an avatar expands mankind's understanding of himself, humanity, and the evolution of mankind on a spiritual level. The evolution of the spirit is said to affect the physical evolution of mankind and is thought to be a way back to the divinity.

bain marie

Named after the female Jewish alchemist Maria Prophetissa, this is said to be a warm alchemical bath (a double boiler container) that is suspended in a cauldron of simmering water. However, as with most alchemical terms, it is also a metaphor for the warm feeling associated with meditation on the road to dissolution or the eradication of the ego.

Baphomet

A mysterious object said to have been venerated by the Templars and thought to be a skull. One possible explanation for the origin of the word could be found in the deserts of Yemen. The people who live there are called the *Al-Mahara*, and they have developed many ways of combating snake poison. The special priests are called *Raaboot* men, and they are said to have learned the secret by transition from father to son. Their legends state that they have immunity from snakebites.

If somebody is bitten, then a Raaboot man is called. He sits by the patient, along with several others, who then chant in a monotone voice "Bahamoot, Bahamoot." The poison is then said to be vomited up or passed out of the body. The Raaboot man then leaves. Is it not possible that "Bahamoot," as a chant for the curing of snakebites, could have made its way through the various cultures and found itself as a word for the head serpent? If nothing else, then the etymology of these two related items is so similar that it again shows in the language of the worldwide spread of serpent worship.

Baqa'

A Sufi term referring to the *Divine Attribute of Everlastingness*. It is opposite to *fana'* or *passing away*. When the Sufi reaches the state of *fana'* he is leaving himself behind and then only the Divine self remains.

Bardo

A Tibetan term meaning simply *between the two*. In essence it is the void. This can be seen in the title of the *Tibetan Book of the Dead*, which is really translated as *The Great Book of Natural Liberation through Understanding in the Between*.

Bel/Baal

A solar god, thought by John Bathurst Deane in his book *Worship of the Serpent Traced Throughout the World* to be an abbreviation of *Ob-El*—the serpent god. Etymologist and historian, Jacob Bryant,, remarks that the Greeks called him *Beliar*, which was interpreted by Hesychius to mean *"a dragon or great serpent."* *Bel* is the Assyrio-Babylonian gods *Enlil* and *Marduk*—being the same as *Baal*.

Beltane could be rendered *Bel-Tan*, both words signifying the dragon/serpent, showing a link across Europe. In fact, *Tan-it* or *Tanit* was the patron goddess of Carthage in Northern Africa, who was also associated with the Tree of Life. Often the Tree is depicted with wavy lines, said to represent serpents. The name *Tanit* means *Serpent Lady*. She is found on many coins from the height of Carthage and is associated with the Caduceus, symbolizing the role of Tanit in life, death, and rebirth. She is basically the same as the Queen of Heaven—Astarte, Isis, and Mary.

birds

The association between birds (or wings) and serpent seems to go back in time many thousands of years. To quote John Bathurst Deane:

> The hierogram of the circle, wings, and serpent, is one of the most curious emblems of Ophiolatreia, and is recognised, with some modifications, in almost every country where serpent worship prevailed.... It may be alleged that all these cannot be resolved into the single-winged serpent once coiled. Under their present form, certainly not; but it is possible that these may be corruption's

of the original emblem which was only preserved accurately in the neighbourhood of the country where the cause of serpent-worship existed; namely, in Persia, which bordered upon Babylonia and Media, the rival loci of the Garden of Eden.

Deane relates these many thousands of images of the winged serpent to the *Seraphim* of the Bible; the fiery and flying serpents. These could also be the origins for the flying dragons, and why Quetzalcoatl was the feathered or plumed serpent. The reason given by Deane for this symbolism is for proof of deity and consecration of a given temple. If this is the case, then temples across the world were consecrated by the ancient serpent with the serpent energy.

bodhicitta

A Sanskrit term meaning *the enlightened mind*.

bodhisattva

A Sanskrit term meaning *the essence of enlightenment or wisdom*, as both are one and the same. In esoteric terms, this is a soul or being who has earned the right to enter nirvana and escape samsara. He or she has become enlightened or illuminated and is a Shining One, but instead of entering Nirvana, he or she has turned back towards this existence to aid humanity.

Buddha

The enlightened or illuminated one who is a bodhisattva. According to New Age traditions, he was the last avatar of the ages of Aries and was the embodiment of wisdom. The serpent was an emblem of Buddha Gautama, the messiah. According to Hindu oral tradition and legend, Gautama had a serpent lineage. Not surprisingly, trees are sacred to Buddhists, as Gautama was enlightened beneath the *bo tree*. In the book *Ophiolatreia*, Hargrave Jennings quotes Captain Chapman, who was one of the first to see the ruins of Anarajapura in India.

At this time the only remaining traces of the city consist of nine temples...groups of pillars...still held in great reverence by the Buddhists. They consist first of an enclosure, in which are the sacred trees called Bogaha.

The basis of the Tibetan healing arts comes from Bhaisajya-guru, Lapis Lazuli Radiance Buddha, the master of healing. The begging bowl is made of lapis lazuli and contains the Elixir of Life. The definition of the Elixir can be found in a story about the Buddha when he passes the night at the hermitage of Uruvela:

The leader Kashyapa warned Buddha that there was only one hut available, and that a malevolent Naga (cobra or serpent) occupied it. Buddha was not concerned and went to the hut. However, a terrific struggle ensued, culminating in the hut bursting into flames. The onlookers drenched the flames, but they had to wait until morning to find out whether Buddha had survived. Buddha emerged with his begging bowl in his arms. Inside was a peaceful, coiled snake. The Buddha had slain the dragon of its fiery notions and emerged with a beneficial result.

chakras

These are the Eastern energy centers in the body (etheric), which run up the spine through the seven endocrine glands. The Kundalini (coiled serpent) energy must be raised upwards through the centers to achieve enlightenment.

channelling

This is a fairly modern term for being able to gain insight from the Otherworld through unknown means. The person may not necessarily know how or why he or she can channel, and may not have undergone training. I propose that this is due to being quantum entangled in the superconscious state to the natural world and is a perfectly natural state of evolution, of which we were once more aware.

circumambulation

To walk or go around ritualistically. The walking or traversing around a sacred spot or monument, such as the Buddhist stupas. The effect is to fix the axis of the world in a particular place and time—thus making that place sacred. The idea is to manifest the creative principle within man. It is believed that these sacred places have a scientific bearing, in that they are often places of high electromagnetic energy, which may link with the energy of the human who has governed his own electromagnetic energy through meditation. It is called *the pilgrimage to the self*, and is seen across the world, most famously at the annual festival of the *Ka'aba* in Islam, where the seven circuits are symbolic of the seven attributes of god—the *Ka'aba* is the black (and therefore void) meteorite that fell to earth and is believed by many to be charged with electromagnetism. The *Ka'aba* or *Ca'abir* is a conical stone (although many say square)—resolved itself into *Ca Ab Ir*—the *Temple of the Serpent Sun*, and is the point of connection between heaven and earth. The cone shape is symbolic of luck, and in the Dionysus myths it was the heart of Bacchus. Conical headdresses were worn by the Dioscuri, Egyptian, and Sumerian kings and priests. In J.C. Cooper's book *An Illustrated Encyclopedia of Traditional Symbols*, Bastius said that the cone and the spinning top shared the same symbolism, and are therefore strongly linked to the enlightenment experience and electromagnetism.

cosmic consciousness

This is the belief that mystics and spiritualists are in touch with a universe that is all and one, and is aware. When we attain this cosmic consciousness we are aware of all things, from all time, from everywhere, all at once. Our external realities of this existence must be cast aside if we are to be able to be conscious of this event of enlightenment. This is the inner reality, the connection to the Divine. In relation to this is cosmic humanity, which sees man as being capable of more than the sum of reality, and of unlimited potential.

daimon

Not the demon of Christianity, but the Inner Teacher, the spirit of the Divine inside each one of us that guides us to perfection. We all have this daimon or daemon, if only we could discover it.

decapitation

This is often found in fables and stories, and relates to the killing of the ego, the mystical death, and a process whereby all that is false is eradicated, thus releasing the Inner Divinity.

deva

A Shining One, angel, or celestial being. Deva's are said to aid mankind with intellectual and spiritual pursuits from their parallel universe. In truth, these are internal Inner Realities that are probably archetypal and visualized as Shining entities due to the physical and mental affects of the enlightenment process. They have physical manifestations in the literal world as real human guides in ages past.

dharma

An Eastern word, dharma is the innermost nature of every individual and is the true being. It is the meaning of life. Man is not acting to his full ability if he does not know his dharma.

double or twin

Every person has his twin within himself. It is simply the opposites discussed elsewhere, the male and female principles. The *monad* is the whole of this. The Tibetans state that our Buddha or enlightened soul within ourselves has, in opposition, the *Devadatta* (the brother). This is the same as *Set*, who is the twin of *Horus/Osiris*; the reason for the twin pillars (between which we must pass in balance) of the Masons and others; the twin Aker jackal or lions of Egypt (Sphinx), between which resides the Great Pyramid; the Ida and Pingala channels of the East that rise up the spine through the chakras towards enlightenment; of Castor and Pollux; and of Romulus and Remus. It can also be broken down further in that each side has its own opposites. Take for instance the Divine Mother, the Holy Spirit or Ghost: she is good and beneficial, but she has herself an opposite other than the Divine Father. This opposite is known as the *Durga*, and is the ferocious aspect of the Divine Mother.

These examples reflect the dual nature of man, seen as dark and light, evil and good, man and woman. Wherever these opposites are to be found, the writer is representing these internal realities. These are the psychological battles that are enacted within us. When we decide to do good and be good, our alter-ego fights the impulse or desire with opposite desires. In essence, good is all those things that are in their correct place, and bad is all those things out of place.

dragon

Taken from the Greek *draco* meaning *seeing*, from his supposed good sight. This we now know to be related to the good internal sight brought to us through the energy of the serpent.

egg

The *egg*, *Cosmic Egg*, or *Cosmogenic Egg* is universally seen with the serpent—as in the symbol of the *Orphic Egg*, which shows a snake wrapped around an egg. From the serpent mound of Ohio to Mithras and Cneph, the egg is associated with serpent worship. According to most scholars, it is the emblem of the mundane elements coming from the creating God. Therefore it is a symbol of the elements of the universe. But there is another reason that the egg relates to early man.

What is an egg? An egg is simply an entry portal into this world. It is a device to give life. And what animal is seen in relation to this unique device and portal? Again, it is the snake—a symbol of the life force—which creates the device that gives life.

Kneph/Cneph was represented as a serpent thrusting an egg from his mouth, from which proceeded the deity *Ptah*, *Phtha*, or *Ptah*—the creative power and father god who is the same as the Indian Brahma.

ego

Psychologically, the ego is the destructive part of ourselves, causing suffering through desires, which lead to us making decisions about our life that are at odds with the Inner Reality of Divinity. We can only eradicate the ego by realizing its effect on us and our errors because of the force of the ego. Once we realize we have ego, we can set about removing it. Buddhists teach that we need to be free from the suffering caused by this element of our lives. Buddha gave us a clear and distinct Eightfold Path to Enlightenment: (1) creative comprehension; (2) good intentions; (3) good words; (4) total sacrifice; (5) good behavior; (6) absolute chastity; (7) continual fight against the Dark Magicians—the alter ego; and (8) absolute patience in all.

elementals

These are believed to be spirits or souls in a lower form of existence than humanity—the spirits of the rocks, animals, plants, and other parts of nature. In ancient times, mystics believe that, as man was closer to nature, he was thereby more capable of perceiving these nature spirits and conversing with them. Names have been given to these elemental spirits, such as *gnomes*, *fairies*, and *elves*. They are spoken of regularly in the texts of Alchemists and Occultists, but are in reality a hidden element. These elementals are the energy signatures of all things as seen through superconsciousness.

It was once believed that mankind could communicate with these elementals and that they aided mankind and even mated with him. However, this is the language of times gone by. In reality, the communication between man and elementals is similar to when animals sense energy signatures, such as before an earthquake, when all the animals disappear, moving upwards towards the hills and mountains. How animals perceive these energy signatures is still a scientific mystery. In this way, the energy signatures, or elementals, communicate with animals. If man, who is nothing more than an evolved animal, could also pick up on these signatures, then he too would be aided by the elementals. The ancient and not so ancient texts that speak of these nature spirits are our only clue as to how mankind can perceive these energy signatures.

epiphany

To experience the revealed God in His Creation. It is spirit manifested in reality. It is the superconscious state seen in ordinary things or through new eyes.

ESP

Extra Sensory Perception, which includes telepathy, clairvoyance, divination, and precognition. Those with this ability may not understand the truth behind their ability, but are (by quirk of fate) able to pick up electromagnetic signature or are quantum entangled to the earth and the cosmic universal consciousness. They are not necessarily in a state of superconsciousness or enlightenment, but are tuned biologically, chemically, and electromagnetically through particle physics. Those who can use ESP and are superconscious can affect the particle world.

etheric body

This is the energy counterpart of the physical body and is an idea manifested across the esoteric, occult, alchemical, and mystical world. It is the body of the chakras, connecting them with a body of energy. These may be vortices of subatomic energy, controlled by the mind once the mind is in control of itself and not confused and sidetracked by the world of external phenomena.

Eye of Dangma

In Sanskrit, *dangma* means *purified soul*. The *Eye of Dangma* is the *Eye of the Purified Soul*. It is the spiritual sight gained by an enlightened or Shining One. This site is that of the superconscious state or altered state of reality, whereby man can perceive the energy signatures of all things, similar to the auras of Kirlian photography.

fall of man

Although believed by millions of Christians, Muslims, and Jews to be a literal event spoken of in Genesis, where Adam and Eve fall from grace, this is a metaphor for the fall of man's higher consciousness to the base nature we know today. The concept of Christ as the Redeemer exists only in the sense that he enabled man to see that there truly was a heaven on earth, achievable now to all mankind, which is the internal dialogue or the inner reality of the self.

fana'

The ego death or the passing away of the self, leaving behind the Divine Self in Sufi tradition. The final element of *fana'* is the *fana' al-fana'*, which simply means *the passing away of the passing away*. This is the stage when the Sufi is no longer even aware of having passed away.

fitrah

This is the pure or prime nature of man in the Sufi tradition. It is the time before man became corrupted by desire, greed, and all manner of evil elements.

Gaia

The goddess of the earth according to Greek legend. Made famous by the scientist James Lovelock, who claimed that the whole earth, including all living organisms, was a single living entity in unison with itself. The concept is not new. Quantum theory is now proving that this is true, and that *all things are one* is a truth. The new term *holism* has been applied to show that all things are interrelated to each other in a series of amazing chemical, biological, electrical, and quantum particle connections.

gnostic

The term given to an individual who claims gnosis or knowledge of his own divinity. According to gnostic belief, the serpent was virtuous and wise. Satan was seen as the elder brother of Jesus, and the serpent was seen as the sign for the savior. The gnostic *Cainites* revered the snake on the tree, and the Ophites used asps and vipers at their sacred ceremonies. The Templars of Scotland in their Ancient Rite venerate the symbol of the serpent wrapped around the Tau-cross. The famous Templar/Masonic *Kirkwall* Scroll, revealed by Andrew Sinclair in his book *The Secret Scroll* is replete with sacred images of the serpent.

guru

A term given to a teacher in Eastern traditions.

Hallaj

An Islamic mystic who truly understood his own inner divinity. He was condemned to death in A.D. 922 following his statement "I am God." His writings are outlawed in the Muslim faith.

haqiqah

A Sufi word for inner reality, from the root *al-haqq*, which means *truth*. The inner reality of ourselves is, in fact, truth—and truth is our inner reality, which can only be gained by *fana'* or the passing away of the self.

hermeneutic

A method whereby man can interpret the symbolic in order to better understand.

hidden treasure

In Islamic tradition, the *hadith qudsi* is the declaration of Allah where He says "I was a Hidden Treasure, so I wanted to be known." Mankind, as reflected images of God, are containers of this hidden treasure, which is the divine self.

himma

Muslim term for the power of the heart. This is the heart within mankind—Divine love.

hierophant

A Greek term for a teacher of ancient mysteries and esoteric myths.

Holy Spirit

Seen as the third person in the Christian Trinity. To modern Christians the Holy Spirit is without gender. However, to other traditions the Holy Spirit was the feminine principle. To Dante it was the husband of the Holy Mother. The Holy Spirit or ghost is the *Fire of Pentecost* seen to inspire the disciples in Acts 2. It is similar to the Kundalini, Solar Force, or Serpent Fire. All of these are names for the same principle. It is more likely that the holy spirit is only complete in the form of the Kundalini, which is masculine, and when in union with the feminine. In symbolism, the gnostics of Christianity saw the spirit as a fish, a lamb, and a dove—all of which were derived from earlier cults, coming from Egypt, Sumeria, and elsewhere.

Horned God

From Pashupati to Pan, the Horned God is seen throughout history in connection with the secret of the serpent. It is Pan who kicks open the cista of Bacchus, revealing the serpent within. Dionysus (Bacchus) is often depicted with horns, and the Bacchanals of Thrace were said to wear horns in imitation of their god. Even Zeus, who transformed himself into a serpent to bring Dionysus to life, was depicted as having horns. The horns are thought to signify the solar aspect of the god—the life-giving aspect. They are also symbolic of the bull. The goat is also associated with the serpent, as Dionysius is often manifested as a goat. The awakening of Moses is symbolized by horns or shining forth. Moses also wields the Caduceus staff and raises the Brazen Serpent of healing for Yahweh in the wilderness.

initiate

A term often misused, but in reality meaning one who undergoes the altering of his own reality to the perception of his own inner self of divinity. There are of course many secret societies and occult groups who claim to have initiates. These initiates undergo various degrees on the road to self-realization. Of course, it can also be said that they undergo manipulation to a distinct way of life and belief system. It is a perfect tool to control the minds of individuals by promising the almost impossible dream of divinity. Few individuals in history can truly claim to have been enlightened, and those who do often live in secrecy.

insan al-kamil

The perfect man, the pure and holy one, or the universal man. This term is used in Sufism for the one who is a fully-realized human being.

jnana

A Sanskrit term meaning *to know* and related to gnosis. Specifically, the term refers to the enlightenment of the consciousness, or wisdom from within. The equivalent Tibetan word *yeshe* means "to know the prime knowledge that has always existed." This reveals the real meaning of the term *gnosis* and jnana as that inherent human and inner wisdom we can find by eradicating the ego.

kabbalah

From the root *KBLH* of the Hebrew language and meaning *to receive*. It is the science of the higher realms, where all superconsciousness is in agreement, as this is the function of our awakened consciousness or superconsciousness. It is the ancient Hebrew system of the internal worlds found within, and can only be understood through the unique symbolic elements of the system and through the eradication of the ego.

karma

The Eastern term for the law of cause and effect. Every action creates or causes another action. Our actions in our current state of existence will cause an effect in our next state of existence.

Kundalini

Meaning *coiled one* and an idea of a coiled serpentine energy, that strives to be reunited with the crown chakra on a system of seven basic chakra or *wheels of energy*, which are located on the human body.

lahut

An Islamic term for the Divine. The opposite is the human or *nasut*.

Lucifer

Although nowadays thought to be a name for the Devil or Satan, the ancient gnostics and mystics never saw it this way. In Latin, *luci*, *lux*, *luce*, or *lucu* means *light; fer* or *fero* means *to bear or carry*. Lucifer is therefore the Light Bearer. In the 4th century there was a Christian sect called Luciferians. One of the early Popes was even called Pope Lucifer. This is the reason why modern-day Christian fundamentalists damn the Masons and others for their deep-rooted belief in the one known as Lucifer. They are not worshipping the Devil, but are instead holding up the Light Bearer as the bringer of wisdom.

manas

The higher spiritual mind of man.

maya

The so-called web of illusion from Eastern traditions. The root is Sanskrit.

monad

From the Latin *monas* meaning *unity; a unit, monad*. Man and woman are the physical manifestations of the spiritual monad; the Divine monad resides in each of us as the Father, Son, and Holy Spirit.

monism

The belief that everything in the universe is made of the same thing, and that metaphysically all things are one and unified.

mukti

A Sanskrit term for *liberation*.

Naaseni

A gnostic sect at the time of Christ called *Naasenians*, or more properly *serpent worshipers*. They considered the constellation of the Dragon as a symbol of their christ.

Nabatheans

A sect from the time of Christ with similar beliefs to the Nazarenes, Sabeans, and Naaseni. They had more reverence for John the Baptist. The Ebionites, those who became the first Christians, were direct disciples of the Nazarene sect.

nadi

A Sanskrit term for the nerve channel of the subtle energies related to the chakra of Eastern tradition.

nafs

A Sufi term for the mind, self, soul, or ego. There are generally seven levels to the *nafs*, similar to the Kundalini. These levels are psychological events or elements of our self that we must move through and overcome to achieve truth. These levels are:(1) the imposing self; (2) the reproachful self; (3) the motivated self; (4) the tranquil self; (5) the happy or content self; (6) the harmonious self; and (7) the fulfilled or pure self.

Naga/Naaga

A Sanskrit term meaning *serpent* (especially *cobra*) that also holds the meaning of tree, mountain, sun, the number seven, wisdom, and initiate. All are symbols and emblems familiar with the worship of the serpent and the enlightenment experience. The Naga are said to reside in Patala, however this has a meaning similar to antipodes, the same name given by the ancients to the Americas. It is a similar term to the Mexican *nagals*, the sorcerers who always kept a god in the shape of a serpent. In Burma they are *Nats*.

Naga is a term for wise men. There is a folk tradition that Nagas washed Buddha at his birth. They are also said to have guarded him and the relics of his body after his death. According to H. P. Blavatsky in *Theosophical Glossary*, the Naga were descended from Rishi Kasyapa, who had 12 wives (therefore, he is the sun), by whom he had numerous Nagas (serpents) and was the father of all animals. Rishi Kasyapa can, therefore, be none other than a progenitor of the Green Man, and this explains the reasons for the appearance of the snake in images of the Green Man and Horned God, such as the Gundestrup Cauldron.

Apollonius of Tyana was said to have been instructed by the Naga of Kashmir. This is the same Kashmir where the serpent tribes became famous for their healing skills. There is a theory that the Nagas descended from the Scythic race. When the Brahmins invaded India, they found a race of wise men that were half gods, half demons. These men were said to be teachers of other nations and instructed the Hindu and Brahmans.

naljor

This is a Tibetan word meaning *holy man* or *adept*, and is connected with the Naga beliefs.

Nazarenes

Also called *Mendaeans* or *Sabaens*, they were a sect of the Essene around the time of Christ. They left Galilee and settled in Syria near Mount Lebanon. They actually call themselves Galileans, even though they said that Christ was a false messiah. They followed the life of John the Baptist instead, who they call the *Great Nazar*. In association with the Ebionites and Nabatheans, they called Jesus the *Naboo-Meschiha* or simply *Mercury*, the great healer of serpentine connection.

nirvana

Eastern tradition holds that we must escape from the constant rebirthing in this plane of existence and go to nirvana (paradise). The term is related to *ni-fana*. Nirvana or *ni-fana* is a place we can all attain, free of the desires of this world and realizing our own inner self or divinity within.

Ophites

A general term, used for one branch of early Christian gnostics, although it is probably too strong to call them Christians in the modern sense. They were also known as the *Brotherhood of the Snake*. According to John Bathurst Deane, the Christian writer Epiphanius said, "the Ophites sprung out of the Nicolatians and Gnostics, and were so called from the serpent which they worshipped." They "taught that the ruler of this world was of a dracontic form" and "the Ophites attribute all wisdom to the serpent of paradise, and say that he was the author of knowledge of men"—linking him to the *Taautus* of the Phoenicians.

They keep a live serpent in a chest; and at the time of the mysteries entice him out by placing bread before him upon a table. Opening his door he comes out, and having ascended the table, folds himself about the bread. They not only break the bread and distribute this among the votaries, but whosoever will, may kiss the serpent. This, the wretched people call the Eucharist. They conclude the mysteries by singing a hymn through him to the supreme father.

The Eucharist mediator is the serpent termed the *Krestos*, as Christ was the mediator on the cross, a symbol and act more ancient than Christ and rooted in serpent worship. The serpent was sacrificed on the sacred tree or *Asherah*. The Ophites were also termed *Sethians* (according to Theodoret) after the Biblical Seth and Egyptian Set, both related to the serpent.

Pharaoh

In the Old Testament and the Koran, the adversary of Moses is Pharaoh, who wants dominion over the Israelites in place of God. Pharaoh is the baseman who must be overcome in order to be in the land or place given by the Divine. The people of the Lord must deny the authority of the baseman to escape and be at peace. Moses is, in Islamic terms, the intellect, which gives one the power of discernment over the ego.

pralaya

Eastern term for the place between the states of existence or death and rebirth. This place exists to give us peace on our journey, and is the same as the Judaic and Christian concept of paradise. It is, in essence, the void.

quintessence

This is the fifth element of the alchemists. It was their description of the energy signature of an ethereal body of the life-force that they encountered in their dreams or hypnagogic states. They believed that they must discover this quintessence to transform or be transformed by it. It is their explanation for the perception of simple nature within the superconscious state.

samadhi

A Sanskrit term used to denote an ecstatic state of higher consciousness. It is the escape from the essence of all suffering. There are levels attributed to samadhi, which depend greatly on who is teaching it.

samatha

In Sanskrit, *sha* means *peace*, and *mata* is *dwelling*. Therefore, somebody who is named Samatha is *dwelling in peace*.

samsara

A Sanskrit term pertaining to the cyclic existence of pain and suffering in which we find ourselves. We must come to an understanding of this in order to escape to Nirvana.

satori

The ecstasy of the mind that has realized true reality.

semen

Often spoken of in alchemy and mystical texts, but misinterpreted as actual physical semen. In fact, it is the term used for the sexual energy of both males and females, and relates more specifically to the union of the Divine opposites within.

shari'ah

The opposite of *haqiqah* in Sufi tradition. Where *haqiqah* is the inner reality of the self, *shari'ah* is the outer reality.

shaykh

A Sufi master. A *shaykh* or *shaikh* is a holy one who has realized his own self and can, therefore, become a guide for others. The female *shaykh* is known as a *shaykha*.

shushumna

Eastern tradition states that this is the fine thread in the center of the spinal column. In ordinary people this is a dark place, but in those seeking wisdom this becomes light or awakened fire—also referred to as the *Kundalini*.

silsilah

This is the Sufi term for the succession of the *Sufi Order* or *tariqah* (which is also the term used for the path between *shari'ah* and *haqiqah* or the outer self to the inner self) as it traces its descent from Muhammad. It is a sacred and holy bloodline from shaykh to shaykh, and is protected within the Sufi Order.

sirr or secret

An Islamic term for the individual's center of consciousness, which is the source of being. Only at this center does one come into contact with the Divine Inner Reality. A fleeting glimpse of the sirr is known as an *al-hal*. A permanent self-realization is known as a *maqam*.

snake/serpent

Said to be androgynous and immortal due to the shedding of its skin. It is said to be from the underworld, due to it emerging from below the ground or slithering from water. It is both a female symbol and moon symbol. It is both a phallic symbol and a solar symbol. It is the yin and yang united in the Tao. It is a symbol of the Tao. It is depicted as a spiral, as ivy, and as the vine. In Iceland, it is referred to as a *skar* or *snokr*. In Danish, the snake is the *snog*. In Swedish it is the *snok*. In Sanskrit it is the *Naga*. In Irish it is *snaig* or *snaigh*. In Hebrew the snake is *nahash*.

sod

Sod is a Hebrew term used for the arcanum. Most modern and ancient words that begin with or end with *s* can be traced back to the word *snake*. (Words such as soul, spirit, or shining are all related.) Sod specifically relates to such mysteries as those of Baal, Bacchus, Adonis, and Mithras. The Hebrews, not surprisingly, had their sod in the Brazen Serpent of Moses, which in all likelihood was the same serpent as the Persian Mithra. The Sodales, or members of the priestly elite or college, were also "constituted in the Idaean Mysteries of the Mighty Mother," according to Cicero in *De Senectute*.

spagira

An alternative name for alchemy, from the Greek *span*, meaning *to extract*. *Agyris* means *to reunite*.

Sufi Path

Although the Sufi Path can vary in number depending upon the writer, Fariduddin Attar's *Conference of the Birds* shows it to have seven stages, similar to the Kundalini.

tanazzulat

This is the Islamic descent from the One Essence as a manifestation of this world. It is a paradox, as the One Essence cannot be manifested in full form, and so whatever is seen manifested is not fully the One Essence. In this way, the One Essence assumes a manifestation that can be known it is not the true One Essence. This can only be seen properly through *theophanic vision*. The theophanic vision can only be mediated by the *himma* or power of the heart. The theophanic mediator sees things on a sensory level above and beyond those ordinary people can possibly perceive. In the Sufi tradition this theophanic vision is known as an ascent to the spiritualised realm. In scientific terms, this is an individual who has entangled with the quantum world—the collective superconscious world. It is the same as the Universal Intellect.

Tau-cross

The T- or Tau-cross has been a symbol of eternal life in many cultures and gives its name to the Bull in the astrological sign of *Taurus* (which also contains *ru*, the gateway). In fact, the Druids venerated the tree by scrawling the Tau-cross into its bark. In the European Middle Ages, the Tau-cross was used in amulets to protect the wearer against disease.

Among the modern Freemasons, the Tau has many meanings. Some say that it stands for *Templus Hierosolyma*, or the *Temple of Jerusalem*; others believe that it signifies hidden treasure or means *Clavis ad Thesaurum—a key to treasure*; or *Theca ubi res pretiosa—a place where the precious thing is concealed*.

The Tau is especially important in Royal Arch Masonry, where it becomes the *Companions Jewel*, with a serpent as a circle above the crossbar—forming the Ankh—with the Hebrew word for serpent engraved on the upright, and also including the *Triple Tau*—a symbol for hidden treasure and made up of eight right angles.

The Tau was also the symbol for Saint Anthony—later to become the symbol for the Knights Templar of Saint Anthony of Leith in Scotland. Saint Anthony lived in the 4th century and is credited with establishing monasticism in Egypt. The story goes that he sold all his possessions after hearing from the Lord, and marched off into the wilderness to become a hermit. On his travels he learned much from various sages in Egypt and developed a large following. He was sorely tempted by the Devil in the form of serpents. In one episode, he follows a trail of gold to a temple that is infested with serpents and takes up residence, needing little food for sustenance other than bread and water. He is said to have lived 105 years. Due to this longevity he is credited with protective powers. All of this is a metaphor for the enlightenment process associated with overcoming serpent energy.

The Order of the Hospitalers of Saint Anthony, who would later take much of the Templar wealth, brought many of Anthony's relics to France in the 11th century, although they were said to have been secretly deposited somewhere in Egypt just after his death.

The Taut or Tau symbolizes the four creative elements of the universe. The symbol of the sun or serpent was added, creating a simple circle or the oval *ru*. This loop above the T-cross created the Ankh, the symbol of eternity. The snake in a circle eating its own tale is symbolic of the sun and immortality, not to mention the point in the cyclic process of creation. Together, the T and O is the perfect symbolical mixture of the four elements and the fifth element. The symbol of the moon was added, turning it into the sign for Hermes/Mercury and showing the Caduceus/Serpent origin. This symbol became the mark or sign that would set the believer aside for saving. In Ezekiel, this is the mark that God will know—the mark on the forehead. As the Victorian historian John Bathurst Deane points out, the Ezekiel passage (9:4) should read, "set a Tau upon their foreheads" or "mark with the letter Tau the foreheads." The early Christians baptized with the term *crucis thaumate notare*. They baptized with the symbol of the snake. And Saint Paul himself, in Galatians 6:17 states, "let no-one cause me trouble, for I bear on my body the marks of Jesus."

This idea of wearing the Tau-cross on the shoulder as a sign would later become part of the Templar markings. The Templars instigated in the worship of serpents. The Merovingians (said by some to be descended from Jesus and a sea serpent or fish god—the *Quinotaur* or *Quino-Tau-r*) were supposedly born with a red cross between their shoulder blades. The Tau cross is also strangely used by those practicing sacred geometry as a "marker" for buried treasure, whether physical or spiritual.

Taautus (Taut)

Said by Eusebius to be the origin of serpent worship in Phoenicia. Sanchoniathon called him the god who made the first image of Coelus and invented hieroglyphs. This links him with Hermes Trismegistus, also known as Thoth in Egypt. Taautus consecrated the species of dragons and serpents; and the Phoenicians and Egyptians followed him in this superstition. Taautus could be a collective social memory of the first group who worshipped the serpent. The idea of Taautus links with the stories of Thoth, who later became a great sage of gnostic and alchemical beliefs. Thoth was deified after his death and given the title the *god of health*. He was the prototype for Aesculapius, and identified with Hermes and Mercury. All healers, teachers, and saviors are associated with the serpent. Indeed, it was as the *healing god* that Thoth was symbolized as the serpent. He is normally represented with the heads of an ibis and baboon.

ta'wil

This is an Islamic term for the vision within the theophanic world, which turns everything visually perceived into a symbolic representation. It is a way for humanity to understand the unknown superconscious world. In terms of the Shaman, this would be symbols devised and taught to the initiates to allow them to better understand the world they are seeing.

tasawwuf

Another term for *Sufism* or *mystical Islam*.

Templars

Friday the 13th of October 1307 was a terrible day for the Knights Templar, as King Philip IV's men descended upon all of the order's French holdings, seizing property and arresting each of its members. Philip owed them huge amounts of money and had no way of paying them back. He secretly hoped that the famous Templar treasure would be his. With the help of his puppet, Pope Clement V, the French king tortured the knights to discover their secrets. Finally, to justify his actions, the knights were accused of heresy, homosexual practices, necromancy, and conducting bizarre rituals such as desecrating the cross—as if to show their lack of faith in this Christian icon.

The most unusual and perplexing evidence they came across however, was the worship of this idol called *Baphomet*. This strange thing—although sometimes referred to as a cat or goat—was generally seen as a severed head. Peter Tompkins in *The Magic of Obelisks* says:

> Public indignation was aroused…the Templar symbol of gnostic rites based on phallic worship and the power of directed will. The androgynous figure with a goat's beard and cloven hooves is linked to the horned god of antiquity, the goat of Mendes.

The list of charges used by the Inquisition in 1308 read:

> Item, that in each province they had idols, namely heads.
>
> Item, that they adored these idols or that idol, and especially in their great chapters and assemblies.
>
> Item, that they venerated (them).
>
> Item, that they venerated them as God.
>
> Item, that they venerated them as their Savior.
>
> Item, that they said that the head could save them.
>
> Item, that it could make riches.
>
> Item, that it could make the trees flower.
>
> Item, that it made the land germinate.
>
> Item, that they surrounded or touched each head of the aforesaid idol with small cords, which they wore around themselves next to the shirt or the flesh.

Some said it was a man's head, but others a woman's head; some said that it was bearded, others non-bearded; some presumed that it was made from glass and that it had two faces. This general mixing of ideas shows where the idea of the head could have come from. That it was a man's head or a woman's, indicates its dual nature—and much like the ancient Celtic heads would incline us to the opinion, that it emerged from part of the ancient head cult. The Celts, it is said, believed that the soul resided in the head. They would decapitate their enemies and keep them as talismans. Probably the best-known head in Celtic lore is that of *Bran the Blessed*, which was buried outside London, facing towards France. It was put there to see off the plague and disease and to ensure that the land was fertile—the same powers that were attributed to the Green Man.

It is also said that the name *Baphomet* was derived from *Mahomet*—an Old French corruption of the name of the prophet Muhammad. Others claim that it comes from the Arabic word *abufihamet*, which means *Father of Understanding*. In the end, the worship of the Baphomet tells us one certain thing—that the Templars were initiates and adepts in the ancient Eastern ways and at the higher levels, in all probability, understood the knowledge. This is seen when we understand that *baphe* means immersion, as in baptism, and *metis* means wisdom. Baphomet, therefore, is truly the immersion of oneself into wisdom, the true inner reality and the true and only divinity.

thermuthis

The rearing cobra goddess of Egypt. She is often depicted suckling a child or nursing children, and this was taken literally in that she became the goddess of little children instead of the obvious nurturing element of the serpent energy related to the Kundalini. In this respect, the link between the serpent child suckling Mother Goddesses and Mary now reveal the true reality of who, or rather what, Mary was representative of.

Tree of Knowledge

Although literally claimed to have been in the Garden of Eden, it is in fact the *Daath* of the kabbalah, the axis mundi, or spine up which rises the serpent.

Tree of Life

Representing the structure of the soul and the universe—the interconnected nature. It is the *Being*, the *Chesed*, or *Inner Man*.

universal intellect

This is the Islamic version of the mind free from the manifestations of this world—free from the impure thoughts associated with the banal reality in which we exist. It is called the Intellect of the Intellect, and is where we can see the hidden in everything. It is the process of true enlightenment.

V.I.T.R.O.L.

An acronym that in Latin means *Visitam Inferorem Terre Rectifactum Invenias Ocultum Lapidum*. This translates to English as *visit the interior of the earth*, which through rectifying you will find the occult stone. Although this can sound completely bewildering to those who do not understand, it does have a simple meaning: The adherent must go inside himself to put right the problems causing suffering, and only then can he obtain the true wisdom of Inner Reality.

Wadjet

Also known as *Wadjyt, Wadjit, Uto, Uatchet, Edjo, and Uraeus*. A predynastic cobra goddess of Lower Egypt who took the title *The Eye of Ra*. She is depicted as a rearing cobra, a winged cobra, a lion-headed woman, or a woman wearing a red crown. She is the protector of Pharaoh. Shown together with *Nekhbet* (who was seen as a woman, a snake, or a vulture), she brings to mind the bird-serpent image of Quetzalcoatl. Wadjet is seen as the fiery Uraeus, anointing the head with flames, similar to the apostles in *Acts* of the Bible. In the Pyramid Texts she is linked strongly with nature. The papyrus plant is said to emerge from her and she is connected to the forces of growth. She is also closely connected to Isis in the form of *Wadjet-Isis in Dep*.

yggdrasil

The cosmic tree of Scandinavia. It is symbolic of the shamanic *world/cosmic tree* and similar to the Tree of Life and Tree of Knowledge. The roots are constantly attacked by the serpent—a reference to the Kundalini serpent said to lie coiled around the base of the human spinal column. The Serpent was known as *nidhogg*, or the *dread biter*. Odin sacrificed himself and hung from the tree for nine nights— showing the resurrective properties of the tree. Odin basically sacrifices his ego with the aid of Kundalini.

zahir

An Islamic term for the outward or exoteric meaning of reality.

zen

A Japanese Buddhist sect seeking enlightenment (of the self) through the spontaneous insights gathered by a single-minded devotion to simplicity. Alternatively, it is insights gained through paradoxes generated by verbal interchange, which often fail to be solved with logic. It is thought to come from *zazen*, which has the meaning of *meditation* or *just sitting*.

Zoroaster

Probably born around 1,500 B.C. in Iran, his teachings are to be found in the *Avesta* and *Gathas*. Zoroastrianism did not prosper until the 6th century B.C., and lasted until it was taken over by Islam in the 7th century A.D. These are believed to have been the wise men of the Christian Bible, who brought gifts to Jesus at his birth. If the Magi saw their gods as serpents, then there is little wonder that they should see and be associated with this serpent-savior born in human form. According to Eusebius in the ritual of Zoroaster, the great expanse of the heavens and nature were described under the symbol of the serpent in the *Ophiolatreia* by Hargrave Jennings. This was doubly mentioned in the Octateuch of Ostanes. Temples were erected across Persia and the East in veneration of the serpent deity.

Appendix B

Timeline of Serpent Worship

Creation	Most creation stories relate how it was a serpent that was involved in the creation. For instance, in Egypt, the sun god *Amun-Ra* emerged from the water as a snake to inseminate the cosmic egg. All life on earth came from this one egg. There is also a remarkable tradition across the globe that there were great wars in heaven, which also involved the serpent deities. All of this points to an original and primary serpent cult, which spread in a migratory pattern across the globe. Then, possibly, there was some kind of major split, and battle ensued between the factions.
2,000,000 B.C.	Stone artifacts discovered in North India said to have been used by hominids.
160,000 B.C.	The earliest known remains of primitive man discovered in Ethiopia in the year 2003. Two shattered skulls, which were highly polished, have been given the name *Homo Sapiens Idaltu*, and are

said to be modern humans with some primitive features. The fact that the heads were polished indicates to scientists that there was some form of ancestor worship in operation—a peculiar and ancient head worship. In a media release from Berkeley University, Professor Tim White of the University of California system says, "They show Africa was inhabited by human ancestors from six million to 160,000 years ago."

100,000 B.C.   *Homo sapiens sapiens* (modern humans) begin migrating to Asia through the Isthmus of Suez.

The Flood   In antediluvian times, the pole of the heavens was said to be the constellation *Alpha Draconis*. In fact, it was the polestar 4,800 years ago, but the idea that it was *Alpha Draconis* points to the belief of serpent rule. In astronomical temples, the Dragon is the ruling constellation at the pole, matching the Greek myth of Draco, who is found near the North Pole.

45,000–50,000 B.C.   Ayer's Rock in Australia is said to have archaeological evidence to prove that man has inhabited and worshipped there for 50,000 years. There are many images upon this rock that might prove that the worship of the snake (and other related symbols associated with it) go back before the end of the last ice age (approximately 10,800 B.C.). There are images of a peculiar Snake People, which are today being used by those with antireptilian agenda (such David Icke, who believe that reptiles invaded earth many thousands of years ago). These snake people are alongside ordinary humans and ordinary animals. There are many spirals, circles, and snake images. Unfortunately, it can be said that these are universal patterns within each one of us, and could therefore emerge anywhere at anytime. There is evidence that people from Australia were part of a trade network 5,000–4,000 B.C.

30,000 B.C. American Indians spread throughout the Americas. Also, Sumerian tablets from this time give us the first pharmacopoeia that we know of. There are many snake-related cures, such as the pouring of heated water over dried watersnake, the *amamashumkaspal* plant, roots of the thorn plant, powdered Naga (an alkali plant), powdered turpentine, and bat feces. We are supposed to rub this into the affected areas with oil and cover with Shakti (although nobody knows what Shakti is).

10,000 B.C. The human population on Earth is 4 million. The total population of Indians is 100,000, making them 2.5 percent of the total. (Note how the Indian population will grow in relation to the rest of the world as time passes). The *Taittirya Brahmana* refers to the rising of *Purvabhadrapada Nakshatra* in the East, indicating an ancient Vedic knowledge of astronomy.

9850 B.C. The *Turin Papyrus* (a King List dated to 1300 B.C., spoken of by Gardiner in 1987 and Smith in 1872) records the installation of the next series of Egyptian kings in 9850 B.C.—close to Plato's dating for Atlantis. The third on the god-king list from Turin Papyrus is *Agathodaemon* or *Su*.

9000 B.C.	Old Europe, Anatolia, and Minoan Crete display Goddess-centered worship. The Minoan matriarchal Goddess is linked with snakes. This is at the same time that standard history tells us cultivation of wild wheat and barley, domestication of dogs and sheep, and the change from food gathering to food production began in Mesopotamia.
7000 B.C.	Oldest known Mesopotamian permanent settlement at Jarmo with crude mud houses, wheat growing, and herding of animals. Trading developed from the Persian Gulf to the Mediterranean.
6000 B.C.	Earliest evidence of village-level civilization at Mehgarh, 125 miles west of the Indus valley. There is evidence of crop farming, producing Asiatic wheat. The site also shows domestication of animals and trade with the West, including copper and cotton from as far away as Arabia.
5000–3000 B.C.	Beginnings of the Indus-Sarasvati civilizations of Harappa (approximately 4000 B.C) and Mohenjo-daro (approximately 2500 B.C) with densely packed villages, extensive irrigation, and a wide variety of crops. Covering more than half a million miles of Northern Indian subcontinent, they are classed as highly artistic and skilled, with images of snakes, unicorns, and other animals being seen in their art for religious purposes. The swastika, thought to be overlapping snakes in the symbol of eternity, is also seen. The earliest signs of Shiva worship (as Pashupati) are discovered to have begun at this time. Shiva is linked with the snake.

4000 B.C.	A period of the rising of Wadjet in Lower Egypt. A Mesopotamian libation vase depicting Caduceus was discovered dating from around this time. Professor Frothingham, in a presentation to the Philological Association and the Archaeological Institute in the 19th century, said that the Caduceus of the Hittites and Babylonians was taken away by the Etruscans, explaining some of the serpent symbolism in Italy. There are also strange similarities between the tale of Ninazu and the Christian world. In *Balbale to Ninazu* 7–15 we find the words "May he make the way straight for you as far as the ends of heaven and earth...."
3500 B.C.	Ziggurat prototype developed at the Temple of Eriddu in Mesopotamia.
3300 B.C.	The beginning of the Mayan calendar.
3100 B.C.	Aryan people inhabit Iran, Iraq, and the western Indus-Sarasvati valley, although some experts say the first wave was 2000 B.C. Aryans are described as having a culture of spiritual knowledge. They probably inherited the serpent-worship beliefs of the Indus civilization. The first known incarnation of Stonehenge in England. From the same period, a *Stele* of the Serpent King found in Egypt has a bas-relief of a falcon in profile above a nearly abstract stroke of a snake. The artifact is now exhibited in the Louvre.
3000 B.C.	People of Tehuacan in Mexico begin to cultivate corn. Arjuna said to have visited Patala and married the daughter of the Naga king. There is also evidence of serpent worship in China during this period. The Manchurian goddess temple shows

fragments from this period of a bear/dragon statue. This confirms that the culture of the serpent with other beasts was already in place. Newgrange in Ireland is also built around this time.

2700 B.C. The worship of Shiva is indicated on seals of the Indus-Sarasvati valley. Shiva is Pashupati—the Lord of the Animals, linked with Cernunnos. The Indus-Sarasvati civilization spreads from Pakistan to Gujurat, Punjab, and Uttar Pradesh.

2500 B.C. Construction of Arbor Low in England began with a mound, said by some to be a serpent. Avebury Serpent in England is constructed. In the Middle East, Dumuzi (or the son of the abyss) emerges as the prototype of the resurrected savior (also called the shepherd), the ever-reviving Sumerian god of vegetation and the very first Green Man. Dumuzi is known for his horned crown of the moon and is both the son and husband of the goddess Gula-Bau. She is seen sitting in front of the serpent in a relief from 2500 B.C. called Goddess of the Tree of Life. Dumuzi is Tammuz, the equivalent of Osiris (born from the mouth of the snake). Osiris is seen as Dionysius in the Greek tongue and Bacchus in Rome, thus proving the ancient link of the serpent with healing.

2400 B.C. The name *Dagan* appears in Mesopotamia. It is a later name for the head of the Philistine pantheon.

2100 B.C. The second stage of Stonehenge, with bluestones from Wales, is moved 135 miles; 90 bluestones are set up in a horseshoe pattern.

2000 B.C.	The Vishnu Purana, the oldest of the Hindu Puranas, speaks of Atala, the White Island, which is one of the seven islands (dwipas) belonging to Patala (the home of the Naga serpent deities). The location of Atala is said to be on the seventh zone, which (according to Colonel Wilford, the translator of the Vishnu Puranas) is 24 to 28 degrees north, and is believed to be the Canary Islands, though this could easily be the starting point of the fabled Atlantis rather than its actual center. In the Bhavishna Purana, Samba made a journey to Saka-Dwipa (an island) looking for Maga (Magi), the worshippers of the Sun/Snake. Riding upon Gurada, the flying vehicle of Krishna and Vishnu he eventually arrived amongst the Magas. The world population is 27 million. India's population is 5 million, making it 22 percent of the world's population. This is also the approximate dating for Stonehenge's third phase, the addition of the familiar topped caps. Stone construction begins at Arbor Low in England. Silbury Hill near Avebury in England is constructed. It is the largest prehistoric mound in Europe, more than 130 feet tall, built over 3 phases, and thought not to be a burial mound.
1600 B.C.	The period of the Minoan Snake Goddess.
975 B.C.	King Hiram of Phoenicia trades with King Solomon and with the port of Ophir. Some say this occurs near Mumbai in India, which would make sense, as India was the center of serpent worship. In John Bathurst Deane's book, he claims that, according to Eusebius, the Phoenicians were

among the earliest serpent worshippers. In fact, he even names the originator of the belief as Taautus.

920 B.C   According to William Harwood in *Mythologies Last Gods: Yahweh and Jesus*, this is the time that the myths of Adam and Eve were laid down as the Genesis story. Solomon's policy of religious toleration allows the raising of the *asherah* tree.

700 B.C.   The Tower of Babylon (built for the God Bel) is said to have been built around this time. According to many sources, it was built in a spiral pattern. Bel may very well come from *Ob-El* or serpent god, and in Greek he is said to be *Beliar*. Taxila, the capital of ancient Punjab, was founded.

500 B.C.   The world population is 100 million. The population of India is 25 million, or 25 percent of the world's population.

4 B.C.   Birth of Apollinus of Tyana—the true Christ who went to India to learn from the King Serpent and was taught in the Temple of Aesculapius, the serpent god of healing. The supposed birth date of Jesus.

A.D. 70   The Temple of Jerusalem was sacked by the Romans. The ark that was there at the time was said to have been full of stones and some badger skins dyed purple. This could not have been the real Ark that is said to have contained the Rod of Aaron, or if it was, then the contents had already disappeared.

A.D. **100**

"The Great Chalice of Antioch is identical in type with the known chalices of the first century of the Roman Empire with their ovoid truncated bowls, their very short stems, their low and exceedingly narrow feet, formed from a horizontal solid disk often turned on a lathe. Their proportions were not developed free hand, but by a minutely worked out geometric system which determined exactly the outline as well as height and width of parts". So said Eisen, who dates the Antioch Chalice to 1st Century A.D., although every other work presented on this chalice dates it to the 6th century. It may be that the additions to the chalice such as the white gold leaf and a second layer of red gold leaf may be confusing things. There is the obvious Christian idea that, because it resembles a 6th century standing lamp, then it must be from the 6th century. Eileen Sullivan of the Metropolitan Museum in New York responded to my questions "regarding the Antioch Chalice. As the museum's Website mentions, the identification of the Antioch Chalice as the Holy Grail has not been sustained, and its authenticity has even been challenged, but the work has usually been considered a sixth-century chalice meant to be used in the Eucharist. Most recently its shape has been recognised as more closely resembling sixth-century standing lamps, its decoration possibly in recognition of Christ's words 'I am the light of the world.' (John 8:12)." Pliny points out that the serpent was a symbol of health for one reason only—that the flesh of the creature "is sometimes used in medicine." Coptic texts, translated from Greek from around this time were discovered at Nag Hammadi in Upper Egypt towards the end of the Second World War. These included fragments of the Gospels of Thomas and the Gospels of Philip and Mary. They make it plain that the Virgin Birth and Resurrection were very much symbolic. They also point out that the Serpent from the Garden of Eden was wise in giving the fruit of knowledge to Adam and Eve.

A.D. 400   the Emperor Theodosius bans pagan rituals, including tying ribbons to trees. This is the same emperor who had his sight restored by a grateful serpent that laid a precious stone on his eyes.

A.D. 500/600   The time of King Arthur. Albert Pike, the Masonic historian, says that the lost word of Masonry is concealed in the name of Arthur. His last name is Pendragon, which means *head dragon*.

A.D. 1150/1200   A branch of the Templars begins to build round churches in Bornholm. In the 12th century, the Sword Knights (a branch of the Knights Templars) was established by the Cistercian friar Theoderik in Riga. These Sword Knights were later to become the Teutonic Knights in Germany. The round churches of Osterlars, Nyker, Olsker, and Nylars were said to have been built defensively, although there is some debate as to the reasoning. According to Erling Haagensen in *Bornholms Mysterier*, all these sites were built upon the familiar Templar sacred geometry. On the wall in the Nyker church there is the Templar symbol of the Agnus Dei, the Lamb of God, with blood pouring from his wound into the chalice. Inside the Olsker church there is an image presumed to be of Saint Olaf surrounded by a circle and 12 stars, holding a serpent in his hand.

A.D. **900–1000**   Mackey's *Encyclopaedia of Freemasonry* tells us that the Druzes settled in Lebanon.

A.D. **1140**   *Secretum Secretorum*, a psuedo-Aristotelean translation of *Kitab Sirr al-Asrar*, a book of advice to kings translated into Latin by Hispalensis and Philip of Tripoli in 1243 dated to this period. This time is thought to be the first showing of the Emerald Tablet of Hermes.

A.D. **1800**   Colonel Meadows Taylor in the Indian *Dakkan* tells of contemporary accounts that the locals, worshipping the Nagas, looked to the snake for healing of disease and pestilence.

A.D. **1896**   In *The Popular Religion and Folk-lore of Northern India*, W. Crooke writes that a census shows over 25,000 Naga form in the northwest province of India, with 123,000 varieties of the snake god Guga and 35,000 votaries of snake gods in the Punjab.

N⊕TES

Introduction

1. From the *Upanishads*, the Sanskrit writings, dating between the 8th and 4th centuries B.C. The word *Upanishads* means literally *to sit beneath*.

2. The Book of Thomas.

Chapter 1

1. Worship of the Serpent. The word *snake* is known in the language of Canaan variously as *Aub*, *Ab*, *Oub*, *Ob*, *Oph*, *Op*, *Eph*, and *Ev*. In the Mayan language, *can* means serpent, as in Cucul*can* the bird serpent. In ancient Sumerian, *snake* is *acan*, and the Scottish also use the word *can* for serpent. Vul*can*, the Roman god of fire, comes from the Babylonian *can* for serpent and *vul* for fire, showing an etymological link across thousands of miles and oceans. Indeed even the very center of the Christian world, the Vati*can*, comes from the words *vatis* for *prophet* and *can* for *serpent*, making the Vatican a place of serpent prophecy.

2. Serpent Worship. Original source from LoveToKnow 1911 Online Encyclopedia © 2003, 2004.

3. The Pelasgian Creation Myth. Original source from *www.ferrum.edu/philosophy/pelasgiancreation.htm*. Adapted from Robert Graves's *The Greek Myths* by Dr. James Luchte.

Chapter 2
1. Michael Talbot. *The Holographic Universe*. Chapter 6: "Seeing Holographically." Harper Collins, 1991.

Chapter 4
1. V.S. Ramachandran and Sandra Blakeslee. *Phantoms of the Brain*. Fourth Estate, 1998.

2. Original source from *http://scienceandreligion.com/mysticism.htm*.

Chapter 5
1. Cruttwell, Charles Thomas. *A Literary History of Early Christianity Including the Fathers and the Chief Heretical Writers of the Ante-Nicene Period*. Charles Scribner's Sons, 1893; and *The Essene Odyssey* by Hugh Schonfield: Element, 1984.

2. Although I state that there are seven chakra levels, it is an oversimplification, as branches of the tradition vary in quantity, mostly agreeing on the basis seven, but then adding other subtle extras as the art becomes more and more complex the higher the initiate travels.

Chapter 6
1. *Dictionary of Phrase and Fable*, Wordsworth, 1993.

2. Sappir is rendered sapphirus in many ancient texts (see the works of Josephus). The stone may not have been the modern sapphire. Theophrastus and Pliny described the sapphirus as a stone with golden spots, which may indicate that it was the lapis lazuli or

Philosopher's Stone, which has elements of pyrite with a golden sheen. The lapis-lazuli was called *chesbet* by the Egyptians and was obtained from some of the oldest mines in the world, dating from as early as 4000 B.C. It was used to make magical amulets and figurines worn by the Egyptian high priests.

3. *The Universal Meaning of the Kabbalah*, Leo Schaya.

4. *Necronomicon*. Simon, 1995

5. *On the Kabbalah and its Symbolism*, Gershom G. Scholem, Routledge and Kegan Paul. London, 1965.

Chapter 7

1. Qodsha/Qadashu. The Holy One is depicted in the British Museum naked, standing with a lion, carrying a mirror and a lotus, and attended to by two snakes. She is often seen with serpents and stars. She dates back at least 3000 B.C. As far as can be worked out, the equivalents in Egypt to these Canaanite deities are as follows: El/Anu is Osiris, Baal is Set, and Asherah is Isis. There are elements of other deities that match those of Horus and even Osiris, Set, and Isis (among others), and it is impossible to pin down this god equal.

2. Original source from *www.geocities.com/SoHo/Lofts/2938.mindei.html*.

3. Sometimes he may also enlist Anat, his sister, who can also approach El and who is very similar in many respects to Asherah.

Chapter 8

1. All of these theories can be found in hundreds of books now, springing originally from the 1980s mega-hit *The Holy Blood and the Holy Grail* by Baigent, Leigh, and Lincoln (Jonathan Cape, 1982). However, here are a few others:

   - *The Head of God*, Keith Laidler. Orion, 1998.
   - *The Temple and the Lodge*, Michael Baigent and Richarld Leigh. Arrow, 1998.

- *The Templar Revelation*, Lynn Picknett and Clive Prince. Corgi, 1998.
- *The Tomb of God*, R. Andrew and P. Schellenberger. Little Brown and Company, 1996.
- *The Second Messiah*, Christopher Knight and Robert Lomas. Arrow, 1998.

2. *The Templar Revelation*, Lynn Picknett and Clive Prince. Corgi, 1998.

3. *The Templars*, Piers Paul Read. Phoenix Press, 1999.

4. According to John Michell in *The Temple at Jerusalem: A Revelation*, Gothic Image.

5. The megalithic yard is said to be the circle divided into 366 parts, as 360 was a mistake on the builder's part. I think that this may be incorrect, as the above evidence shows a remarkable knowledge— so remarkable that to make such a mistake seems implausible. It may be one of two things, a tilt in the earth's axis, leading to a 366-day year and, therefore, upsetting the ancient measuring systems, or a bending of the 366 to 360 to obtain the perfect number. Of course, it may be that the symbolic 360-degree circle overtook the actual measurements.

6. *The Templars*, Piers Paul Read. Phoenix Press, 1999.

7. Ibid.

8. Emerald Tablet. A legendary object engraved in Phoenician by the fabled Hermes Trismegistus, with a secret message only to be seen by the initiated Shining Ones. Circa A.D. 1200, a Latin version became available, thus preventing the masses from reading it and allowing the clergy (and mostly copied and printed by the clergy, who damned the book) the almost sole rights to its secrets. The main sentence, which has been taken from the book is "that which is above is like that which is bellow," and this has been shortened to "as above, so below."

9. Josephus. *Antiquities VIII*, 3:4.

Chapter 9

1. "Confession of Faith" of a Polish Cabalistic Sect known as Soharites, 19th century. Taken from the *New Baptist Magazine*, April 1927.

2. *The Splendour that was Egypt*, Margaret A. Murray Book Club Associates, 1973.

3. Ibid.

Chapter 10

1. *The Holy Bible: The Great Light In Masonry, King James Version, Temple Illustrated Edition*. A J Holman Company, 1968.

2. *Masonic Holy Bible, Temple Illustrated Edition*. A J Holman, 1968.

3. *Encyclopaedia of Freemasonry*, Albert Mackey, Charles T. McClenachan, Edward L. Hawkins, William J. Hughan. The Masonic History Company, 1973.

4. *Encyclopaedia of Freemasonry*, Albert Mackey, Charles T. McClenachan, Edward L. Hawkins, William J. Hughan. The Masonic History Company, 1973.

5. *The Great Secret or Occultism Unveiled*, Eliphas Levi. Samuel Weiser Inc., 2000.

6. *Comte de Gabalis: Discourse on the Secret Sciences and Mysteries, in Accordance with the Principles of the Ancient Magi and the Wisdom of the Kabalistic Philosophers* by Abbe N. de Montfaucon de Villars. Now in print with Kessinger Publishing, Montana, U.S.A.

7. *Clef universalle des sciences secrets*, P. V. Piobb, as quoted in *A Dictionary of Symbols* by J. E. Cirlot.

8. *Libellus Iv.25 from Corpus Hermeticum*, dating to around 2nd or 3rd century A.D.

BIBLIOGRAPHY

Abdalqadir as-Sufi, Shaykh. *The Return of the Kalifate*. Cape Town: Madinah Press, 1996.

Ableson, J. *Jewish Mystics*. London: G Bell and Sons Ltd., n.d.

Andrews, R., and P. Schellenberger. *The Tomb of God*. London: Little, Brown and Co, 1996.

Ashe, Geoffrey. *The Quest for Arthur's Britain*. London: Paladin Press, 1971.

Bacher, Wilhelm, and Ludwig Blau. *Shamir*. *www.jewishencyclopedia.com*.

Baigent, Leigh. *Ancient Traces*. London: Viking Press, 1998.

———. *The Elixir and the Stone*. London: Viking Press, 1997.

Baigent, Michael, and Richard Leigh, and Henry Lincoln. *Holy Blood and the Holy Grail*. London: Jonathan Cape, 1982.

———. *The Messianic Legacy*. London: Arrow, 1996.

———. *The Dead Sea Scrolls Deception*. London: Arrow, 2001.

———. *The Temple and the Lodge*. London: Arrow, 1998.

Balfour, Mark. *The Sign of the Serpent*. London: Prism, 1990.

Balfour, Michael. *Megalithic Mysteries*. London: Parkgate Books, 1992.

Barber, Malcolm. *The Trial of the Templars*. Cambridge: Cambridge University Press, 1978.

Barrett, David. *Sects, Cults and Alternative Religions*. London: Blandford, 1996.

Barrow, John. *Theories of Everything*. London: Virgin. 1990.

Basham, A.L. *The Wonder that was India*. London: Collins, 1954.

Bayley, H. *The Lost Language of Symbolism*. London: Bracken Books, 1996.

Bauval, R. *The Orion Mystery*. Oxford: Heinemann, 1996.

Beatty, Longfield. *The Garden of the Golden Flower*. London: Senate, 1996.

Begg, E. *The Cult of the Black Virgin*. London: Arkana, 1985.

Begg, E. and D. Begg. *In Search of the Holy Grail and the Precious Blood*. London: Thorsons, 1985.

Blaire, Lawrence. *Rhythms of Vision*. New York: Warner Books, 1975.

Blavatsky, Helene P. *Theosophical Glossary*. Whitefish, Mont.: Kessinger Publishing Ltd., 1918.

Borchert, Bruno. *Mysticism*. Maine: Samuel Weiser, Inc., 1994.

Bord, Colin and Janet Bord. *Earth Rites: Fertility Practices in Pre-Industrial Britain*. London: Granada Publishing,1982.

Bouquet A.C. *Comparative Religion*. London: Pelican, 1942.

Boyle, Veolita Parke. *The Fundamental Principles of Yi-King, Tao: The Cabbalas of Egypt and the Hebrews*. London: W & G Foyle, 1934.

Brine, Lindsey. *The Ancient Earthworks and Temples of the American Indians*. London: Oracle, 1996.

Broadhurst, Paul and Hamish Miller. *The Dance of the Dragon*. Cornwall: Mythos Press, 2000.

Bryant, N. *The High Book of the Grail*. Cambridge: D. S. Brewer, 1985.

Bryden, R. *Rosslyn – a History of the Guilds, the Masons and the Rosy Cross*. Rosslyn: Rosslyn Chapel Trust, 1994.

Budge, E. A. Wallis. *An Egyptian Hieroglyphic Dictionary Volume 1*. Dover, Dover Publications: 1978.

Butler, E.M. *The Myth of the Magus*. Cambridge: Cambridge University Press, 1911.

Callahan, Philip. *Paramagnetism: Rediscovering Nature's Secret Force of Growth*. Austin, Tex.: Acres, 1995.

―――. *Ancient Mysteries Modern Visions: The Magnetic Life of Agriculture*. Austin, Tex.: Acres, 2001.

―――. *Nature's Silent Music*. Austin, Tex.: Acres, 1992.

Ceram, C. W. *Gods Graves and Scholars: The Story of Archaeology*. London: Gollancz, Sidgwick, and Jackson, 1954.

Coles, John. *Field Archaeology in Britain*. London: Methuen, 1972.

Campbell, Joseph. *Transformations of Myth Through Time*. London: Harper and Row, 1990.

Cantor, N.F. *The Sacred Chain*. London: Harper Collins, 1994.

Carr-Gomm, Sarah. *Dictionary of Symbols in Art*. London: Duncan Baird Publishers, 1995.

Cavendish, Richard. *Mythology*. London: Tiger Press, 1998.

Carpenter, Edward. *Pagan and Christian Creeds: Their Origin and Meaning*. London: Allen and Unwin Ltd., 1920.

Castaneda, Carlos. *The Teaching of Don Juan*. London: Arkana, 1978.

Childress, David. *Anti-Gravity & The World Grid*. Stelle, Ill.: Adventures Unlimited Press, 1987.

Chadwick, N. *The Druids*. Cardiff: University of Wales Press, 1969.

Churchward, Albert. *The Origin and Evolution of Religion*. Whitefish, Mont.: Kessinger Publishing Ltd., 1997.

Churton, Tobias. *The Golden Builders*. Lichfield: Signal Publishing, 2002.

Clarke, Hyde and C. Staniland Wake. *Serpent and Siva Worship*. Whitefish, Mont.: Kessinger Publishing Ltd., 1877.

Collins, Andrew. *Twenty-First Century Grail: The Quest for a Legend*. London: Virgin, 2004.

———. *From the Ashes of Angles, The Forbidden Legacy of a Fallen Race*. London: Signet Books, 2004.

———. *Gods of Eden*. London: Headline, 1998.

———. *Gateway to Atlantis*. London: Headline, 2000.

Cooper, J.C. *An Illustrated Encyclopaedia of Traditional Symbols*. London: Thames and Hudson, 1978.

Croker, Thomas Crofton. *Legend of the Lakes*. N.p, 1829.

Crooke, W. *The Popular Religion and Folk-lore of Northern India*. Whitefish, Mont.: Kessinger Publishing Ltd., 1997.

Cumont, F. *The Mysteries of Mithra*. London: Dover Publications, 1956.

Currer-Briggs, N. *The Shroud and the Grail; a modern quest for the true grail*. New York: St Martins Press, 1987.

David-Neel, Alexandria. *Magic and Mystery in Tibet*. London: Dover Publications, 1929.

Davidson, H. R. Ellis. *Myths and Symbols of Pagan Europe*. Syracuse, N.Y.: Syracuse University Press, 1988.

Davidson, John. *The Secret of the Creative Vacuum*. London: The C. W. Daniel Company Ltd, 1989.

De Martino, Ernesto. *Primitive Magic*. Dorset: Prism Unity, 1972.

Devereux, Paul. *Secrets of Ancient and Sacred Places: The World's Mysterious Heritage*. Beckhampton: Beckhampton Press, 1995.

———. *Shamanism and the Mystery Lines*. London: Quantum, 1992.

———. *Symbolic Landscapes*. Glastonbury: Gothic Image, 1992.

Dinwiddie, John. *Revelations—the Golden Elixir*. Writers Club Press, 2001.

Dodd, C.H. *Historical Tradition of the Fourth Gospel*. Cambridge: Cambridge University Press, 1963.

Doel, Fran and Geoff Doel. *Robin Hood: Outlaw of Greenwood Myth*. Temous, 2000.

Duckett-Shipley, Eleanor. *The Gateway to the Middle Ages, Monasticism*. Ann Arbor, Mich.: University of Michigan Press, 1961.

Dunstan, V. *Did the Virgin Mary Live and Die in England?* Rochester, N.Y.: Megiddo Press, 1985.

Davies, Rev. Edward. *The Mythology and Rites of the British Druids*. London: J. Booth, 1806.

Devereux, Paul. *Places of Power: measuring the secret energy of ancient sites*. London: Blandford, 1999.

Devereux, Paul and Ian Thompson. *Ley Guide: The Mystery of Aligned Ancient Sites*. London: Empress, 1988.

Dunford, Barry. *The Holy Land of Scotland: Jesus in Scotland and the Gospel of the Grail*. N.p., n.d.

Eliade, Mircea. *Shamanism: Archaic Techniques of Ecstasy*. Princeton, N.J.: Princeton University Press, 1964.

Ellis, Ralph. *Jesus, Last of the Pharaohs*. Cheshire: Edfu Books, 2001.

Epstein, Perle. *Kabbalah: The Way of the Jewish Mystic*. Boston: Shambhala Classics, 2001.

Ernst, Carl. *Venomous Reptiles of North America*: Washington D.C.: Smithsonian Books, 1992.

Evans, Lorraine. *Kingdom of the Ark*. London: Simon and Schuster, 2000.

Feather, Robert. *The Copper Scroll Decoded*. London: Thorsons, 1999.

Fedder, Kenneth and Michael Alan Park. *Human Antiquity: An Introduction to Physical Anthropology and Archaeology*. Mountain View, Calif.: Mayfield Publishing, 1993.

Ferguson, Diana. *Tales of the Plumed Serpent*. London: Collins and Brown, 2000.

Fergusson, Malcolm. *Rambles in Breadalbane*. N.p., 1891.

Fontana, David. *The Secret Language of Symbols*. London: Piatkus, 1997.

Ford, Patrick. *The Mabinogi and other Medieval Welsh Tales*. Berkeley: University of California Press. 1977.

Fortune, Dion. *The Mystical Qabalah*. Maine: Weiser Books, 2000.

Foss, Michael. *People of the First Crusade*. London: Michael O'Mara Books, 1997.

Frazer, Sir James. *The Golden Bough*. London: Wordsworth, 1993.

Freke, Timothy and Peter Gandy. *Jesus and the Goddess*. London: Thorsons, 2001.

Gardner, Laurence. *Bloodline of the Holy Grail*. London: Element, 1996.

————. *Proof – Does God Exist?* California: Reality Entertainment, 2006.

Gardiner, Samuel. *History of England*. London: Longmans, Green, and Co., 1904.

Gascoigne, Bamber. *The Christians*. London: Jonathan Cape, 1977.

Gerber, Richard. *Vibrational Medicine*. Santa Fe: Bear & Company, 2001.

Gilbert, Adrian. *Magi*. London: Bloomsbury, 1996.

Goldberg, Carl. *Speaking With The Devil*. London: Viking, 1996.

Gould, Charles. *Mythical Monsters*. London: Senate, 1995.

Graves, Robert. *The Greek Myths: 2*. London: Pelican, 1964.

Gray Hulse, Tristan. *The Holy Shroud*. London: Weidenfeld and Nicolson, 1997.

Guenther, Johannes Von. *Cagliostro*. London: William Heinemann, 1928.

Hagger, Nicholas. *The Fire and the Stones*. London: Element, 1991.

Hanauer, J.E. *The Holy Land*. London: Senate, 1996.

Hancock, Graham. *The Sign and the Seal*. London: Arrow, 2001.

Halifax, Joan. *Shaman: the Wounded Healer*. London: Crossroad, Thames and Hudson, 1982.

Harbison, Peter. *Pre-Christian Ireland*. London: Thames and Hudson, 1988.

Harrington, E. *The Meaning of English Place Names*. Belfast: The Black Staff Press, 1995.

Hartmann, Franz. *The Life of Jehoshua The Prophet of Nazareth: an occult study and a key to the Bible*. London: Kegan, Trench, Trubner & Co, 1909.

Heathcote-James, Emma. *They Walk Among Us*. New York: Metro, 2004.

Hedsel, Mark. *The Zelator*. London: Century, 1998.

Howard, M. *The Occult Conspiracy*. Rochester, N.Y.: Destiny Books, 1989.

James, E.O. *The Ancient Gods*. London: Weidenfeld and Nicolson, 1962.

Jennings, Hargrave. *Ophiolatreia*. Whitefish, Mont.: Kessinger Publishing Ltd., 1996.

Johnson, Buffie. *Lady of the Beast: the Goddess and Her Sacred Animals*. San Fransisco: Harper and Row, 1988.

Jones, Alison. *Dictionary of World Folklore*. New York: Larousse, 1995.

Kauffeld, Carl. *Snakes: The Keeper and the Kept*. London: Doubleday and Co., 1969.

Kendrick, T. D. *The Druids*. London: Methuen and Co., 1927.

King, Serge Kahili. *Instant Healing: Mastering the Way of the Hawaiian Shaman Using Words, Images, Touch, and Energy*. Los Angeles: Renaissance Books, 2000.

Knight, Christopher and Robert Lomas. *Uriel's Machine: Reconstructing the Disaster Behind Human History*. London: Arrow, 2004.

Knight, Christopher, and Robert Lomas. *The Second Messiah*. London: Arrow, 1997.

Laidler, Keith. *The Head of God*. London: Orion, 1999.

———— *The Divine Deception*. London: Headline, 2000.

Lapatin, Kenneth. *Mysteries of the Snake Goddess*. Boston: Houghton Mifflin Company, 2002.

Layton, Robert. *Australian Rock Art: a new synthesis*. Cambridge: Cambridge University Press, 1986.

Larson, Martin A. *The Story of Christian Origins*. Village, 1977.

Leakey, Richard and Roger Lewin. *Origins Reconsidered*. London: Doubleday, 1992.

Le Goff, Jacques. *The Medieval World*. London: Parkgate Books, 1997.

Lemesurier, Peter. *The Great Pyramid Decoded*. London: Element, 1977.

Levi, Eliphas. *Transcendental Magic*. London: Tiger Books, 1995.

Lincoln, Henry. *Key to the Sacred Pattern*. Gloucestershire: Windrush Press, 1997.

Loye, David. *An Arrow Through Chaos: how we see into the future*. Rochester, N.Y.: Part Street Press, 1983.

Lyall, Neil and Robert Chapman. *The Secret of Staying Young*. London: Pan, 1976.

MacCana, Proinsias. *Celtic Mythology*. New York: Hamlyn, 1992.

Mack, B.L. *The Lost Gospel*. London: Element, 1993.

Maclellan, Alec. *The Lost World of Agharti*. London: Souvenir Press, 1982.

Magin, U. *The Christianisation of Pagan Landscapes*. in The Ley Hunter No. 116, 1992.

Mann, A.T. *Sacred Architecture*. London: Element, 1993.

Maraini, Fosco. *Secret Tibet*. London: Hutchinson, 1954.

Matthews, John. *Sources of the Grail*. London: Floris Books, 1996.

————. *The Quest for the Green Man*. Newton Abbott: Godsfield Press, 2001.

Maby, J. C. and T. Bedford Franklin. *The Physics of the Divining Rod*. London: Bell, 1977.

McDermott, Bridget. *Decoding Egyptian Hieroglyphs*. London: Duncan Baird Publishers, 2001.

Meij, Harold. *The Tau and the Triple Tau*. Tokyo: H.P., 2000.

Michell, John, and Christine Rhone. *Twelve-Tribes and the Science of Enchanting the Landscape*. Grand Rapids, Mich.: Phanes PR, 1991.

Milgrom, Jacob. *The JPS Torah Commentary: Numbers*. New York: Jewish Publication Society, 1990.

Moncrieff, A. R. *Hope, Romance & Legend of Chivalry*. London: Senate, 1994.

Morgan, Gerald. *Nanteos: A Welsh House and its Families*. Llandysul: Gomer, 2001.

Morton, Chris and Ceri Louise Thomas. *The Mystery of the Crystal Skulls*. London: Element, 2003.

Muggeridge, Malcolm. *Jesus*. London: Collins, 1975.

Nilsson, M. P. *The Minoan-Mycenaean Religion and Its Survival in Greek Religion*. Oxford: Lund, 1950.

Oliver, George. *Signs and Symbols*. New York: Macoy Publishing, 1906.

O'Brien, Christian and Barbara Joy. *The Shining Ones*. London: Dianthus Publishing Ltd., 1988.

Oliver, Rev. George. *The History of Initiation*. Whitefish, Mont.: Kessinger Publishing Ltd., 1841.

O'Neill, John. *Nights of the Gods*. N.p., n.d.

Opponheimer, Stephen. *Eden in the East*. London: Orion, 1988.

Orofino, Giacomella. *Sacred Tibetan Teachings on Death and Liberation*. London: Prism-Unity, 1990.

Pagels, E. *The Gnostic Gospels*. London: Weidenfeld and Nicolson, 1979.

Paterson Smyth, J. *How We Got our Bible*. London: Sampson Low, n.d.

Pennick, N. *Sacred Geometry*. Chievely: Capall Bann, 1994.

Picknett, Lynn and Clive Prince. *The Templar Revelation*. London: Corgi, 1998.

Piggot, Stuart. *The Druids*. London: Thames and Hudson, 1927.

Pike, Albert. *The Morals and Dogma of Scottish Rite Freemasonry*. Richmond, VA: L.H. Jenkins, 1928.

Plichta, Peter. *God's Secret Formula*. London: Element, 1997.

Plunket, Emmeline. *Calendars and Constellations of the Ancient World*. London: John Murray, 1903.

Powell, T.G.E. *The Celts*. London: Thames and Hudson, 1968.

Rabten, Geshe. *Echoes of Voidness*. London: Wisdom Publications, 1983.

Radin, Dean. *The Conscious Universe*. London: Harper Collins, 1997.

Randles, Jenny and Peter Hough. *Encyclodepia of the Unexplained*. London: Brockhampton Press, 1995.

Read, Piers Paul. *The Templars*. London: Phoenix, 1999.

Rees, Alwyn, and Brynley. *Celtic Heritage*. London: Thames and Hudson, 1961.

Reid, Howard. *Arthur—The Dragon King*. London: Headline, 2001.

———. *In Search of the Immortals: Mummies, Death and the Afterlife*. London: Headline, 1999.

Richet, C. *Thirty Years of Psychic Research*. New York: Macmillan, 1923.

Rinbochay, Lati, Locho Rinbochay, and Leah Zahler, and Jeffrey Hopkins. *Meditative States in Tibetan Buddhism*. London: Wisdom Publications, 1983.

Rohl, David. *A Test of Time: The Bible—from Myth to History*. London: Arrow, 1995.

Roberts, Alison. *Hathor Rising: The Serpent Power of Ancient Egypt*. Rottingdean, East Sussex: Northgate, 1995.

Roberts, J.M. *The Mythology of the Secret Societies*. London: Granada, 1972.

————. *Antiquity Unveiled*. N.p.: Health Research, 1970.

Robertson, J. M. *Pagan Christs*. London: Watts, 1903.

Rolleston, T. W. *Myths and Legends of the Celtic Race*. London: Mystic P, 1986.

Russell, Peter. *The Brain Book*. London: Routledge, 1980.

Schaya, Leo. *The Universal Meaning of the Kabbalah*. N.J.: University Books, 1987.

Schele, Linda, and Mary Ellen Miller. *The Blood of Kings: Dynasty and Ritual in Maya Art*. New York: Braziller, 1992.

Scholem, Gershom G. *On the Kabbalah and Its Symbolism*. London: Routledge & Kegan, 1965.

Schonfield, Hugh. *Essene Odyssey*. London: Element, 1984.

————. *The Passover Plot*. London: Hutchinson, 1965.

Schwartz, Gary, and Linda Russek. *The Living Energy Universe*. Charlottesville, Va.: Hampton Roads Publishing, 1999.

Scott, Ernest. *The People of the Secret*. London: The Octagon Press, 1983.

Seife, Charles. *Zero: The Biography of a Dangerous Idea*. London: Souvenir Press, 2000.

Seligmann, Kurt. *The History of Magic*. New York: Quality Paperback Book Club, 1997.

————. *Signs, Symbols and Ciphers*. London: New Horizons, 1992.

Simpson, Jacqueline. *British Dragons*. London: B. T. Batsford and Co, 1980.

Sinclair, Andrew. *The Secret Scroll*. London: Birlinn, 2001.

Sharper Knowlson, T. *The Origins of Popular Superstitions and Customs*. London: Senate, 1994.

Smith, M. *The Secret Gospel*. London: Victor Gollancz, 1973.

Snyder, Louis L. *Encyclopaedia of the Third Reich*. London: Wordsworth, 1998.

Spence, Lewis. *Introduction to Mythology*. London: Senate, 1994.

———. *Myths and Legends of Egypt*. London: George Harrap and Sons, 1915.

Stephen, Alexander M. *The Journal of American Folklore*. January/March, 1929.

Stone, Nathan. *Names of God*. Chicago: Moody, 1944.

Sullivan, Danny. *Ley Lines*. London: Piaktus, 1999.

Talbot, Michael. *The Holographic Universe*. London: Harper Collins, 1996.

Taylor, Richard. *How to Read a Church*. London: Random House, 2003.

Temple, Robert. *The Crystal Sun*. London: Arrow, 1976.

———. *Netherworld: Discovering the Oracle of the Dead and Ancient Techniques of Foretelling the Future*. London: Century, 2002.

Thiering, Barbara, *Jesus The Man*. London: Doubleday, 1992.

———. *Jesus of the Apocalypse*. London: Doubleday, 1996.

Thomson, Ahmad. *Dajjal the Anti-Christ*. London: Ta-Ha Publishers Ltd., 1993.

Thomson, Oliver. *Easily Led: A history of Propaganda*. Gloucestershire: Sutton Publishing, 1999.

Toland, John. *Hitler*. London: Wordsworth, 1997.

Tolstoy, Nikolai. *The Quest for Merlin*. London: Little, Brown and Co., 1985.

Tull, George F. *Traces of the Templars*. London: The Kings England Press, 2000.

Vadillo, Umar Ibrahim. *The Return of the Gold Dinar*. Cape Town: Madinah Press, 1996.

Villars, de, Abbe N. de Montfaucon. *Comte de Gabalis: discourses on the Secret Sciences and Mysteries in accordnace with the principles of the Ancient Magi and the Wisdom of the Kabalistic Philosophers*. Whitefiesh, Mont.: Kessinger Publishing Ltd., 1996.

Villanueva, J. L. *Phoenician Ireland*. Dublin: The Dolmen Press, 1833.

Vulliamy, C. E. *Immortality: Funerary Rites & Customs*. London: Senate, 1997.

Waite, Arthur Edward. *The Hidden Church of the Holy Grail*. Amsterdam: Fredonia Books, 2002.

Wake, C. Staniland. *The Origin of Serpent Worship*. Whitefish, Mont.: Kessinger Publishing Ltd., 1877.

Walker, B. *Gnosticism*. Wellingborough: Aquarian Press, 1983.

Wallace-Murphy, Hopkins. *Rosslyn*. London: Element, 2000.

Waters, Frank. *The Book of the Hopi*. New York: Ballantine, 1963.

Watson, Lyall. *Dark Nature*. London: Harper Collins, 1995.

Weber, Renee. *Dialogues with Scientists and Sages: Search for Unity in Science and Mysticism*. London: Arkana, 1990.

Weisse, John. *The Obelisk and Freemasonry*.Whitefish, Mont.: Kessinger Publishing Ltd., 1996.

Wheless, Joseph. *Forgery in Christianity*. N.p., Health Research, 1990.

Williamson, A. *Living in the Sky*. Norman, Okla.: University of Oklahoma Press, 1984.

Wilson, Colin. *The Atlas of Holy Places and Sacred Sites*. London: Doring Kindersley, 1996.

———. *Beyond the Occult*. London: Caxton Editions, 2002.

———. *Frankenstein's Castle: The Double Brain—Door to Wisdom*. London: Ashgrove Press, 1980.

Wilson, Hilary. *Understanding Hieroglyphs*. London: Brockhampton Press, 1993.

Wise, Michael, Martin Abegg, and Edward Cook, *The Dead Sea Scrolls*. London: Harper Collins, 1999.

Within, Enquire. *Trail of the Serpent*. N.p., n.d.

Wood, David. *Genisis*. London: Baton Wicks Publications, n.d.

Woods, George. Henry, *Herodotus Book II*. London: Rivingtons, 1897.

Woolley, Benjamin. *The Queens's Conjuror*. London: Harper Collins, 2001.

Wylie, Rev. J. A. *History of the Scottish Nation, Volume 1*. 1886.

Zollschan, G.K., J.F Schumaker, and G.F. Walsh, *Exploring the Paranormal*. London: Prism Unity, 1989.

Other References

Dictionary of Beliefs and Religions. London: Wordsworth, 1995.

Dictionary of Phrase and Fable. London: Wordsworth, 1995.

Dictionary of Science and Technology. London: Wordsworth Edition, 1995.

Dictionary of the Bible. London: Collins, 1974.

Dictionary of the Occult. London: Geddes and Grosset, 1997.

Dictionary of World Folklore. London: Larousse, 1995.

Web References

www.gardinersworld.com

www.serpentgrail.com

www.theshiningones.com

www.philipgardiner.net

www.radikalbooks.com

www.elfhill.com

www.handstones.pwp.blueyonder.co.uk

www.sacredconnections.com

www.pyramidtexts.com

INDEX